CONFIDENTIAL MEMO

Badge No. 1197: Carrie McCall

Rank: Sergeant

Skill/Expertise: Superior investigative skills, uncanny cop instincts, innate ability to charm and disarm

Reason Chosen for Assignment: A looker with a black mark on her otherwise sterling record, McCall's the perfect choice to play "lover" to partner Linc Reilly's "lawbreaker" in an undercover sting designed to get her *real* close to the suspected rogue cop.

Badge No. 0730: Lincoln Reilly

Rank: Sergeant

Skill/Expertise: Seasoned undercover operative, disciplined and dangerous

Reason Chosen for Assignment: The best of the best, but a cop believed to have lost his way—but not his need for the love of a woman....

Dear Reader,

What better way to start off a new year than with six terrific new Silhouette Intimate Moments novels? We've got miniseries galore, starting with Karen Templeton's *Staking His Claim*, part of THE MEN OF MAYES COUNTY. These three brothers are destined to find love, and in this story, hero Cal Logan is also destined to be a father—but first he has to convince heroine Dawn Gardner that in his arms is where she wants to stay.

For a taste of royal romance, check out Valerie Parv's *Operation: Monarch*, part of THE CARRAMER TRUST, crossing over from Silhouette Romance. Policemen more your style? Then check out Maggie Price's *Hidden Agenda*, the latest in her LINE OF DUTY miniseries, set in the Oklahoma City Police Department. Prefer military stories? Don't even try to resist *Irresistible Forces,* Candace Irvin's newest SISTERS IN ARMS novel. We've got a couple of great stand-alone books for you, too. Lauren Nichols returns with a single mom and her protective hero, in *Run to Me*. Finally, Australian sensation Melissa James asks *Can You Forget?* Trust me, this undercover marriage of convenience will stick in your memory long after you've turned the final page.

Enjoy them all—and come back next month for more of the best and most exciting romance reading around, only in Silhouette Intimate Moments.

Yours,

Leslie J. Wainger
Executive Editor

Please address questions and book requests to:
Silhouette Reader Service
U.S.: 3010 Walden Ave., P.O. Box 1325, Buffalo, NY 14269
Canadian: P.O. Box 609, Fort Erie, Ont. L2A 5X3

Hidden Agenda
MAGGIE PRICE

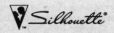

INTIMATE MOMENTS™

Published by Silhouette Books

America's Publisher of Contemporary Romance

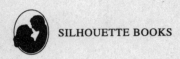 SILHOUETTE BOOKS

ISBN 0-373-27339-8

HIDDEN AGENDA

Visit Silhouette at www.eHarlequin.com

Printed in U.S.A.

Books by Maggie Price

MAGGIE PRICE

turned to crime at the age of twenty-two. That's when she went to work at the Oklahoma City Police Department. As a civilian crime analyst, she evaluated suspects' methods of operation during the commission of robberies and sex crimes and developed profiles on those suspects. During her tenure at OCPD, Maggie stood in lineups, snagged special assignments to homicide task forces, established procedures for evidence submittal, even posed as the wife of an undercover officer in the investigation of a fortune-teller.

While at OCPD, Maggie stored up enough tales of intrigue, murder and mayhem to keep her at the keyboard for years. The first of those tales won the Romance Writers of America's Golden Heart Award for Romantic Suspense.

Maggie invites her readers to contact her at 5208 W. Reno, Suite 350, Oklahoma City, OK 73127-6317. Or on the Web at http://members.aol.com/magprice.

To tough guys with soft hearts

Chapter 1

"Good morning. Can you tell me where I can find Lieutenant Quintana?"

The smoky voice pulled Lincoln Reilly's attention from the Selective Enforcement Unit's coffeemaker, a half-opened packet of sugar gripped between his thumb and fingers. It wasn't often his mind snapped off. But it did as he took in the petite woman with a mass of copper-red hair and cool blue eyes in a face created to grab a man's attention.

As was whatever smoldering perfume she wore.

Although he'd been out of the loop a couple of years where women's fashions were concerned, something told him the sea-foam-green sweater and slacks that hugged her curves were up-to-the-minute in style.

The gold Oklahoma City P.D. sergeant's badge and holstered Smith & Wesson 9mm automatic clipped to her waistband had him jerking his mind back to business.

He made sure none of the effort showed as he met her

gaze, thinking she damn well didn't look like a run-of-the-mill female cop. "Quintana's office is there," Linc said, angling his head. "The one with the glass panel looking out onto the squad room."

"Thanks. So what's it like working in the SEU?"

"It's a job." Linc dumped the contents of the sugar packet—then another—into his coffee. It was Monday morning; he had endured a hellish weekend with people who brought back memories that ripped at his soul. With his thoughts so dark, he was in no mood for chitchat. Further, the Selective Enforcement Unit—SEU—operated in its own sphere. The squad worked autonomously, involved in undercover operations that most police employees never knew about. The redhead's badge had gained her access to the third floor of the nondescript building that housed OCPD's undercover units. That's *all* it would get her, unless she had a legitimate need to know about personnel or operations.

"I'll ask Quintana," she murmured, then tipped her head at Linc's coffee mug. "You know, that could be your problem."

He turned to face her, noting the top of her head barely reached his shoulders. "What problem?"

"Surliness. All that refined sugar you dumped in your coffee contains a mountain of additives. You should try stevia."

He knitted his brows. "What the hell is stevia?"

"A natural sweetener made from a plant extract." When she shook back her hair, that wild, reddish mane slithered around her shoulders, her breasts. "I take my coffee black, in case you were planning to ask."

"Knowing that, my day is complete." The unwelcome stirring of his system had him feeling just perverse enough to take a sip from his mug instead of offering to get her a cup.

Apparently unoffended, she extended her right hand. "I'm Carrie McCall. Transferring from Patrol to the SEU."

His gaze flicked to her hand while he caught another whiff of her scent that was as hot and steamy as the contents of his mug. Dammit, he had to get the hell away from her. He didn't want a reminder of how a certain woman's looks, voice, *scent* had the power to pull him in.

"Linc Reilly. Excuse me while I run out and pick up some stevia." Turning his back on her, he headed across the squad room. By the time he reached his desk, she had sauntered—that was the only way to describe the slow, loose swing of her hips—halfway to Quintana's office.

Linc settled into his chair, noting all conversation in the squad room had ceased. He glanced around. It didn't surprise him to see every pair of male eyes tracking McCall's progress.

"Who's the babe?"

Linc shifted his attention to the cop at the desk across the aisle. In an unofficial vote of all the PD's undercover units, Tom Nelson had won the title of worst dressed. Today's stained sweatshirt and threadbare jeans looked disreputable, as did his dark, rumpled hair and unkempt beard. Propped back in his chair, his scuffed loafers on the desk, he held a report in one hand and a donut in the other. He had his eyes glued on the door to Quintana's office through which McCall had just disappeared.

"Her name's *Sergeant* McCall," Linc answered. "Transferring in from Patrol."

"Hallelujah." Nelson pounded a fist against his heart. "About time this office got some worthwhile scenery."

Linc raised a brow. "We've got two women in this unit. If Annie or Evelyn hear you, they'll grind you into dog meat." Linc frowned at Annie Becker's desk. His partner always beat him to work, but he'd seen no sign of her this morning.

"Our gals are attractive," Nelson conceded. "Just nothing like the McCall sisters."

"Sisters?"

"You know Grace Fox? Ryan Fox's widow?"

Linc sipped his coffee, and scowled when he found himself thinking about the additives he was consuming. "I've met Grace."

"She's the oldest. I heard the youngest sister is a few months out of the academy, but I haven't run into her yet. If she's as seriously gorgeous as the other two, mamma mia."

Linc shook his head. Nelson's looks were as memorable as a telephone pole, but that didn't stop him from viewing himself as the department's answer to Casanova. "Keep talking like that, you'll get slapped with a sexual harassment suit."

"Nah." Nelson's toothy grin lent charm to his bearded, gaunt face. "All I did was pay the McCall sisters a compliment."

"Some women wouldn't view it that way," Linc said as he unlocked his desk and pulled out a file folder.

"Reilly's right, Nelson." The derisive voice coming from just behind Linc stiffened his spine. "And we all know he's an *expert* in looking out for a woman's best interests."

Jaw locked, Linc swiveled his chair around. The detective who stood inches away was a little over six feet tall, with black hair, olive skin and deep-set eyes guarded by heavy brows.

After his lousy weekend, a run-in with Don Gaines was not going to lighten his mood, Linc thought. "Don't talk around the subject, Don. You got something to add, say it to my face."

Gaines sipped his coffee. "I've made my feelings clear."

"Crystal." Linc didn't add that he agreed with the man who had once been as close as a brother. He, Lincoln Reilly, had put work above his wife and in the process got her killed. "Since rehashing old ground won't change things, I suggest you switch subjects or move on."

Nelson's scuffed loafers hit the floor, his wary gaze darting between both men. "I was just mouthing off about women. Talking garbage. I didn't mean to get this thing started again."

"This *thing* is ongoing," Gaines commented, then glanced toward their boss's office. "As for Carrie McCall, you'd better watch what you say, Nelson. She might look like a piece of fluff, but she's got the rep of being a good street cop who can kick butt whenever it's necessary."

"Thanks for the tip," Nelson muttered as Gaines turned and headed toward his desk. "Sorry, Linc." Nelson raked a hand across his beard. "I don't know what else to say."

"Nothing to say," Linc swivelled his chair around. "Not your fault, Tom." *It's mine.*

As if reading Linc's thoughts, Nelson leaned forward. "Not yours, either, buddy."

"Yeah." Linc's voice remained steady while anger and guilt boiled inside him. He didn't need a reminder of what he had carried like a ten-ton stone on his conscience every day, every night, every cursed second for the past two years. He had as good as killed Kim. Because he had not put her first, she had died horribly. If he had been a better husband, she would be alive. If he had been a better cop, he would have dug up something on the slime in the ski mask who'd kidnapped, raped and murdered her. As it was, Linc knew only what the grainy surveillance tape at the crime scene had picked up.

But he did, *finally*, have something, he reminded himself. After two years of searching for the white male with a snake tattoo on his forearm, the bastard had been spotted. Once. That one sighting had been enough to give Linc a place to start. He would find the slime. Find him, and make him pay.

Linc eased out a breath. The pain he'd endured since Kim's death had taught him that tormenting himself over what couldn't be changed was futile. So, while he waited for his partner, he opened the file and scanned the notes he and Annie had compiled on a string of murders that had begun a year and a half ago.

Unlike Kim's, these homicides held no personal undertones. His and Annie's interest had merely spiked when they realized six do-wrongs handled by various detectives assigned to the SEU had wound up murdered. Linc himself had dealt with four of the victims. All had been career criminals who preyed on innocent citizens and had sidestepped punishment in the criminal justice system. All had died the way Linc would have expected: ambushed and head-shot in apparent incidents of street violence. Still, his cop's instincts had him wondering if there was something more about the killings than what appeared on the surface. He simply didn't know.

"Reilly!"

Linc looked up, saw Quintana leaning out of his office door.

"Yeah, Lieu?"

"Need to see you. And bring an extra cup of coffee." Quintana glanced across his shoulder, then looked back at Linc. "Black. Make sure there's no sugar in it."

Eyes narrowed, Linc checked the glass panel on Quintana's office. The coppery-red flash he caught through the open miniblinds told him Carrie McCall was now seated in a visitors chair.

Setting his jaw, Linc slid the file into the drawer and locked it. Damn if the woman hadn't gotten that cup of coffee out of him after all.

Even without looking toward the office door, Carrie McCall knew the instant Linc Reilly stepped inside. She'd felt the same sizzling awareness when she'd spotted him at the coffeemaker. She had spent a week studying his file. Learning about the man. Yet none of that had prepared her for the electric current that had zipped through every nerve in her body when she came face-to-face with her prey.

Forcing the cadence of her breathing to remain even, she told herself her reaction was to be expected. After all, she was under strict orders to get close to Reilly. Take him down for murder, if the evidence was there. He was her first undercover assignment—one that was risky at best. Dangerous at worst.

Carrie kept her attention centered on Lieutenant John Quintana, sitting at the tidy desk in front of her. SEU's commander was a toughly built, compact man in his mid-fifties who gazed at her with serious, dark-brown eyes. The stark bareness of the office walls and nondescript tan mini-blinds at the window were in direct contrast to Quintana's starched white shirt, red tie, blue blazer and gray slacks. He looked comfortable and competent. By all accounts, Quintana was an experienced, solid supervisor who commanded the respect of his troops.

Carrie understood that—it had always been vitally important she earn the respect of her fellow officers. But if Quintana knew the real reason she'd been placed in his unit, his esteem would not be among the things she earned.

Although her shoulders were as stiff as wire, she kept her expression relaxed as she smiled at Quintana. "I'm looking forward to working in your unit, Lieutenant. After more than five years in patrol, I'm ready for a different type of police work."

''You'll get that here.'' Quintana glanced up, then gestured at chair beside hers. ''Reilly, have a seat. Linc Reilly, this is Carrie McCall.''

Turning her head, Carrie watched the man stride toward her. Six foot four, powerfully built, yet rangy and lean. His hair was pitch-black, edging toward renegade length. He had a sharp-cheeked face with a street-smart look about it and the exotic golden eyes of a tiger that no woman drawing breath would overlook. Including her. That lean, rangy body was clad in snug, worn jeans, and a red fisherman-style sweater, its sleeves shoved up to reveal muscular forearms.

The man made an impressive package. A dangerous one, too, if he was the cop who'd coolly executed six people.

''Your coffee,'' Linc said. ''Black. No additives.''

''Thanks.'' Because of his earlier refusal to shake her hand, she set the cup on the lieutenant's desk and offered hers again. ''Pleasure to meet you, Sergeant Reilly.''

He kept his eyes on her face as his fingers engulfed hers. ''Likewise, Sergeant McCall.''

She might as well have touched a lightning bolt, Carrie thought, as an electric shock flashed through her system. It took every bit of her willpower not to jerk from his hold.

Telling herself she would deal later with her overall brainless reaction to the man she was here to investigate, she forced a cool smile. ''That errand you mentioned you needed to run must not have taken you long.''

His fingers tightened, as did his smile. ''Not long enough.''

Since he made no move to loosen his grip, she had to tug her hand from his.

Quintana frowned. ''You two know each other?''

''Met at the coffeemaker,'' Linc replied, and turned. ''Did you need me for something other than beverage delivery, Lieu?''

Quintana stabbed a finger toward the chair angled beside Carrie's. ''Have a seat.'' He waited until Linc complied, then asked, ''What's the status of the crackdown on The Hideaway?''

Carrie sensed Linc's hesitation. She didn't have to wonder why—when she received her assignment, she had done her research. Selective Enforcement was an undercover unit that worked closely with Intelligence and primarily targeted career criminals. Their work was sensitive and could adversely impact numerous investigations—even get people killed—if information leaked. By necessity, SEU operated as a highly compartmentalized unit. The cops assigned there were even closemouthed with each other. Officers who were friends might not know the specifics of what each other was working on. And certain questions that fell outside the need-to-know area automatically generated suspicion. Good detectives were habitual, generic snoops, but this unit called for cops who were very localized snoops. Which meant Carrie was going to have to be careful in how she ferreted out the evidence she'd been sent there to obtain.

Seconds ticked by before Linc said, ''Annie and I will make our first visit to The Hideaway tomorrow night. I'll write you a status report on everything that's been done so far.''

Quintana shook his head. ''Give me an oral report. Now.''

Linc slid Carrie a look, then remet his boss's gaze. ''Like we planned, guys from Intelligence have been watching The Hideaway's parking lot. They've photographed employees and customers, compiled a list of tag numbers off their vehicles. When I get the list, I'll have dispatch run twenty-eight checks off those tags. Once they give me the name of each vehicle's registered owner, I'll have background checks on each name run through the

CCH and NCIC,'' Linc continued, referring to the department's Computerized Criminal History and the National Crime Information Center computers. ''That'll give Annie and me an idea of the people we'll be dealing with at The Hideaway. From that, we'll firm up our final plan on how to play the assignment.''

Quintana nodded. ''How many visits you figure it'll take to pile up enough citations to raid the place?''

''Five or six, depends on what we find once we're inside. We need enough violations to shut the place down permanently. Hopefully, Annie and I will have everything we need so the raid can go down before Thanksgiving. I can't promise that, though.''

''Sounds good, Reilly. Except one thing.''

''What?''

''Annie's no longer working with you on this. McCall is.''

Linc shifted his weight. ''Look, Lieu, we know from my informant there's lots of illegal activity at The Hideaway. Some we're only guessing about at this point. My partner and I have to observe the violations, identify who's doing what, then write up nightly reports. Anything inaccurate listed in the arrest warrants, any screw-ups during the bust could mean the entire case gets tossed. We also have to be careful how we interact with The Hideaway's customers and employees—most who probably don't know the definition of 'upstanding citizen.' Annie's good, she's got experience at all aspects of this kind of operation.''

''I agree with you, Reilly.'' A frown drew Quintana's dark brows together. ''Thing is, Annie's snagged an assignment to the new Homeland Security task force. Captain Vincent called me at home this weekend to let me know.''

Linc ran a hand through his hair. "How long will she be gone?"

"As long as the task force wants her. You're teamed with McCall, starting with The Hideaway operation. Bring her up to speed so she'll be ready by tomorrow night."

"You're the boss." Linc's expression might have remained impassive, but his tone rang in Carrie's ears like cold steel.

Quintana nodded, then locked his gaze with hers. "McCall, I had a talk with Captain Vincent. He's studied your file, says he has confidence in your abilities. Which means he doesn't put much stock in what that patrol cop's wife accused you of."

Heat surged into Carrie's cheeks while her internal defenses snapped up like a drawbridge. Although the department leaked like a sieve, she had hoped her former lieutenant—who *knew* she'd been an innocent victim of circumstance—had managed to keep the damn incident under wraps. Apparently not. Great.

Crossing his arms over his chest, Linc angled his head toward her. Carrie didn't have to look at him to feel his intense scrutiny. Which made her cheeks burn even hotter.

"I assure you, Lieutenant, that woman's accusation was unfounded. I did nothing inappropriate."

For Carrie, the knowledge that the wife of one of her fellow patrol officers had stormed the *chief's* office to make her unfounded accusations was a continuing cause of mortification. And because her pride was still raw, she added, "I take my work seriously, Lieutenant. The last thing I would do is engage in on-duty lip-lock sessions in the back seat of some patrol car."

Despite telling herself not to, she glanced at Linc. He stared back at her. Noncommittal. Cop face. Unyielding.

Quintana tapped a pencil against his desk in a sharp staccato rhythm. "McCall, the bottom line here is that the mayor's office has gotten calls from a citizen wanting this crackdown on The Hideaway. That makes it high profile. Lots of media and political attention at the end. Anything gets screwed up, some—maybe all—of the people we collar walk. That happens, there'll be hell to pay. It won't go over well if inappropriate action on some cop's part screws up this operation.''

Carrie's nerves tensed. Working an attention-getting case while it was imperative she maintain a low profile was the last thing she needed. But she had orders to get close to Reilly, and The Hideaway was his case. She had no choice.

''You don't need to worry about me, Lieutenant.'' Years ago she'd gotten involved with another cop. When that relationship ended in disaster, she'd made it a rule to avoid romantic entanglements with all cops. As far as Carrie was concerned, that rule was set in stone.

''Good.'' Quintana plucked a key off his desk then stood. He moved around the desk, handed Carrie the key as she rose. ''We had a man retire last month so you get his desk. He cleared out his paperwork, but I'm not sure what supplies he left. You need anything, get with my secretary. Evelyn's got paperwork you need to fill out.''

''I'll see her first thing.'' Carrie accepted the key, then picked up the foam cup of coffee she had yet to sample.

''Reilly, point out the empty desk to McCall.''

''Sure.'' If he had a problem being harnessed with a new partner, it didn't show in his face as he stepped back to let her pass out of the office ahead of him.

The squad room was a long rectangle, with a row of grime-streaked windows high up on one wall that let in the gloomy November sunlight. Metal desks stuck out from the walls like boat slips; those placed in the center of the room butted up against each other, front to front.

All desks had identical telephones, computers and ancient rolling chairs.

Carrie noted the room's backwash of noise changed to a murmur when she stepped into view. She sensed eyes watching her while she followed Linc through the maze of putty-colored desks. Any cop new to a unit was a subject of curiosity. In normal circumstances, she would have had to prove herself before she could expect anything other than surface acceptance. That wouldn't happen here. She'd be yanked from the SEU the instant she ferreted out the evidence that Internal Affairs needed to file charges against Linc Reilly.

If the evidence even existed.

Linc paused at a metal desk as run-down looking as all the others. The nearby wall held a cork bulletin board loaded with yellowed fliers, notes, cartoons and bureaucratic memos.

"This is it," he said, then flicked his gaze to the cup in her hand. "Guess you didn't want coffee after all."

"You're right, I didn't." She sat the foam cup aside and met his gaze. His golden-brown eyes looked a little harder than the floor beneath her feet.

"Look, Reilly, I'm sure you've got major concerns over taking on a new partner while you're involved in a high-profile investigation."

A muscle in his cheek jerked, but his eyes stayed level. "That sums it up."

"Your concerns are understandable," she persisted. "I don't have delusions of grandeur. I'm not supercop, out to prove how good I am at taking down bad guys. The bottom line is, I've never worked undercover. I want to learn as much as you're willing to teach me. All I ask is that you give me a chance."

"Fair enough," he said, his expression impassive.

"Hey, Reilly, you got a call on line three."

The voice that had Linc glancing across his shoulder belonged to a dark-haired detective with a scraggly beard who sat at a paper-piled desk on the far side of the squad room.

"Put it on hold," Linc said, then looked back at Carrie.

"After I take this call, I'll introduce you around the squad. Then I'll head to Intelligence to get those photos and tag numbers from The Hideaway. I'll drop the list of car tags off at dispatch. The run should be ready by early afternoon. We can get together then and I'll bring you up to speed on what we've got so far."

"Thanks, Reilly."

"Don't thank me, McCall." He smiled now, a quick, powerful strike. "You screw up, I'll be right there in your face."

"I don't plan to screw up."

"Then we shouldn't have a problem."

The usual hubbub of ringing telephones, raised voices, rattling coffee cups and clicking computer keys restarted when Carrie settled at her desk. She kept Linc in her sights as he headed across the squad room. His sure, determined walk sent the message he was a man who possessed total confidence in himself and his abilities. Since she was still puzzling over her own reaction to him, she could attest to the power of his physical presence.

Taking a deep breath, she shifted her thoughts to another aspect of the man. Other officers had told her that in a pinch, he was fearless, the type of partner they wanted next to them when there was trouble. It was rumored Reilly could be as ruthless as the dopers, robbers, gang members and killers who had it in for the cops.

Nothing wrong with that, Carrie conceded. Sometimes a cop survived solely because he was as hazardous as the scum with whom he dealt. Problems surfaced when that ferocity pushed a cop to dole out his own form of justice. Became a self-appointed death squad. An avenger.

Had the vicious murder of his wife transformed Reilly into one of those cops? Had the pain and trauma—and no doubt, the guilt—he had suffered transformed him into a rogue who had become judge, jury and executioner?

Before leaving the SEU, Carrie would know the answers to those questions.

Chapter 2

Linc had decided to bring Carrie McCall up to speed in the drab, windowless interview room that jutted off the main squad room. With various printouts, photographs, rap sheets, mug shots and the detailed plan he'd drawn up for the operation at The Hideaway, they had a mountain of paperwork to go over. The scarred table in the room's center was big enough to spread out everything. What he hadn't factored into the equation was that the interview room was small enough to take on an intimate edge when he enclosed himself there with a woman who wore a kick-a-man-in-the-gut perfume.

What the hell had he been thinking? he silently berated himself while watching her leaf through surveillance photos. Her gaze was intense, her demeanor serious as she examined the pictures of people and vehicles that had shown up in The Hideaway's parking lot over the past nights. Just because she was all business didn't change the fact she looked like a million dollars, with her perfect face and that mass of coppery hair that slid with each subtle movement past her shoulders to her breasts.

A cool, composed, sexy million dollars.

He averted his gaze to one of the bare walls, painted an institutional green. It annoyed him that just by sitting across a table from him she could deflect his attention from the case that should have his total concentration.

"From the outside, The Hideaway looks like a good-size place," she commented while shuffling the photos.

He felt an additional twist of irritation when it took his thoughts a second to click off her and on to business. In the two years since Kim's death, he had barely noticed any woman, much less had one seemingly take over his mind.

In a flash of intuition, he knew that no matter how his new partner handled this assignment, even if she made no mistakes, she was going to give him a great deal of trouble.

The sort of trouble he didn't want or need.

"The Hideaway was once a farmhouse that's been enlarged," he said finally. "There's a main bar room for drinking and dancing. Another for playing pool, with a handful of smaller rooms jutting off it. I've got a layout of the interior which we'll go over."

"I never heard about this place while working patrol." She glanced up from the photos, her blue eyes intense. "I rode one of the far northwest districts and The Hideaway is way southeast, so that's probably why. How long has it been in operation?"

"Long enough for people who live in the area to complain about the drunk and speeding drivers, loud music and everything else that goes along with a place like that."

"Why not put a couple of traffic units out there to pull over the customers after they drive off? Cite the bar owner for noise violations? Things like that."

"We did. Then one day a thirteen-year-old boy took a

detour by The Hideaway and found skin magazines in the Dumpster.''

''Thirteen years old?'' Carrie angled her chin. ''Don't tell me that young man complained about the content of the magazines.''

''Actually, he believed he'd struck gold, until his mother found them under his mattress. She confronted the kid and he 'fessed up to where he'd found the stuff. She called the mayor's office, threatening fire and brimstone if the city allowed—and I quote—that 'den of sin' to continue operating. The mayor's up for re-election and the woman promised to get her church's congregation to campaign against him if he didn't take action. The mayor called the chief and ordered him to do whatever it takes to shut down The Hideaway.''

''Do we have any idea what all is going on there?''

''Gambling, illegal liquor distribution, live sex acts.''

''Sounds like quite the party place.''

''An understatement. About the same time the irate woman called the mayor, one of my snitches gave me a tip about the activity going on there. I sent a report to Quintana.'' Linc kept his expression neutral. He had no intention of telling his new partner about the covert role he'd played in engineering this assignment. He had finally caught the scent of his wife's killer, and it led to The Hideaway. ''When the order to shut down the bar came from the chief, Quintana assigned the case to me since I already knew about the place.''

''So, how do you have this operation set up?''

''Quintana and I agreed that if a couple of guys went in to scope out The Hideaway, they'd get viewed as either holdup men or cops. Either way, all criminal activity would stop while the unknowns were there. That happened, we'd have nothing to make arrests on.''

''And the mayor gets *real* unhappy.''

"Exactly. On the other hand, a man and woman go in and cozy up to each other, they're viewed as married, or maybe just messing around. Takes the heat off."

"Makes sense," she said, looking back at the photos. "From the dress of people, I'd guess the place gets a mix of clientele. Some cowboy wannabes, construction worker types. Blue-collar guys. And pickup trucks are the vehicle of choice for the majority."

"Right on all points." Linc gestured toward the stack of criminal history sheets the Records Bureau had compiled from his list. "Over thirty percent of the people who own those pickups have felony convictions. A couple of robberies. Assaults. Burglaries. Indecent exposure. Like you said, a real mix."

Carrie nodded. "So, the dress of the day for us is jeans and boots."

Linc took in her stylish sea-foam-green sweater, the trendy gold chain looped at her neck, the matching earrings. If she even owned a pair of jeans, they probably had some designer logo stitched on the butt. "The *right* kind of jeans and boots, McCall. The basic rule of appearance in any undercover operation is look like what you're supposed to be, not what some movie or TV show tells you undercover cops look like."

Crossing her forearms on the table, she leaned in. "You tell me what you want me to be, Reilly. That's what you'll get."

What he wanted her to be was *gone*. To take her hot, steamy scent and that husky, just-had-sex voice and get the hell away from him. He knew that wasn't going to happen.

"You can't walk in there looking like some fashion plate," he said, aware that his voice had taken on an edge. "What you need to be specifically is something you and I have to talk about. Since we don't know each other and have no idea of each other's interests, the way for us to play this is as a couple who's been out on a few dates. That way it'll ring true if we know only surface details about each other. We'll say we're both new in town, met a few days ago in a checkout line at Wal-Mart.''

''Do we have jobs yet?''

''I don't. When I was in college, I spent summers working as a roofer, so I know the lingo. My story is that I'm looking for a roofing job. It's November, so those are scarce. No one's going to question why I haven't found work.''

''What about me?''

''What about you, McCall? Your family has cops out the wazoo.'' Since that morning, he'd found out her grandfather and father were retired OCPD. She not only had two sisters on the force, but three brothers. It turned out that Linc had gone through recruit school with Bran McCall. ''Do you have any job experience other than wearing a badge?''

''My mother owns a landscape nursery. Growing up, I worked there weekends and summers. I can talk plants, flowers and sod with an expert and not get tripped up.''

Linc gave her a thin smile. ''That how you know about… What the hell is that stuff you told me to put in my coffee?''

''Stevia.'' Shaking her hair back, she sent him a smug smile. ''A perennial shrub of the aster family. *Asteraceae*, to be exact. It tastes sweet, but has no calories.''

''You'll impress all the beer guzzlers at The Hideaway with that kind of information.''

She slid him a look from beneath her lashes. ''I don't expect my goal is to dazzle anyone with my mental capabilities.''

Not when she could walk into a room and have every

man around instantly fantasizing about getting her underneath him.

"You're right," Linc conceded. "Still, knowing as much as you do about the nursery business is a good cover in case you run into some expert on petunias."

"Do I have a job here?"

"Do most garden centers hire during this time of year?"

"No. They operate with a skeleton crew."

"Then you haven't snagged a job, either. That tightens our cover. We're unemployed, but still have money to party every night. We drive nice cars, which we'll borrow from the department's asset forfeiture inventory. All that gives the impression we're not above doing something against the law to get our funds. And to spend them on illegal activities."

"Like maybe you paying to engage in a 'live' sex act with one of The Hideaway's working girls?"

"Like that." He leaned back in his chair. "This is another advantage to my going in with a female partner. I'll sure as hell let any of the working girls proposition me. Name their price. That'll get them busted during the raid. Since I've got you with me, I'll decline all offers. Don't want to mess up my deal with you by having a roll with some other woman."

"Where have you been all my life, Reilly?" she asked dryly. "My heart's all aflutter, knowing my boyfriend is so devoted."

"*Lover*, McCall. I'm going in as your lover, and you mine. That means we do a lot of hand holding. Touching. Dancing. You think you can do a convincing acting job?"

"Like I told you, I'll be exactly what you want me to be." She pursed her glossed lips. "Our deep commitment to each other clearly means I have to turn down any men who come on to me."

"That's the idea." Testing her, Linc leaned in. "With

your looks, you'll get offers that involve a hell of a lot more than a lip-lock session in the back seat of a patrol car.''

Irritation flicked in her eyes. ''*No* lip-lock session took place. That rookie's idiot wife got jealous and couldn't handle him riding with a female partner. It's my bad luck she took her fictional story to the chief. Who then gave my lieutenant orders to separate me from the idiot's husband. The next day, I was transferred out.''

That McCall didn't hesitate to defend herself pleased Linc. In undercover work, an easygoing personality that was sometimes punctuated by a strong showing of a refusal to let oneself get run over could be very effective.

''Let's get back to that flood of offers you'll receive,'' he began. ''When a guy comes on to you, lays a hand on you, tell him I've got a hair-trigger temper. Make sure he knows if anybody touches my woman, I believe in big-time payback.''

''So, do you have a hair-trigger temper? Believe in big-time payback if someone messes with your woman?''

For some reason, Linc sensed the question was just as loaded as the Glock holstered at his waist. ''Doesn't matter. As long as people at The Hideaway believe I do.''

''Well, *lover* boy,'' Carrie cooed in a husky voice that slid over his senses. ''I'll try not to rile you up. I wouldn't want to find out about your temper firsthand.''

''That's wise, *sweet thing*.'' Linc was fast becoming aware that Carrie McCall could stir him up just by being in the same room. ''While we're on the subject of getting riled, is there a man who'll have a problem with your spending the next handful of nights with me?''

''No.''

''How about some hulking cop who'll thump me with a sap just for dancing with you?''

"You don't have to worry, Reilly. I have this ironclad rule about not getting involved with other cops."

"Guess that rookie's wife didn't know about your rule."

"Guess not. Your questions work both ways. Is there someone who'll have a problem when you cozy up to me at The Hideaway?"

Linc looked down at the reports spread on the table while emotion scraped at him. At one point he'd had a life outside the job. A woman he couldn't wait to go home to. He would forever carry her blood on his hands.

"There's no one." He looked up in time to see compassion flash in Carrie's eyes.

"I'm sorry," she said quietly. "I know what happened to your wife."

"Yeah."

"I thought there might be someone…recent."

"No." He never again wanted a real life. He had his job, a safe place in which he hid his grief in the ruts of routine.

"Okay." Easing out a breath, Carrie looked back at the stack of photos in front of her. "So, our undercover personas are new to Oklahoma City. How'd we wind up at The Hideaway?"

His new partner asked good questions, Linc thought. When you worked undercover, you needed a believable reason to be wherever you showed up. You could die if you didn't have one.

"There's a dive motel about a mile south of there," he said. "The Drop Inn. After I snagged this assignment, I rented a room on a weekly basis. I told the clerk I was new in town and asked where I could get some booze, food and action. He told me about The Hideaway."

"Are you staying there during the operation?"

"Off and on, in case someone decides to check on me. When I don't stay there, it'll look like I went home with you. It will help our cover if you're seen at the Drop Inn with me. We can go into the office and I'll ask the clerk some question. We'll want him—and anyone else watching—to see you go into my room. We'll stay a while, leave the bed looking like we really are lovers.''

"When do we start?"

"Tomorrow night. Does that give you time to get whatever clothes you'll need?"

"You think I work at my Mom's nursery in designer jeans? Think again, Reilly. I dig in the dirt, haul bags of manure and peat moss. I've got plenty of appropriate clothes." Leaning back, she steepled her fingers. "Of course, if our undercover personas are engaging in illegal activities, we'd have money for nicer clothes. I'll have to think about my wardrobe. Maybe wear quality stuff I could have bought in a consignment shop."

When he remained silent, she asked, "Am I off base on the clothes deal?"

"No, you made a good point." He angled his chin. "I'm trying to picture you wielding a shovel. Hoisting bags of manure. The image won't gel."

"Proves you don't know anything about me."

"That's a fact." He didn't want to, either. Unfortunately, this assignment required him to get to know her.

Just then the door swung open. Linc's shoulders tensed instinctively when Don Gaines stepped in.

The detective's dark, deep-set eyes flicked from Carrie to Linc, then back to Carrie. "You'd be Carrie McCall." Stepping to the table, he offered his hand. "I'm Don Gaines. I was out of the squad room when you got introduced around."

Carrie offered a smile and her hand. "Nice to meet you."

Gaines looked back at Linc, handed him a message slip.

''I took a call from a detective in Tulsa. He wants to talk to you about a homicide they had over the weekend.''

Linc bit back a curse when he read the victim's name. Arlee Dell had a mountain of priors by the time his name came up as a suspect in a series of home invasions Linc investigated. He'd pulled Dell in a couple of months ago, but could never prove his connection with the crimes, so he'd walked. Linc suspected Dell pulled another invasion two weeks ago where an elderly couple had been tied up, tortured and strangled.

Linc met Gaines's gaze. ''Thanks, I'll give the cop a call.''

''He said Dell was shot,'' Gaines added. ''Twice in the heart, once in the head.''

Linc tightened his jaw. The man who had once been his closest friend was a good, thorough cop. Had Gaines also picked up on the fact that over the past year and a half a number of scum handled by SEU cops had wound up shot in the head? If so, Gaines would know Dell was victim number seven.

A knot settled in Linc's gut as his mind worked. In college, Gaines had been crazy about Kim; though she'd chosen Linc over him, his feelings for her had never cooled. Gaines blamed Linc for Kim's death. He would like nothing better than to see Linc pay for what had happened to her. Was that why Gaines had gone out of his way to deliver the phone message? Linc wondered. Because he wanted Linc to *know* he'd connected the killings that had commenced one month after Kim's body had been found tossed in a ditch?

While his mind continued its systematic, methodical analysis, Linc felt a cold realization settle inside him. Suspicion. As a cop, he lived with it, always casting as wide a net as possible, encompassing every possibility, distasteful or not. Which was why he now found himself wondering if the deep loathing Gaines felt for him had, over time, taken on an intensity so dark that Linc had failed to see it. Was Gaines so obsessed with making Linc pay for Kim's death that Gaines had decided to make *him* a mark for the murders?

After all, Kim's killer had never been found. The bastard had escaped justice, just as the now-dead seven other maggots had. It was possible a grieving husband might begin a killing spree to avenge his wife. If that husband were a cop, he would know how to get away with those murders. The last of which occurred during the past weekend. Somewhere in Tulsa. Linc had spent the weekend with Kim's family in Claremore, a twenty-minute drive from Tulsa.

Linc's sense of unease gathered strength when he remembered sitting at his desk last Friday, telling Tom Nelson his weekend plans. Gaines could have overheard the conversation. He knew where Kim's parents lived.

Linc lifted his eyes from the message slip. He could read nothing in Gaines's face. Linc couldn't afford to trust, to discount, to filter possibilities through a screen of denial the way most people did. He'd learned a long time ago that the simple truth of the world was that people, even otherwise decent people, regularly did rotten things to others. Now, Linc needed to figure out a way to find out if Gaines had allowed himself to step over the line. If he'd become one of the people they had both spent their lives pursuing. If his bitterness over losing Kim to the man who he blamed for her torturous murder burned so hot he would commit seven homicides with the intention of pinning them on his former friend.

Gaines nodded to Carrie. "Hope to work with you soon."

"Same here."

Gaines flicked Linc a look before walking out.

"That homicide sounds serious," Carrie commented.

Linc's shoulders felt like high-tension wire, and a stone had lodged in his chest. "Isn't every homicide?"

"*Real* serious. If the head shot came after the victim was already dead, doesn't that sound like the work of a pro?"

McCall might be his new partner, but she was an outsider. Linc had no intention of discussing this with her. What he did plan to do was find out what the hell was going on. And who was behind it. And if he was some bastard's intended patsy.

A sick, seething anger swirled in his gut.

"Work of a pro," he repeated, a slash of the anger sounding in his voice. "You gain that expertise watching Mafia movies?"

Her eyes went as cold as winter. "I'm not some green rookie, so spare me the attitude. I've snagged calls to enough homicide crime scenes to know how to spot the work of a pro."

"Maybe you should have transferred to Homicide."

"No." Now her eyes were as deep and dark and potent as her voice. "I'm right where I should be."

"I need to return this call, then go by Quintana's office."

"Fine."

Rising, Linc scrubbed a hand over the back of his neck. He wasn't exactly sure what was going on, but he now felt its dark, menacing presence aimed directly at him. His new partner, however, wasn't to blame for whatever problems he had, he reminded himself.

"Sorry about the attitude, McCall. Didn't mean anything by it."

"No problem." She shrugged. "I've got a tough hide."

He skimmed his gaze down her face, her throat, elegant

and thin. Her hide didn't look so tough to him, he thought as he headed out the door. It looked like cool, creamy silk.

Two hours later Carrie had a headache that was almost off the chart. She knew it was partly due to the stacks of printouts, mug shots and reports piled on the table in front of her. Her brain had simply overloaded on the names and images of people who frequented The Hideaway. Then there was the stress that came from spending time in close proximity to the man presently seated across the table.

She cast him a quick glance. Linc sat in silence, studying a report, his jaw set, the look in those intriguing golden eyes disturbingly detached.

After returning, he had not alluded to what the Tulsa detective told him about the homicide. Nor mentioned why he'd swung by Quintana's office after that. Carrie hadn't asked. Couldn't ask. The last thing she dared do was show too much interest in what might be another killing of a do-wrong whom an SEU cop had handled. Linc specifically.

Just then he laid the report aside and met her gaze. She sought out the man behind those dark eyes, eager to determine his level of involvement in the murders, but saw nothing revealed.

"We've put in a full day," he said. "Let's meet here tomorrow afternoon and review things. After that, we make our first visit to The Hideaway."

"Sounds good." Before she could rise, he placed a hand over her wrist.

"Sorry about that spurt of attitude earlier."

Carrie stared at his strong, firm hand while ordering herself to ignore her jittery stomach. "You already apologized."

"So I did. See you tomorrow."

The November sky hung like a curtain of gray velvet as Carrie made her way to the parking lot where the biting wind swirled paper and leaves into small cyclones. Her teeth chattering from the cold, she steered her sporty little lipstick-red MG out of the lot, drove five blocks, then stopped at a pay phone.

At home she downed extra-strength aspirin, showered, ate dinner, then climbed back into the MG and headed to Penn Square Mall. The digital clock on the dash glowed an eerie green eight when she pulled behind a black van that sat idling in the lot's shadowy perimeter.

She shoved open the door and stepped out into wind so cold it felt like a razor slashing against her face. The van's passenger door swung open just as she reached it.

"Slide in here, Sergeant, before you catch your death."

Shadow obscured the face of the woman sitting in the driver's seat. From their previous meetings, Carrie knew Captain Patricia Scott habitually wore her salt-and-pepper hair twisted into a severe topknot. She had a strong, intelligent face with a network of lines pulling at the flesh around her eyes. Scott had been a cop for twenty-five years, the last three spent as commander over the OCPD's Internal Affairs Division.

"So, McCall, how'd your first day in the SEU go?"

Carrie lifted a shoulder, the gesture masked beneath her thick sweater and heavy coat. "I'm there under false pretenses, investigating another cop…"

"No one said it would be easy."

Carrie stared out the windshield at the sea of cars parked beneath the mall's security lights. Working Internal Affairs was not an assignment she would have picked. It had been thrust on her when the rookie's wife made her accusations about Carrie and her husband to the chief. At the same time, IA had needed a female cop to go undercover. The rat squad had been a convenient place for Carrie to get transferred.

"We went over this, McCall," Scott continued. "If a

cop turns vigilante and starts killing people, we have to stop him."

Nodding, Carrie remet the captain's gaze. "Did you have time to find out about the Tulsa homicide after I called?"

Scott plucked a file from between the bucket seats. "All I had to do was mention the specifics of the shooting— two shots to the heart, one to the head, and they knew what homicide I was calling about. Arlee Dell is the victim's name."

"Does his murder match the others?"

"Yes. Dell has a rap sheet thick enough to use as a booster seat for a kid. Priors for seven felony convictions, including rape, attempted rape, assault and stalking."

"Nice guy. What's his connection to Linc Reilly?"

"He hauled Dell in for questioning about home invasions, but didn't have enough evidence to hold him. A similar invasion occurred two weeks ago where an elderly couple was tortured and strangled. Dell is—was—Reilly's prime suspect."

"Sounds like Dell's life's work was harming people."

Scott gazed at Carrie through the inky shadows. "Dell is the seventh person to die over the past year and a half who's been handled by an SEU detective. This isn't a co-incidence. The shootings are too efficient. Never any witnesses. No collateral damage. Never any cops close by— at one incident, patrol units were decoyed away from the area by a bogus call to 911. Clearly, the shooter preplans his getaways. All that's left at each scene is a dead scumbag, shot at least once in the head."

"Scumbags who would continue to pull maybe forty or fifty bad crimes a year," Carrie added, mentally reviewing the rap sheets in the file IA had given her. "I can't work up remorse over the Avenger's choice of victims."

When Scott tilted her head, a shadow fell across her face like a veil. "The Avenger?"

Carrie nodded. "That's what I've pegged him. Or them. It could be two cops capping the bad guys. A team."

"Either way, your Avenger handle is a good one," Scott stated. "McCall, no one expects you to feel remorse over evil people dying. I don't. It's *how* they're dying that's the problem. IA's job is to make sure cops don't step over the line. If we don't keep a lid on things, you can bet some citizen board will get formed to do it for us. Most cops prefer IA watching over them than civilians who have no idea what it's like dealing with human garbage. It's when a cop breaks the law while dealing with the garbage that we step in. We have to."

Carrie massaged her right temple. Talking about her covert assignment had stirred her headache back to life. "You're right. I just don't like lying about what I'm doing."

"Hopefully you won't have to for long. And you're right—we might have a team of cops doing these hits. But when you run the dead guys against the cops who handled them, Reilly's name keeps coming up. Too many times for it to be a coincidence. So, right now he's our focus. What's your take so far on him?"

He's dark, moody and sexy as hell. That her physical impression of the man was the first thing to pop into her head had Carrie struggling against a nagging unease. Then there was her over-the-top response to his touch that had alarm bells shrilling in her head.

"Reilly's thorough," she began. "He has the undercover op we start tomorrow night totally mapped out. He insisted we go over the concept today at least five times. We'll do that again tomorrow. I doubt the man leaves anything to chance."

"Neither does the Avenger," Scott murmured. "How

did he react when Gaines delivered the message about the Tulsa murder?''

Carrie paused, considered things. The instant Gaines walked in, she had felt the weight of tension in the room. She sensed Linc stiffen; Gaines had stood as rigid as a flagpole. Some sort of conflict existed between the men, she was sure. Since she had no idea what had caused it, she decided to keep the observation to herself for the time being.

''Reilly didn't outwardly react when Gaines told him about the murder,'' Carrie responded. ''I tried to get him talking about it after Gaines left. He wouldn't. If Reilly's the Avenger, he won't be tripped up. And the last thing he'll ever do is confess. The only way to nail him is to catch him in the act.''

''That's why you're assigned to work with him. Get close to him.''

''I'll only get so close,'' Carrie blurted.

Scott studied her while silence stretched. ''If you're informing me you won't sleep with Sergeant Reilly, I never intended for you to,'' she finally said.

''Just wanted to make that clear.'' Carrie pressed her lips together. She *knew* sleeping with Reilly wasn't in her job description. So where the hell had her comment come from?

''Glad that's settled.'' Scott opened the armrest between the seats, pulled out a small metal box and handed it to Carrie.

In the weak beam from a far-off light, Carrie saw the brand name of a well-known throat lozenge printed across its top. ''You think I have a sore throat?''

Scott smiled. ''That's what someone will think if they spot that in your purse. There's clay inside to make impressions of keys. You get Reilly's house key, press both sides of it into the clay.''

Carrie stared at the box. "Once I get the impression, how do I get the key made?"

"Bring the box to me. I know a vice officer who has a connection who will make the key overnight. Discreetly."

"Are you sure my going into Reilly's house is legal?"

"This makes it legal," Scott said, handing her an envelope. "It's a covert entry warrant for your search. It authorizes you to hunt for certain evidence. If you find anything linking Reilly to the murders, photograph it, then leave. Write a report detailing what you saw and where it's located."

"What about notice? Doesn't Reilly have to be notified that a search has occurred?"

"For this type of warrant, the courts have a procedure for delaying notification up to seven days after the search."

Carrie closed her eyes. "I don't like the idea of going into another cop's house. What if Reilly isn't the Avenger?"

"What if he is? At some point an innocent person is going to get hurt. We've got to find the Avenger, McCall. If it isn't Reilly, fine, but we have to *know*."

Carrie's cop brain told her what she was doing was right. Still, in her heart she felt a tug of guilt, a ripple of unease.

"Reilly's house is alarmed," Scott continued. "We could send in a guy to disable it and do the search, but there's a chance Reilly has some fail-safe measure to alert him if someone screws with the system. Plus, he lives in an older housing addition so neighbors are home during the day. Some guy messing around outside the house will get noticed."

"I can't exactly ask Reilly his alarm code."

"True." Scott reached into the pocket of her coat. "If

you wind up at his place and he has to enter the alarm code, use this.''

Carrie studied the small recorder Scott handed her. ''How do I get his code with a tape recorder?''

''That's a high-power recorder. Keep it in your pocket and activate it when Reilly enters his alarm code. The recorder will pick up the tones. One of the department's tech guru's will translate the beeps into the code.''

''Slick,'' Carrie murmured.

''Once you have the key and the code, you drop by Reilly's house when you know he's tied up somewhere else. If you find anything that connects him to these homicides, we take him down. End of story.''

''Just like that.''

A few moments later Carrie slid back into her MG. She started the engine, let it idle while the taillights of Scott's black van disappeared into the night.

Instead of driving away, Carrie shifted her thoughts back to that afternoon. She wished she hadn't seen the flash of grief in Linc's eyes when she mentioned his wife. The man who had kidnapped her, then raped her over a span of days before killing her was still free. A man who was as evil as seven others who no longer presented a threat to innocent citizens.

Carrie figured half the people in the city would cheer the Avenger if they knew he had prevented hundreds of violent crimes. Saved the lives of uncountable decent people. Hell, a part of her cheered him!

She clenched her gloved fingers around the steering wheel. No, she thought. She carried a badge, she wasn't allowed to think like that. Murder was murder.

She'd been ordered to take down a killer. That's what she intended to do. If Linc Reilly was that killer, so be it.

Chapter 3

The following evening, Linc watched his new partner slide into the passenger seat of the hunter-green SUV he'd checked out from OCPD's asset forfeiture inventory. Firing up the engine, he noted with relief she'd forgone her come-and-get-me perfume for their first visit to The Hideaway. All he could smell on the crisp November air was the aroma of soap and skin.

A half hour later, he decided the warm, natural scent of woman that slid around him—*into him*—was far more enticing than anything bottled. Damn near erotic, he amended as he whipped the SUV into The Hideaway's parking lot, gravel crunching beneath its wheels.

"What is it about macho guys and pickup trucks?" Carrie asked while scanning the vehicles crowding the lot. "Clue me in, Reilly. Do guys believe that driving a pickup enhances testosterone production?"

Linc took a measured breath, which failed dismally at easing the tightness in his gut. "The macho drug dealer who owned this SUV must not have thought so.'' He killed the powerful engine, then gazed out the windshield through the frozen twilight. In the yellowish glow of the sodium-vapor lights that illuminated the lot, he counted about ten pickup trucks to every car. ''Neither do I,'' he added. ''My personal vehicle is a Cadillac Allanté.''

''Cops don't count,'' she said, flicking down her visor and popping open the cover of the vanity mirror. She fluffed her dense, wild hair, the mirror's bright light enhancing the gold and fiery-red accents. Studying her, Linc noted she'd used a heavy hand tonight when applying her makeup. Instead of giving her a cheap look, however, the smoky eyeshadow, dark liner and emergency-exit-red lipstick enhanced the smoldering, alluring mystique she must have been born with.

He scowled, annoyed he felt a glimmer of curiosity over her last comment. ''Why doesn't the kind of vehicle a cop drives count?''

''They're armed. On the macho scale, a cop packing a gun is equal to some redneck civilian driving a pickup truck.''

''McCall, that has got to be the biggest pile of…''

Linc let his voice trail off when a going-to-rust blue Chevy rumbled into the slot on the SUV's passenger side. Seconds later a burly man with dark hair pulled back in a ponytail climbed out of the Chevy. Shoulders hunkered beneath his denim jacket against the cold, he lumbered toward the bar's entrance.

''Recognize him from the mug shots you studied?'' he asked.

''Howard Klinger. a.k.a. Howie Kling.'' Carrie snapped off the mirror. ''He has priors for larceny. Was once nabbed on a residential burglary charge, which got reduced to possession of stolen property.''

''Good memory, McCall.''

''Comes from all those years riding patrol. You have to keep track of the baddies and what they're up to.''

''Yeah.'' Linc also possessed a cop's honed memory. One that enabled him to picture in detail the portion of a snake tattoo captured two years ago on a grainy surveillance tape. He was haunted by the possibility that the tattoo had been one of the last things his wife had seen. Most nights he jerked awake in a cold sweat, half expecting to see the dark, slippery tail of the snake slithering beneath the closet door. Recently, a snitch had seen a pool player at The Hideaway with a similar tattoo. If Linc didn't spot Kim's killer on this visit, the assignment he'd engineered for himself gave him the luxury of spending as many nights at the bar as necessary until the bastard showed.

''Where'd you go, Reilly?''

He slicked his gaze across the SUV's front seat. Carrie sat unmoving, studying him with the open scrutiny of a cop.

''Just running over the details of this assignment one last time,'' he stated. ''Ready to get started?''

''Ready.'' Leaning, she nudged her purse under the seat. ''So I don't have to keep track of it all night,'' she explained.

''Where's your gun?''

''Inside my left boot.''

He looked down, saw she had on black leather boots with low, spiky heels. ''No cowboy boots for you, McCall?''

''I put a lot of thought into image, and decided to go with my own unique look. Since our undercover personas have money to burn and no jobs, I opted for a mix. Jeans and silk. Toss in a little faux fur.'' She shook back her hair. ''What's the verdict, Reilly? Like the combination?''

His gaze moved down her short, mink-look fur jacket to the black jeans that molded her trim butt and slim legs.

"The look works for me," he answered calmly, even as his blood stirred. "What are you packing in your boot?"

"A .25 baby Browning. How about you?"

He shifted his left leg, felt the reassuring hardness of the automatic secured in the leather insert he'd had sewn inside the top of his left boot. "Brought my .380 Sig. Let's go."

What had been on Reilly's mind? Carrie mused as she slid out of the SUV into the dark, cold air. She doubted it had been their assignment as he'd claimed. She could think of nothing about a covert bar investigation that would set his mouth in such a grim line and transform those yellow-gold eyes into hard, cold chunks of amber.

Her thoughts scattered the instant Linc settled an arm around her waist and nudged her against his side. When her shoulders did an instinctive jerk, he glanced down.

"We're hot for each other, remember?" he asked while bass rhythm coming from the bar thumped on the night air.

"Right."

His arm tightened on her waist. "You need to get used to this."

"No problem." Despite the layers of clothing they both wore, she was aware of the strength in his arm, of the hardness of his thigh against her hip. The faint, spicy fragrance of his aftershave made her insides clench. She gave silent thanks he didn't know about the little flips going on in her stomach.

Flips that had no business being there, she told herself. It wasn't like he was someone she could consider jumping into a relationship with. The man had maybe murdered seven people. Even if he turned out to be as innocent as a virgin, he was a co-worker. Her *partner*. She'd learned the hard way the pitfalls of getting romantically involved with another cop.

She swallowed around a knot of tension as she and Linc crunched their way across gravel through the sea of vehicles. To get her mind off her flipping stomach, she focused on the structure coming into view.

Linc had mentioned The Hideaway's management had set up shop in a vacant farmhouse. The place hadn't totally lost the look, Carrie judged when they advanced up the steep steps leading to an old-fashioned wraparound porch. She checked both ends, half expecting to see a wooden swing hanging from ceiling hooks.

"Want to bet about a zillion drunks have toppled down those narrow steps?" Linc asked.

"I'll pass." The weathered boards beneath her feet vibrated with music. "You'd rake in all the chips on that one."

"I know." Grinning, he raised a shoulder beneath his scarred bomber jacket. "I only wager on sure things."

A red glow from the neon beer signs hanging in the front windows angled across his face, highlighting day-old stubble. In the crimson light he looked sexy, rugged and a little ruthless.

The flips in Carrie's stomach transformed into somersaults. Why did the cop she'd been ordered to investigate have to be the type of man who lured her like a moth to a blowtorch?

When Linc pulled the door open, a wall of sound and a cloud of smoke hit them. "After you," he said over the noise.

Inside, a bouncer with huge biceps looked them up and down. A red bandana topped his shoulder-length blond hair; he wore black pants and a sweatshirt with the sleeves razored off. Carrie pictured him lying on a weight bench, straining beneath a barbell loaded with iron plates the size of tractor tires.

"No cover charge for chicks," the bouncer said over

the racket of pool games, loud talk and a country tune crooning from the jukebox. He nodded toward Linc. ''Men pay twenty bucks.''

''Sure thing.'' Linc tugged the department-supplied flash roll from the front pocket of his snug Levi's.

Stepping away, Carrie slid off the faux-mink jacket she'd picked up that morning in a trendy consignment shop. Through the smoke-laden air she noted the glint in the bouncer's eyes when Linc peeled a twenty off the thick layer of bills.

''You charge all male customers to get in?'' Linc asked.

''Not the regulars.''

''How many visits do I have to make before I'm a regular?''

The bouncer's mouth curved, more sneer than smile. ''I'll let you know.''

''First rip-off of the night,'' Linc murmured when he joined Carrie.

''Get the feeling the Incredible Hulk runs the complaint department?'' she asked. ''Grouse about something, and see how fast he pounds you into dust.''

''I'll try to avoid that.'' Wrapping his hand around hers, Linc threaded a path for them through a maze of occupied tables.

His touch reactivated the somersaults in her stomach. *Get real, McCall,* she told herself, and shifted her attention to her surroundings.

As Linc's sketch had shown, the long, polished bar spanned one entire wall, booths another. Tables filled the rest of the main room, surrounding a spacious dance floor, presently packed with couples waltzing to the country tune oozing from the jukebox. Through an archway Carrie glimpsed several pool tables, each with a rectangular light fixture suspended above it. Beyond the pool tables was a wall dotted with closed doors. Linc's snitch had said those were the small rooms where The Hideaway's working girls entertained clients.

Just as they reached the far end of the crowded bar, two men slid off their stools and tossed bills beside their empty glasses. Carrie draped her jacket across the back of one stool while Linc did the same to the one beside it. The location afforded them a view of both rooms. She noted Linc doing a slow survey of the men gathered around each pool table.

"What'llitbe?" The bartender wearing a T-shirt with a beer company logo barely glanced at them while he filled a pitcher from a beer tap. A jagged scar ran through his lower lip halfway to the tip of his stubbled jaw.

Looking back, Linc settled his hand on Carrie's thigh. "Want your usual?"

She could swear she felt the heat of each of his fingers seep through her jeans. "Not when the evening's still young." Even to her own ears her voice sounded low and throaty. "I'll start with something tame."

Linc tucked a finger under her chin and gave her a slow smile that had her throat clicking shut. "Babe, so far I haven't found one tame thing about you."

While Carrie struggled to breathe, he ordered a diet soda and a beer. It's an act, she reminded herself.

When the bartender placed their orders in front of them, Linc peeled a twenty off the roll of bills and tossed it onto the bar. "Keep the change," he said.

"Thanks." Interested now, the man slicked them another look. "New in town?"

"I just moved here last week," Linc said, and dipped his head toward Carrie. "Same goes for her. I'm staying at the Drop Inn. The night clerk said I'd find good food here."

"Hamburgers are great. The five-alarm chili will set you on fire."

"And some action."

The bartender grabbed a whiskey bottle from in front of the dingy mirror that ran the length of the bar. "What sort?"

Smiling, Carrie leaned in. "What's your name, handsome?" She already knew the answer. The jagged scar on his lower lip had still been raw in the mug shot she'd studied.

"Zack." He filled one glass with whiskey, then another.

Aitken. She mentally added his last name while reviewing the misdemeanor gambling arrests on his record. "Well, Zack, I'm Carrie. My friend, Linc, and I are looking for all sorts of action." She gave him a wink. "What do you recommend?"

Zack glanced toward the opposite end of the bar where customers were feeding coins into several tabletop video games. "We've got video poker. Pool. And lots of friendly folks."

Linc sipped his beer. "If I want to play video games, I'll go to an arcade."

Zack gave them another once-over. Carrie knew she and Linc wouldn't get an invitation to participate in illegal activities until they'd been checked out. She'd wager the Drop Inn's night clerk would soon receive a call about Linc.

"You folks keep dropping by," the bartender said. "You might find more interesting stuff to do down the line."

"Fair enough," Linc said, then turned to Carrie. "Want to play pool?"

"You go ahead." Their plan was to split up part of the time during each visit and try to spot as much illegal activity as possible. "I'll try the video poker Zack suggested," she added. By law, Oklahoma did not allow games of chance that paid off in cash winnings. Gaming machines were legal only if the players racked up points that netted additional free games. Raising a shoulder, she glanced at the dance floor. "If I get bored with poker, I bet I can find some cowboy to give me a whirl."

Easing in, Linc curled a hand around the side of her throat while his eyes locked with hers. "When you find that cowboy, babe, make damn sure he understands you're mine."

Her mouth went dry while arousal twined through her belly. The spicy scent of his aftershave was like a drug pumping into her system, spiking her pulse. For a mindless instant she wondered what it would be like to have his hands slicking over her bare flesh, to feel those perfect, white teeth scraping down her throat.

Her throat in which her pulse currently thrummed against his palm. The knowledge he could feel her response to him snapped sanity back into place. What was she doing? What in heaven's name was she doing? She was a cop, on the job. *He* was her job.

With an alarm blaring in her head, her instinct was to jerk away from his touch, his scent. Since doing so might blow their cover, she eased back until his hand slid from her throat.

Linc said nothing, only watched her with his fascinating gold-brown eyes that had desire thickening around her like a spider's web.

Carrie forced both a smile and an evenness into her voice. "I just had a thought."

"What?"

"I'll want to freshen up after I dance." She held out her hand. "Why don't you give me the key to the SUV so I can get my purse?"

"I'll get it for you."

"Sugar, I don't want to have to keep track of it now,"

she countered, keeping her hand out. "I'll just slip outside when I'm ready."

He pulled his jacket off the back of the stool, dug in the pocket for the key. "If you're sure," he said, dropping it into her palm.

"I'm sure." She wrapped her fingers around the key. The ring held only the key to the vehicle, but she had seen Linc toss the key ring he usually carried into the glove box. That ring surely held his house key. Once he was immersed in his pool game, she would slip outside and make a clay impression.

He rose off the stool. "See you, babe."

"Count on it, sugar."

"Wanna 'nother game?" the heavyset biker with a Fu Manchu mustache asked while handing Linc a crumpled twenty-dollar bill.

"Some other night," Linc said over the sound of billiard balls smacking together. He had spent the past hour playing pool while covertly checking men's hairy forearms. He'd seen an uncountable number of tattoos, but none that resembled the coiled tail of a snake. His two-year search for Kim's killer had led him to The Hideaway, but he'd known it would have been too much to ask to spot the bastard his first night there.

After replacing his cue in the holder bracketed to the wall, he snagged the beer he'd been nursing and strode toward the archway. He was vaguely surprised at the impatience burning through him. He'd always possessed the patience of a hunter, capable of hunkering down and waiting as long as it took to get what he wanted. That was one reason undercover work had been such a natural fit. What had changed? he wondered. Why did he feel a gnawing urgency to get the hell away from this place and not look back?

He paused when he stepped into the main room. The air was gray with cigarette smoke and seemed to shimmer with the music. Narrowing his eyes, he did a slow reconnaissance of the packed dance floor. Seconds later he caught a flash of fiery hair in the pulsating mass of bodies.

Earlier, he'd felt the softness of that auburn mane when he pressed his palm against Carrie's throat. He'd been tempted to grab a handful of thick, silky fire, tug her chin back…

Then do what? he asked himself. See what it took to get her pulse beating harder than it already had been? He scrubbed a hand over his stubbled jaw. The spike in her heartbeat didn't necessarily mean she felt an attraction to him. This was her first undercover assignment, her nerves had to be working overtime. His weren't, though. Attraction was exactly what he'd felt with his hand on her throat, his mouth inches from hers while he breathed in the scent of soap and woman.

Dammit! He didn't welcome the attraction, had no intention of acting on it. He needed to concentrate on finding Kim's killer. Period. Problem was, he couldn't get his mind off the possibility his one-time best friend—or maybe someone else—had decided to make him the fall guy for seven murders!

Sipping his beer, Linc scrolled his thoughts back to that afternoon. After calling the Tulsa homicide cop, he had gone to see his boss. He'd laid out everything for Lieutenant Quintana—from the pattern that all seven dead men had SEU files to the fact that *he* had spent the weekend in close proximity to the Tulsa murder. Grim-faced, Quintana seemed convinced Linc had nothing to do with the killings, and indicated he would start the matter up the chain of command. His boss's reaction somewhat eased Linc's mind. Still, he had to keep up his guard in case he'd been targeted for a frame. With so much on his plate, he did not need the added complication of dealing with a new partner. Especially one who made his system churn.

A young cowboy swirled Carrie into view just as the song ended. The noise level dropped so fast it was almost like turning deaf. Linc saw the man whisper something in her ear; Carrie tipped her head back and laughed.

Linc set his beer aside and moved their way, not at all surprised she'd found a dance partner. Reaching her, he slid his arm around her waist, then turned his attention to the cowboy. He was in his early twenties, of medium height, broad shoulders, narrow hips, dressed in jeans and a denim work shirt, its sleeves shoved up on well-developed forearms.

"Time for me to claim my lady," Linc said, and caught the flash of disappointment in the man's eyes.

The cowboy shifted his gaze back to Carrie. "It was my pleasure, red."

"And mine." She offered her hand. "You take care, West."

"Will do." He gave her a smile with a dose of low-voltage charm. "Hope to see you around here again."

"Count on it."

Linc watched the cowboy melt into the crowd, then looked at Carrie. She had pulled her hair up with one hand and was fanning her bare neck with the other. The color was high in her cheeks, her hair damp at the temples.

She looked like she'd just engaged in a bout of hot sex and might be willing to jump back into bed for more.

The image had him grinding his teeth. "Looks like that cowboy is a real admirer of yours, *red*."

"His name is West Williams," she said, her voice a low whisper. "I don't remember seeing information on him in our files. Do you?"

"No. Think he has a record?"

"My instincts tell me he's a good guy, but I'll run him."

She settled a hand on his arm. "We should dance. Over by the jukebox. There's something going on with one of the booths. I can't figure out what it is."

"All right."

The jukebox sparked back to life with a husky-voiced country singer torching a love song. Linc slipped his arms around Carrie, thinking he would have preferred a rowdy tune that required little touching. Trying to ignore the way her body meshed with his, he guided her over the wooden floor with smooth, intricate steps.

"You're a good dancer," she said against his ear.

"I figured you were waiting for me to step on your toes."

She angled her head back to look up at him. Her mouth was red and wet and curved in genuine puzzlement. "What brought that on?"

Without thinking, he tangled his fingers with the tips of her hair. It was a shame, a damn shame, he thought, that she felt so incredibly good in his arms. "Could be the way your nails are digging into my shoulder."

"Oh." Her hand flexed open. "Sorry."

"It's just a flesh wound." They reached the side of the dance floor closest to the long row of booths, most of them occupied. Linc bent his head so that his cheek brushed hers, his mouth close to her ear. Heat pulsed off her flesh and he wondered if her skin tasted as creamy as it smelled. "What am I looking for?" he asked.

"Check out the booth in the corner," she said, swaying with him. "The one with the reserved sign on it."

The slow song melted away into another with a quicker tempo. Linc splayed his fingers against her back and continued moving in the same steady rhythm while he watched the booth. Minutes later he said, "I've seen two men and one woman slide into the booth at separate times. Each sits there for a short time, then leaves."

Carrie nodded, the light from the jukebox touching her cheek with gold. "While I've been dancing, I've counted a dozen people do the same thing," she whispered. "A waitress never comes by to see if they want to order anything." She shrugged. "Any guess about what's going on?"

"Not yet." When the song ended, he drew away, but kept her hand in his. "How about we try out the booth?"

"You're reading my mind."

She slid in first, he followed. "It's too dark to see much," she said seconds later. Against his side, Linc felt her body shift while she patted her hand against the wall. "All I feel is some sort of padded piece of wood," she said.

"What size is it?"

"About the dimensions of a chair arm."

"Does it move?"

"Can't get it to budge." Carrie met his gaze. "Those people wouldn't have sat here and then left without a reason. They had to have picked up something. Or left something. Maybe both. There's no other explanation."

"Drugs and cash, maybe." Linc swept his gaze upward, spotted a camera, its lens aimed at them. "We're on film," he said. "Let's go outside and look at the other side of that wall. Maybe we can spot some sort of sliding panel."

"Good idea."

Linc smiled when a rail-thin waitress wearing tight jeans and a white T-shirt scurried toward the booth. "Two beers—"

She cut him off with a shake of her head. "I'll be happy to serve you at another table." She patted the small sign at the table's edge. "This one's reserved."

"Sorry," Linc said, rising. "Didn't notice."

"No harm done." She ran a damp rag over the tabletop. "You folks find another spot and I'll bring those beers."

Carrie slid out of the booth. "Listen, sugar, all that dancing just caught up with me. How about passing on those beers and taking me home?"

"Sure, babe." He slipped the waitress a few dollars, telling her they'd be back the next night.

Minutes later they were outside, following the beam of Linc's small penlight while they crept toward the rear of The Hideaway.

He didn't care that the air was as cold as a morgue fridge. In retrospect, it was far preferable to the heat that had surged through him while Carrie swayed in his arms. If he hadn't felt a gnawing curiosity about what the deal was with the back booth, he would have made up some excuse to halt their dancing a lot sooner.

As it was, he planned to take a long, cold shower when he got to his room at the Drop Inn.

"See anything?" His words were almost soundless as he swept the penlight's beam over the rear corner of the building.

"Nothing." Carrie's breath made tiny puffs of steam on the cold air. Narrowing her eyes, she stepped in for a closer look.

Holding the beam steady, Linc glanced sideways. Bare bulbs dangling from ancient fixtures affixed to the roof's eaves illuminated the rear of the old house. The bulbs tossed shadows in every direction along the graveled access that ran the length of the structure. A few feet from where he and Carrie stood was a back door and wooden porch with several steps leading down from it. A Dumpster sat angled to one side of the porch. Beyond the Dumpster, another bare bulb illuminated a weathered, storm-cellar-type door that butted against the building's foundation. Door to the basement, Linc surmised. The shiny hinge and padlock securing the door glinted beneath the light.

Linc shifted his gaze back to Carrie. As if searching for

the trigger of a secret panel, she used her gloved fingers to prod the building's rough-planked exterior. "None of the waitresses even looked at any of the people I spotted in that booth while I was dancing," she whispered. "Then you and I plop down, and a waitress is on us like white on rice. Something's definitely going on with that booth."

"Yeah, I—"

Hearing a faint creak, Linc froze. In his peripheral vision he saw the back door swing open.

He shot Carrie a look to make sure she'd heard. Standing motionless, she watched the door with eyes as sharp as broken glass.

Adrenaline charging his system, Linc clicked off the penlight. A half second later, the bouncer stepped into view. His muscled arms looked rock hard as he stood in the pool of light illuminating the small porch. With one thick-fingered hand wrapped around the porch rail, he turned his head, his gaze conducting a slow sweep of the area.

Although pockets of shadows engulfed the corner of the building, Linc saw nothing that would provide cover. If he and Carrie tried to sneak away, their footsteps would sound like crunching echoes on the gravel lot.

He knew only seconds remained before the bouncer turned his gaze in their direction. Knew, too, only one explanation for his and Carrie being there would keep their cover intact.

Linc locked a hand on her wrist and jerked her against him.

"Play this out," he ordered in a low, urgent murmur then crushed his mouth down on hers.

Chapter 4

Holy cow, was all Carrie could think as bolts of sensation shot through her body.

In the part of her brain that still functioned, she accepted that Linc's wrenching her into his arms and crushing his mouth down on hers had been the sole way to keep their cover intact when the bouncer stepped out of The Hideaway's back door. But, holy heaven, her comprehending Linc's motive hadn't stopped her pulse from spiking, her knees from going weak and something hot erupting inside her.

Automatically her gloved hands came up to his shoulders and locked tight. Her pulse thundered in her ears. It was all she could do not to hum with pleasure as his mouth moved against hers, hot, hungry, devouring. Her defenses a mere memory, she parted her lips beneath his and savored his dark, reckless taste.

He held her so closely her breasts were flattened against his chest. The heat of his body seeped through the layers of clothing between them. She shuddered as the scent of his cologne wrapped around her, warm and masculine.

Time became elastic, stretching beyond awareness as pleasure speared inside her. Desire flowed through every cell of her body. She thought hazily she could stand there all night—the rest of her life—enveloped in his arms, wrapped in this erotic, sensual cocoon of heat.

''What the hell you doin'?''

The hulk's gruff shout jerked Carrie's head back. She dragged in a shallow, ragged breath. Her legs felt like jelly; inside her gloves, her palms were sweating. Her heart pounded so hard she could feel her pulse throbbing under her skin. Her entire body felt sensitized. No man had ever affected her like this, taken her so far with only a kiss.

''Don't lose your cool,'' Linc cautioned in an almost inaudible whisper, his breath stirring the hair at her temple.

Waaaaaaaay too late, she thought.

Keeping one arm wrapped around her shoulders, he gave the hulk a sardonic look. ''Man, what the hell does it look like we're doing?''

Beneath the porch light, the bouncer appeared a hundred times more menacing than he had while collecting their cover charge inside the bar's front door. Carrie could almost read the thoughts going on behind his hostile glare. Of course it looked like he'd stumbled over hot-to-trot lovers. With the show he'd seen, no way would he think what had been going on between her and Linc was pretense.

But how could it be pretense when they had actually been on the verge of swallowing each other?

She had been on the verge, she amended, and slowly lifted her gaze. Linc watched the bouncer, his expression cool and focused, his exotic golden eyes impassive.

He had been acting. Their kiss had rocked her to her toes, yet Linc's performance had solely been in the line of duty. The realization she had actually kissed him back sent panic wafting up her spine. She knew the emotion wasn't due to fear from the hulk, but because the pleasure that had sung along her nerves while she'd been engulfed in Linc's arms was far from safe.

Linc Reilly wasn't even in the same ballpark with safe! He was her assignment. The possible suspect in seven murders. For her own sake, she had to remember that.

Hulk's mouth curled with derision. "What it looks like is you're gettin' yourself a piece of that redhead. What I want to know is why *here?*" He surged off the porch, boots pounding down the wooden steps. "You lookin' for something back here?"

Linc's gaze sharpened on the man advancing toward them through the long fingers of shadow. Easing his gloved hand up, he settled his palm against the back of Carrie's neck. Against her side, his body felt like a solid, protective wall.

"Listen, pal," Linc began, "the lady and I were just..." He flicked Carrie a cocky look. "Talking. Right, babe?" The pressure of his fingers against her neck was the only indication Carrie had that, inwardly, he was as taut as a coiled spring.

"Talking?" She rolled her eyes. "Sugar, this big, strong man here strikes me as being too smart to fall for such a lame line." Raising her shoulders beneath her jacket, she sent the bouncer a sassy look. "You're right, handsome. We're back here in the dark because I am looking for something."

"Yeah?" His breath puffed like steam on the icy air. "Exactly what are you lookin' for?"

"A good time," she cooed, snuggling against Linc's side. "This man promised to show me one. *He* wanted to drive to the Drop Inn, but I..." Her lashes did a demure slide downward. "Well, *I* didn't want to wait so I lured him back here in the dark for a little privacy.'' She flipped a wrist. ''Hope we haven't caused you too much trouble.''

Sneering, the hulk gazed at her as if she were some hot cream puff who would start squealing if he laid a hand on her. What he didn't know was she had a Browning in her left boot and, despite his size, she could disable him with one blow to the trachea.

''Back of the bar's a restricted area,'' Hulk said finally. ''You're trespassin'. Don't let me catch you here again.''

''You won't,'' she said lightly, then sent Linc a meaningful smile. ''Sugar, now that my blood's cooled, it's way too frigid out here for my taste. I'm ready to head over to your room, if you still want.''

Tugging her head back, he poised his mouth over hers. ''Yeah, babe, I want. I want the hell out of you.''

Minutes later Carrie wondered how she'd managed to walk across the parking lot to the SUV when she felt shakier than she had after chasing down her first fleeing felon.

''Close call,'' Linc observed as he slid behind the wheel.

''Yes.'' Waiting for her nerves to level, she stared out the windshield. In the glow of the widely spaced lights, it appeared there were even more vehicles packed into the lot than when they'd arrived.

''You handled Mr. Steroid like a pro,'' Linc commented. The SUV's engine roared to life when he twisted the key.

If only she had handled her response to her partner with equal skill, Carrie thought. Mortification balled in her stomach at the knowledge it had taken just one kiss for Linc to light her up like a Christmas tree.

She closed her eyes. He had caught her off guard, was all. Had carried pretense further than she'd been prepared to take it. Her system hadn't been ready for the sudden onslaught of sensation. She'd be ready next time.

Don't let there be a next time. As it was, just being in

the man's vicinity made her feel like a woman rushing headlong over the verge of safety into the unknown.

Shifting in his seat, Linc rested his shoulders against the driver's door. "Why so quiet, McCall?" The shaft of light angling across his face lent him a compelling, reckless look.

"Just going over all that went on tonight," she answered. "We need to get to the Drop Inn and write reports on what we observed and who we observed doing it."

"That's on the agenda." Pulling off his gloves, he shoved a hand through his dark, wind-ruffled hair. "Look, McCall, what happened back there—"

"Was the only thing we could do to keep our cover intact."

"That's right." His expression was a study in calm, as if they'd shared nothing more exciting than a drive in the country. "What happened is an example of undercover work where you don't just need a story and a reason to be somewhere, you need a *damn good* story and reason." He paused. "I just want to make sure you're okay with it."

Being human, the knowledge that her kiss had no apparent effect on him scraped her pride. "Your concern is noted, Reilly, but you can relax," she said dryly. "You're not the first man to kiss me."

"Well, there's breaking news," he said, matching her tone. He reached out an utterly steady hand and flipped on the heater fan. "Like I said, you played things right. Everything."

"Thanks." As long as Linc believed her reaction had been as big an act as his, she didn't feel so exposed. So vulnerable.

She changed the subject by nodding toward the rusting blue Chevy still parked beside the SUV. "Howard Klinger went into the bar the same time we did," she said while warm air flowed out of the dashboard's vents. "I never saw him inside. Did you?"

"No. I looked for him when we were at the bar, then after that, while I played pool. I never caught sight of him."

"Don't you think that's strange?"

"More than. An ex-con with a knack for dealing in stolen property walks into a bar then turns invisible. We need to find out what Howard Klinger, a.k.a. Howie Kling is up to."

"And where he goes to do whatever he's up to."

Linc rested a wrist over the steering wheel. "While you were searching for a panel on the bar's outside wall, I noticed a wooden staircase on the back of the building. Lights were on in a couple of rooms on the second floor. Howie could have been upstairs, doing whatever."

Carrie pursed her mouth. "Maybe the bouncer pitched such a fit because he didn't want us to see anyone using those stairs."

"Makes more sense than his being so concerned just because we were trespassing on The Hideaway's private property."

"True." She frowned. "Do you think Howie has something to do with whatever's going on in that back booth?"

"Anything's possible. We need surveillance on the booth."

"A camera?"

"That's what I'm thinking."

"Any idea how to get one in there?"

"No, but I know a cop in Vice who'll know. You ever work with Wade Crawford?"

"My sister Morgan has. I remember her saying Crawford's so smooth he could charm a nun into a hot trance."

"Well, I've definitely missed seeing that side of him." Leaning, Linc popped open the glove box.

Carrie held her breath when he nudged aside his key ring. After making the mold of his house key, she had attempted to replace the ring and the keys in the same position she'd found them. She began breathing again only after Linc retrieved his cell phone and closed the glove box's door.

He gave her a look. "If I set up a meeting with Crawford tomorrow, think you can manage to keep from falling under a hot trance?"

"I promise to control my libido." She was having enough problems doing that where her current partner was concerned.

While Linc made the call, Carrie fished her purse from under the seat. Beneath her fingers she could feel the outline of the small metal box that held the clay imprint of Linc's house key.

"Crawford's tied up most of tomorrow," Linc said after ending the call. "The earliest he can get with us is around seven tomorrow night." As he spoke, Linc put the SUV into gear. "He's installing cameras at a place not too far from my house, so that's where we'll meet. Okay with you?"

"Sure." Carrie tightened her fingers on her purse. If she played things right, tomorrow night might be her chance to get the code to Linc's alarm system.

He gave her the address, then added, "Once we're done with Crawford, you and I will head back here for our second night of fun."

Carrie fastened her seat belt. "When did the lieutenant over in asset forfeiture say he'd have my car ready?"

"Why?" Linc flicked her a look as he steered toward the lot's exit. "You don't like the way I drive?"

"Now that you mention it, you could use remedial training," she tossed back. If they had driven separately tonight, she would be driving to the Drop Inn alone. *Away from him.* Which would give her system time to settle.

"But I asked because your ops plan calls for each of us to have a vehicle," she explained. "If I don't always show up at the bar at the same time as you, the working girls will be more apt to hang around you. Even if you turn down a proposition for sex, a couple of bills will buy you some of their time. Might be a way to find out about what's going on behind the scenes."

"Glad you remember my plan, McCall."

"What about my vehicle?"

"Asset Forfeiture just took possession of a classic red-and-white Corvette." His mouth curved. "I figured you'd look at home in a car like that, so I put your name on it. You can pick it up tomorrow. That okay with you?"

"Peachy," Carrie said. She would drive a garbage truck if it gave her some distance from the man.

The following night Linc had just dumped a handful of kibble into the bowl on the kitchen floor when the doorbell rang.

"*Bon appétit*, fuzz face," he muttered to the Siamese that had spent the past five minutes weaving around his ankles. Hunger was the only reason the damn cat got near him.

Wiping his hands on the dish towel he'd slung over one shoulder, he swung open the front door. And faced the woman who had robbed him of sleep throughout the previous night.

Thoughts of her had, anyway.

This evening Carrie wore the fake mink jacket over a black turtleneck sweater and a red leather skirt that showed ample creamy thigh. She'd bundled her hair up into a disheveled twist; in the porch light, it glowed the color of flames. Subtle hues of smoke and teal emphasized her blue eyes, making them seem huge as she gazed coolly up at him.

"It's freezing out here," she said, her low, throaty voice a smoky puff on the night air. "You going to invite me in?"

"Yeah." When he swung the door wide open, he glanced out at the driveway. The Corvette looked like a sleek bullet beneath the light over the garage door. "Enjoying the car?"

"Drives like a dream." She slid out of her jacket. "Since it's the only vehicle in the driveway, I take it Wade Crawford isn't here?"

"He called." When Linc stepped closer to take her jacket, he got a whiff of her straight-to-the-glands perfume. Great, he thought. Just great.

Squaring his shoulders, he moved a few feet into the dark-paneled living room. He draped the mink across the back of the deep-cushioned wing chair where he'd left his own scarred bomber jacket. "Crawford's running a few minutes late. I've got everything he'll need on The Hideaway laid out on the coffee table in here."

Carrie's gaze swept over the leather volumes crammed into the bookshelves on both sides of the brick fireplace, the twin hunter-green leather couches that faced each other from either side of a coral area rug.

Her intense study of her surroundings gave Linc the opportunity to skim his gaze down her back, her tight rear, her legs that a man might picture in his dreams. If only he'd managed to get any sleep last night, he damn well might have pictured them in his own. As it was, he had lain awake in his ratty room at the Drop Inn, telling himself his blood-churning response to their kiss had been a matter of simple, unbridled lust. A man wanting a woman. Nothing complicated, and sure as hell nothing emotional.

Carrie McCall had stirred him up, and his body had responded. Big-time.

He was only human, after all. She'd stood in his arms trembling, her body sending erotic shudders against his that had shot need straight to his loins. And when her lips parted beneath his… How the hell could he have *not* responded?

"You have good taste, Reilly," she said. Her fingertips swept over the plaid throw that draped the back of the couch nearest her. "Very good taste."

"My wife gets the credit. It was her house when we got married. I just moved in."

Carrie gazed back at him, her expression straightforward with no hint of pity. "She had a knack for decorating."

"That's what she did for a living. She was a decorator. A damn good one."

"In the McCall family, my sister Grace got all the interior design skills. After her husband died, she sold their place and moved in with Morgan and me. Our house feels like a warm, comfortable nest now, and it's all Grace's doing."

Making no comment, Linc jammed his thumbs into the front pockets of his jeans. Everyone handled the death of a spouse differently. *He* had stayed in this house with the damn cat Kim had doted on because it was a way to hold on to his wife. Still, he couldn't take some of the memories. He'd had to close off the entire second story because just walking up the staircase and stepping into the bedroom he and Kim had shared had been like plunging a knife into his chest, over and over. For the past two years he'd slept on the couch in the downstairs study, living in a handful of rooms like a monk, trying to empty the guilt and anguish that came with having Kimberly's blood on his hands.

And now here he stood, looking at the woman who, in one erotic sweep, had stirred him back to life.

He hadn't given a second thought to setting up the meeting here with Wade Crawford. It had just been a matter of logistics. That was before he'd spent the night plagued by thoughts of Carrie McCall; before he'd thought about what it would feel like watching her in the home he'd shared with Kim. Before he'd realized what it might be like to have every breath he took filled with Carrie's seductive scent.

He fisted his hands. Feeling attracted to another woman was not what he wanted. What he wanted was to continue channeling his time and energy into hunting down the tattooed bastard who'd kidnapped, raped and murdered his wife. Then there was his concern over the possibility someone had decided to frame him for seven murders. He had a damn full plate without adding his unwanted feelings for his new partner to the mix.

When Carrie moved to one of the bookshelves, her heels clicked against the dark-oak floor. Linc's gaze snagged on her bare toes that peeked out from under the red leather tops of a pair of backless slides. He scowled. "You plan on dancing in those shoes?"

She looked over her shoulder. "I have before."

"McCall, I want you armed whenever you're at The Hideaway."

She turned, her eyes locked on his. "I am armed."

He slicked his gaze down her snug turtleneck, the red leather skirt. "Garter holster?" he asked, doing his best not to picture where against her creamy thigh the holster nestled.

"Good guess." She moved across the room to where he stood. "Did you cook tonight?"

"Why, do you smell smoke?"

Her answering laugh slid beneath his skin like quicksilver. "No." She flicked a finger against the kitchen towel draped over his shoulder. "You look domestic, is all."

"I fed the cat," he said, pulling the towel off his shoulder. "Dumping food into a bowl is about the extent of my culinary skills. How about you?"

"I barely even know my way to the kitchen. Morgan's the cook in our family. To her, following the instructions in a gourmet recipe is child's play."

He lifted a brow. "Grace decorates. Morgan cooks. What's your speciality?"

She tossed her hair back. "I've always seemed to have a way with men."

"Another newsflash," Linc said just as the doorbell rang. He lobbed the towel onto a chair on his way to the hallway. He answered the door and motioned Wade Crawford inside.

As if giving credence to Carrie's comment about her speciality, the Vice cop zeroed in on her with a blinding grin.

"Don' know why you and I have never worked together," Crawford commented while his hand engulfed Carrie's. The man was in his early thirties, tall, lean and lanky. He wore jeans and a gray hooded sweatshirt, and his long, coal-black hair was lashed back with a leather thong. His slow, deep drawl bespoke his Louisiana heritage.

Linc noted Crawford kept his hand wrapped around Carrie's while his gaze took her in, head-to-toe, in obvious appreciation. Yeah, Linc thought darkly. She sure as hell had a way with men.

Carrie returned Crawford's smile. "You worked with my sister Morgan a couple of months ago."

"Right, she and Alex Blade were undercover together. I heard she got hurt on that job. How's she doin'?"

"Fine, she's working swing shift in Patrol now. And she and Alex just announced their engagement."

"Not a surprise. Before I snapped to how things were between them, I told Blade I was hopin' to spend time with Morgan. He about ripped a hole in my throat."

"There's true love for you," Carrie murmured.

"Yeah." Crawford dipped his head. "Thing is, I'm more into 'seize the moment and have a good time.' How about you?"

A surge of emotion—feeling dangerously territorial— had Linc taking a step forward. "How about you both put a lid on your libidos before you go into some sort of trance?" he asked, shooting Carrie a pointed look. And because he didn't care to give credence to the emotion scraping at him, he added, "At least until after we take care of business."

Carrie gave him a smooth smile. "Sure thing." She slid off her shoes and curled into one corner of the nearest couch.

Fifteen minutes later Linc finished briefing Crawford on The Hideaway investigation.

The Vice cop leaned to study the floor plan spread on the coffee table between the couches. "So, you and McCall settle in the back booth," he mused. "In less than a minute a waitress is on you like a heat-seeking missile, shooing you away."

"Exactly," Linc said. "McCall and I figure the booth is used as a drop-off and pickup point for illegal property. Probably drugs. We need to figure out how the system works."

Linc shifted his gaze to Carrie. The Siamese was now curled on her lap, its face tucked into its tail. "Can you think of anything about The Hideaway I left out?"

"No," she said, then looked at Crawford. "There's a sense that plenty of stuff is going on behind the scenes.

It'll take time before Linc and I are privy to what all that is.''

All business now, Crawford nodded. "So, let's figure out how we can get some of that stuff on tape." Using a pen, he pointed to a spot on the drawing. "This is the booth you're talking about, right?"

Linc shifted beside him to get a better view. "Yes."

The pen's tip moved. "And this is the jukebox?"

"Correct."

"Any idea what brand it is?"

"Don't have a clue," Linc said. "Do you, McCall?"

"No. I can check while we're there tonight."

"That'd be good," Crawford said. "The juke sits at a good angle for a camera to get shots of activity in the booth."

Stroking a hand along the cat's back, Carrie raised a brow. "You thinking about planting a camera on the jukebox?"

"*Inside* it," Crawford said. "Call me with the brand of the juke and I'll get the schematics. There'll also be a service sticker somewhere on the jukebox. You see them stuck on all sort of vending machines—For Service, Call This Number. I need the repair company's name and phone number, too."

"Then what?" Linc asked.

"I'll program a special coin implanted with a microchip. One of you drops the coin into the slot on the juke, and the chips makes the electronics go crazy. We'll time things so when that happens, I'll be set up in a van in The Hideaway's parking lot. When the juke goes haywire, you make noise about how it stole your money. I monitor outgoing phone calls. When the repair number gets dialed, I'll intercept the call." Crawford shrugged. "Next day I'll show up, retrieve the coin, fix the jukebox and plant a camera inside, aimed at the back booth. Piece of cake."

Carrie frowned. "Don't you need a warrant for all that?"

Crawford lifted a shoulder. "Not for the camera. The Hideaway is a business with a surveillance system already installed, so there's no expectation of privacy. No different, really, than if you walk in wearing a mini-camera hidden in a belt buckle or piece of jewelry. Intercepting the phone call is another matter that a judge will have to approve, but I don't think there'll be a problem. The department has received numerous complaints about the activities going on at The Hideaway. Some citizens are up in arms over it. The two of you sat in that booth and tried to figure out what's going on, but you got warned off. To do that again would put you and the operation in danger. We list all those facts in the paperwork we present to a friendly judge, and request permission to intercept only the one call to the jukebox repair company. I'm ninety-nine percent sure we'll get the judge's okay."

Crawford glanced at his watch. "Got to get back to the surveillance cameras on Vice's numbers racket." He rose. "That all I need to know about The Hideaway?"

Linc stood. "The bouncer looks like he can break bricks with his face."

"I'll be sure to make nice with him," Crawford said with a grin. "Don't bother seeing me out," he added before disappearing into the hallway.

When the door clicked shut, Linc looked back at Carrie. She'd risen off the couch and slid on her heels. The Siamese was awake now, gazing up at her with adoring eyes.

Linc grabbed his jacket. "That sorry fleabag won't give me the time of day unless she's hungry."

"I can't imagine what her problem is." When Carrie stroked the cat's neck, a purr that sounded like a miniature outboard motor filled the room. "I don't get it, Reilly.

How could she possibly be immune to that wild, irresistible charm of yours?''

"One of life's great mysteries," he commented as he slid on his jacket. "Let's hit The Hideaway." He lifted her jacket off the chair and held it up by its shoulders.

"Quite the gentleman," she said as she crossed to him.

"Yeah." When he slipped the jacket onto her shoulders, his right hand grazed her nape. Electricity seemed to snap through him, tightening his insides. Against his knuckles he felt her quick shiver.

He settled the jacket onto her shoulders, letting his hands rest there. With her hair swept up, he had a perfect view of the long, slender arch of her neck. Guilt knotted his gut when he found himself fighting the urge to lower his head, scrape his teeth along that silky stretch of flesh. Logically he knew he was free to feel, to move on. And though he conceded it was nothing more than pure lust jolting through his system, feeling anything for another woman added weight to the blame he carried over Kim's death. If he had been a better husband, she'd be alive today. Period. Having failed one woman so totally, he had no plan to ever move on to another.

Only when Carrie stepped forward with a jerk did he realize he still had his hands on her shoulders. After freeing herself from his touch, she turned to face him. A tiny flash of nerves sparked in her eyes.

He angled his chin. "Ready to go to work?"

She clenched her hands, unclenched them. "Yes."

"I need to turn off a couple of lights. I'll meet you at the front door."

"Fine."

She was in the entry hall, staring at the alarm panel when he rounded the corner a few seconds later. A faint line formed between her brows when she met his gaze.

"Something on your mind, McCall?"

A look crossed her face he couldn't read, a quick shadow. ''Nothing. Just anxious to get to work.'' She slid her hands into the pockets of her jacket and waited while he stabbed in the alarm's code.

Amber Grove

Amber certainly had. She'd recently read it three or four...[illegible]...and appreciated its words. She ran her fingers carefully...[illegible]...folder and slipped what he needed in the...[illegible]...

Chapter 5

Three days later, Carrie balanced a paper plate in one palm while leaning across the scarred table in the Selective Enforcement Unit's small interview room. "Linc didn't tell me today is his birthday," she commented, while plucking a fork out of a jumbled pile of plastic utensils.

"That's Reilly for you," Tom Nelson said. Leaning back in a chair, the scruffy detective popped another bite of chocolate cake into his mouth. "Doesn't like anybody making a fuss over him. Did you notice your partner's quick exit back to his desk the minute he saw the cake?"

"I caught that," Carrie said, slicing a bite off the sliver of cake she'd cut for herself. Earlier the squad's secretary, Evelyn, had lured Linc into the interview room on the pretense of needing help to hunt for a report. When he walked in and saw the squad gathered around the table laden with a cake ablaze with candles, something akin to annoyance flashed in his eyes. He'd blown out the candles, said a terse, "Thanks, guys," then returned to his desk, claiming he needed to make a phone call.

Savoring the blend of chocolate cake and strawberry icing, Carrie watched Nelson flick crumbs off his faded T-shirt. He was a slightly built man whose dark hair, beard and clothing forever looked as if he'd been caught in the eye of one of Oklahoma's infamous tornadoes. His face was plain and nondescript, yet saved from obscurity by a toothy grin.

Although her specific assignment was to find out if Linc was guilty of the seven Avenger murders, Carrie had reviewed background information on all the SEU detectives. She knew Nelson had also dealt with one of the murdered do-wrongs. Knew, too, that a few years ago the affable cop had been accused of planting evidence in the home of a suspected serial rapist. The allegation had never been proven. Still, if it were true, Carrie knew it was within the realm of possibility Nelson had jumped from setting-up career criminals to killing them.

Leaning a jeans-clad hip against the table, she decided to take advantage of her first opportunity to chat with the man.

"So, what's with Reilly?" she asked. "Does he hate turning a year older so much he can't act like he appreciates your wife baking him a cake?"

When laughter broke out on the other side of the cramped room, Carrie glanced up. Lieutenant Quintana and several detectives stood in a cluster, chatting.

Nelson glanced across his shoulder at the group, grinned, then looked back at Carrie. "Nah, Linc appreciates the effort. You can bet he'll give Susan a call to thank her for the cake. Maybe even send her flowers. He just won't talk about doing it." A crease formed between Nelson's bushy brows. "My bringing the cake was probably a bad idea."

"Why?"

"His wife's birthday is a couple of days from now."

Nelson scrubbed a hand over his face. "*Was*, I should say. I'd forgotten that until I walked in here with the cake and Evelyn reminded me. Linc and Kim always went away together for a long weekend to celebrate their birthdays. They sometimes waited and took extra days off around Thanksgiving. This is a lousy time of year for Linc."

"Wasn't she murdered on Thanksgiving Day?" Carrie asked quietly.

"That's when they found her body. Two years ago."

Carrie glanced toward the door. She could see a wedge of the squad room, caught the backwash of noise from the cops who'd returned to their desks. She wondered if Linc had retreated to his, or if he'd needed to put more space between himself and the reminder of Kim's death. Carrie could only imagine what agonizing memories the birthday cake had stirred inside him.

"You meant well," she said, meeting Nelson's gaze. "I'm sure Linc knows that."

"Yeah."

A shrill chirp filled the air. Everyone in the room glanced at the display on their own cell phone.

"Mine," Nelson said. He answered, told the caller to hold, then stood and nodded toward the remains of the cake. "Guess we just need to give Linc more time."

Nodding, Carrie watched him disappear through the door.

"It's a damn shame Kimberly Reilly didn't have more time to live."

The hard-as-quartz voice coming from just behind her had Carrie's stomach lurching. Turning, she discovered Don Gaines had moved from the group of cops at the far side of the room. The tall detective with black hair, olive skin and deep-set eyes clearly had no problem letting her know he'd eavesdropped on the end of her conversation with Tom Nelson.

Her mind scrolled back to her first day in the SEU when Gaines gave Linc the message about the Tulsa murder of the Avenger's seventh victim. Carrie had watched the men face each other while something akin to ill will sparked in the air. Now Gaines's expression was almost unnerving in its coldness. Gauging from the tone of his remark about Kimberly Reilly, Carrie wondered if Linc's wife could be the cause of that ill will.

She set her plate aside. "I'm sure everyone wishes Kim Reilly were still alive."

"Some more than others." Gaines looked down at her with grim assessment. "Are you and Reilly getting along as partners?"

"You bet." She forced a smile. "Linc's honing his pool-playing skills, and I've learned every country dance there is."

"I guess you've been hitting the dance floor together?"

"We're undercover as a couple." Carrie shrugged. "Couples dance. Why do you ask?"

"Wouldn't be the first time partners wound up getting cozy."

Her shoulders stiffened when memories of the kiss she and Linc shared flooded back, sharp and swift and hotly erotic. Then there was the scalding desire that had shot beneath her skin the night at his house when he'd helped her on with her jacket and his knuckles brushed her neck. Still, the fact she experienced a primal, physical zing whenever she got around Linc didn't mean they were "getting cozy."

She cast Gaines a cool-eyed look. "I have no idea why you made that last comment, Sergeant Gaines."

"Why don't you call me Don?"

"Why don't you stop dancing around whatever message you're trying to send me and say what you mean."

"All right. It would be a huge mistake for you to get involved with Reilly."

She kept her eyes on Gaines's while uneasiness drifted through her. "A mistake for other than the obvious reasons?"

"Yes. I'd be concerned about any woman, whether she was a cop or not, who wound up with Reilly." He crossed his arms over his chest. "It's his fault she's dead."

Carrie blinked. For an instant her mind centered on the Avenger murders, but none of the victims had been female. She shook her head. "Who?"

"Reilly's wife. Kim."

Her spine as taut as a bowstring, Carrie glanced over to see if Quintana or any of the other detectives had overhead the remark. Her sense of unease heightened when she discovered she and Gaines were the only people left in the small room. "That's a serious accusation, Sergeant Gaines."

"A true one."

"Really? I heard Mrs. Reilly went out of town alone and walked in on a gas station robbery. That the hijacker killed the clerk first, then her."

"Days later. You heard right."

"How can you justify telling me her death is Linc's fault?"

"Her family had a reunion planned in Claremore," Gaines said, referring to the town a two-hour drive north. "Reilly gave Kim his word he'd go with her, then backed out. According to the surveillance tape at the gas station, she walked in right after the bastard shot the clerk. She ran out, but he grabbed her, kidnapped her. Raped her who knows how many times. Two days later he dumped her in a ditch."

Kim's death was not Linc's fault. But Carrie had no intention of debating the point with Gaines. Instead, she wanted to find the reason for the obvious loathing he felt for Linc.

"Kimberly clearly meant a lot to you."

"We dated. She was a beautiful woman." A splinter of pain worked its way into his voice. "She deserved a hell of a lot better out of life than what she got."

You loved her, Carrie realized. "Better than a husband who promised to take her somewhere then changed his plans?"

"If Reilly had cared about her, he would have driven her to Claremore. She'd still be alive. Her death is on him."

"Do you truly think Linc didn't care about her?"

"You tell me. What do you think of a man who buries his wife in the cheapest plot at the cemetery?"

Carrie opened her mouth to comment, but couldn't find the words.

Gaines stepped closer. "I've got no agenda, Carrie. Consider yourself warned, is all. Reilly's good at telling a woman what she wants to hear. Turns out you can't trust what he says."

Just then movement in the doorway caught Carrie's eye. She turned her head and saw Linc standing there. His eyes were intent, unnervingly watchful, his expression a cop mask of studied neutrality.

Even as she gave thanks he was too far away to hear her conversation, Gaines said, "Speak of the devil."

"Hey, partner." She smiled while dread curled in her stomach. "Need me for something?"

Linc glanced at Gaines, then remet her gaze. "Wade Crawford called. He has the coin ready."

"The coin," she repeated, trying to get her thoughts to click back into place.

"The coin fitted with microchips." Moving into the room, Linc halted a few inches from her. "The one that'll screw up the jukebox at The Hideaway. I told Crawford you and I would come downstairs to his workshop. The three of us need to decide how we want to run things.''

''All right. When do we go see him?''

''Now.'' Linc gave Gaines a stony look. ''That is, if you're finished 'speaking of the devil' to my partner?''

''I'm done.'' Gaines gave Carrie a curt nod. ''Watch your back,'' he said, then turned and strode out the door.

''Linc, I—''

''We'll talk on our way downstairs.''

Minutes later Linc stepped into the stairwell behind her. ''Let's talk here.''

''All right.'' Carrie moved to one side of the landing. When the door swung shut, silence dropped around them like a stone. The stairwell was unheated and the cold air bit through her heavy sweater.

Linc leaned against the metal railing, his distinctive tawny-gold eyes locked with hers. His dark jeans and black turtleneck emphasized his grim expression. ''I've got a good idea of what Gaines laid on you,'' he said evenly. ''I'll deal with him later. For now I figure I've got some damage control to do with you.''

''Damage control?''

''We won't work out as partners if we aren't honest with each other, McCall. I don't want you to have misgivings about me.''

Her gaze slid from his while a mix of guilt and paranoia tightened her throat. Had he somehow found out she was IA, investigating him on suspicion of seven murders? Was his comment some vague innuendo meant to let her know he *knew?*

No, she thought grimly. If Linc knew, he would probably have his hands locked around her throat right now.

She moved her gaze back to him, and froze. His eyes had narrowed on her face and looked hard as granite. Fear zipped through her at the possibility he had somehow read her mind.

"Is…something wrong?"

He studied her for a clutch of seconds. "I'm waiting for you to comment on your encounter with Gaines."

"I know you weren't close enough to overhear what he told me," she pointed out. "So why do you think you know what he said?"

"I didn't have to overhear him, because he's said the same thing to my face often enough." Linc crossed his arms over his chest. "He told you Kim's death was my fault."

Carrie nodded slowly. "Yes."

"I don't talk about what happened to my wife. But you and I need to work together, so if you have questions about what Gaines told you, ask."

Carrie looked at him, incredulous. "Okay, here's my first one. Since you know Gaines is going around accusing you of causing your wife's death, why haven't you bashed in his face?"

"Because he's right. I'm at fault."

"I've heard enough about the case to know what happened. You weren't even *there*."

"That's the point. I wasn't *there*. I'd promised to take her to her family reunion and backed out."

"Ever consider that if you'd walked into that gas station with her, you might be dead, too?"

"If I had been there, that bastard wouldn't have laid a hand on her," he said, his voice toneless. "I wasn't with her, so she's dead. Blame's on me."

When Carrie remained silent, he angled his chin. "I figure you've got more questions."

She had a job to do. She couldn't afford to think of him as anything more than an assignment. Still, gazing across the stairwell's landing, she didn't just see a cop who maybe went around offing bad guys. She also saw a man whose wife had had every right to walk into a gas station without being kidnapped, raped and murdered. A man who could never accept her death as just some hard lesson of fate. So he'd placed all the guilt for what had happened at his own feet.

Carrie didn't want to admit that something about Linc was starting to call to her in far more than a physical sense. Given their situation, just the thought frightened the hell out of her.

"Questions, McCall?" he prodded.

Shoving a hand through her hair, she asked the first thing that came to mind. "Why does Gaines hate you?"

"We both dated Kim. She chose me. Before you ask, no, there wasn't anything between her and Gaines after that, although he would have liked that. When she told him she was going to marry me, he told her he'd wait for her as long as it took for her to realize what a mistake she was making."

"And when she died," Carrie theorized, "so did any chance he perceived he had with her. Which is your fault, too."

"Bingo." Linc raised a shoulder. "In college Gaines and I were best friends. Hard to imagine that now."

How far had Gaines's bitterness toward Linc taken him? Carrie wondered. All along, Kimberly Reilly's death had been thought to be the motive for her husband's suspected crime spree. Nothing Carrie had found out today changed that. But what about the Avenger himself? Had the murders been committed not by Kim's husband but her spurned lover? A lover intent on making the man she had chosen over him pay for her death?

Carrie rubbed at the center of her forehead where a headache had begun to brew. With so many thoughts whirring in her mind, she couldn't recall if Gaines had personally handled any of the Avenger's victims. Either way, Gaines had full access to all of the SEU's file.

"You okay?" Linc asked.

"A headache, is all."

"Crawford probably has aspirin in his workshop." Linc glanced down the stairwell. "Any more questions before we head to the basement?"

"Maybe." Carrie leaned a shoulder against the wall and felt the coolness of the cinder blocks seep through her sweater. "There's a scenario I'd like to lay out for you, get your opinion on."

"I'm listening."

"A male and female cop meet at a restaurant on their dinner break. After the meal, the female cop excuses herself to go use the rest room. The male cop says he'll wait outside for her. In the parking lot he stumbles on a stoned junkie boosting a car. The junkie gets off a shot before the male cop can even unholster his weapon. He's dead before he hits the ground. If his companion had been with him, could she have saved him? Is it her fault he's dead just because she took a side trip to the rest room?"

Shoving off the railing, Linc closed the space between them. "Why do you think I needed to hear about Ryan Fox's murder?" he asked softly.

"Because my sister went through hell blaming herself for his death when she wasn't even *there*." Thinking about her brother-in-law's murder and the baby Grace miscarried soon afterward tightened Carrie's throat. "Sound familiar?" she managed.

"No." Linc's eyes darkened with the hint of temper that sounded in his voice. "My situation's different."

"I know that's how you see it," Carrie countered unabashed. "Kim was your wife, and you feel like you let her down. Maybe you did because you didn't drive her that day. But her death isn't your fault. Any more than Grace had anything to do with Ryan's murder. It just happened.''

''I told you I'd answer your questions,'' Linc snapped. ''I didn't say anything about letting you analyze my life. If you have anything else you need to ask to make it easier for you to work with me, do it now. Otherwise, this conversation is over.''

Carrie's chin came up a notch. ''You're a tough guy, Reilly. Grace got her nose out of joint, too, when I told her that wallowing in undeserved guilt was bad for her. If I hadn't gone though what I did with my sister, I'd be like everybody else, walking on eggshells when the subject of your wife's death comes up. I just happen to know that doesn't do you one bit of good in the long run. What you need is—''

She jolted when Linc slapped his palms against the cinder blocks on either side of her head and skewered her with those compelling brownish-gold eyes. ''Sweetheart, you have no idea what I need.''

His sudden closeness had the breath backing up in her lungs and her pulse throbbing hard and quick. She could feel the heat of his body, smell his woodsy cologne, something virile and strong. His broad chest was inches from her nose.

''What Grace needed...'' When her voice went raspy, Carrie cleared her throat. ''What Grace needed was some sessions of grief counseling with the department's shrink. They did her a world of good. You should try it.''

Linc slowly leaned in, halting only when his lips were an inch from hers. ''I'm not Grace,'' he said, his breath a warm wash against her flesh.

''So I've noticed.''

The hovering kiss stirred a reckless energy inside Carrie. She could think of several reasons why she should duck under either of his rigid arms and step away. They were all very practical, very logical, very sane reasons. She stayed put for only one impractical, illogical and insane reason: She wanted to taste him again. Wanted his hot, demanding, tempting mouth on hers. Wanted his hands pressed against her flesh while a fireball of heat roared through her veins.

Just then the door swung open and Lieutenant Quintana stepped onto the landing. Linc pushed off the wall and moved back, but not before their boss got an eyeful.

Quintana looked stiff-necked and forbidding in his black suit and blood-red tie while his narrowed glare sliced from Linc to Carrie then back to Linc. "You told me the two of you had a meeting with Crawford."

"That's where we're headed," Linc said mildly.

"Looks to me like you took a damn detour."

Linc shrugged. "We had things to talk over."

Quintana's deepening scowl told them what he thought of Linc's explanation. "McCall, you assured me I wouldn't get saddled with the same kind of sex-bomb behavior that got you transferred out of Patrol."

Embarrassment burned Carrie's face, and she wished she could melt into the wall. "What Linc said goes, Lieutenant, we were just talking. Sir." She didn't want to think about what might have happened if their boss hadn't swung through the door.

"Get back to work," Quintana ordered. "And not on each other," he added as he headed down the staircase.

Linc expelled a short, explicit curse. Carrie sagged against the wall and listened to the strident clang of Quintana's footsteps pounding down the metal stairs.

"That wasn't good," she muttered.

Linc slid her a look. "There's a point we agree on."

Desperate to regain control, she shoved away from the wall. "Look, apparently we're attracted to each other."

"Apparently," he agreed.

''We're partners,'' she persisted. Several years ago she'd gotten involved with a cop who worked her same shift. Memory of the resulting pain and hurt was enough to freeze every bit of hot need Linc's presence instilled in her. The knowledge of how willing she'd been to step into his arms put the fear of God into her. As did the awareness she had somehow begun to care for him in a way no work partner ever should. Certainly in a way no Internal Affairs cop should ever feel about her quarry!

''We're working undercover, Linc. Our getting involved is too dangerous, we could get careless.'' She closed her eyes, opened them. ''One of us could get hurt.''

''You're right,'' he concurred, his mouth settling into a grim line. ''Our getting involved is a bad idea for a lot more reasons than just the job.'' His eyes remained on hers as he raked his fingers through his dark hair. ''So, we agree to back off. Concentrate on what needs to be done. To be smart.''

''Yes,'' Carrie concurred, hoping her unsteady legs would hold out long enough to get her downstairs to Wade Crawford's workshop. ''Totally smart.''

Chapter 6

"Lights, camera, action," Wade Crawford said the following night when he ducked into the back seat of Linc's idling SUV.

In the driver's seat, Linc watched the front of The Hideaway where two bikers chatted in the frigid night air while swilling beer from long-necked bottles. Earlier that evening, he had spotted the two men playing pool with some slovenly-looking associates. Although all had ham-size forearms littered with tattoos, none of the tattoos were of a snake.

Linc felt a nerve-aching frustration stirring inside him. Already he'd spent a week at The Hideaway and had gotten no closer to finding the tattooed bastard who'd murdered his wife. His and Carrie's undercover assignment to observe enough violations to shut down the bar would last only so long.

"Hey, Reilly, you with me?" Crawford asked.

"Yeah." Linc angled to get a view into the back seat

where the Vice cop had settled. In anticipation of the meeting, Linc had parked the SUV beyond the reach of the sodium-vapor lamps. The laptop computer balanced on Crawford's thigh provided the only source of light inside the vehicle. With the windows tinted dark, no passerby could see in.

"I wasn't sure you could pull it off," Linc said while studying the monitor. "But that camera you planted in the jukebox has a perfect line of sight on the back booth."

"I'm wounded you doubted my ability," Crawford said in his slow drawl. Light from the computer gave his self-righteous expression an eerie glow.

"Your job skills were never at issue," Linc countered dryly. "I just thought the blond waitress who hung all over you while you worked might have diverted your attention."

"Tanny?" Crawford grinned. "She wasn't a problem. I had to distract her for a couple of minutes while I slipped the camera inside the juke, is all. Did that by promisin' to take her out on her night off."

With the SUV's heater now blowing warm air, Linc pulled off his leather gloves and tossed them onto the dash. "All in the line of duty, right?"

"I live to serve. You ready for instructions on this?"

"Ready," Linc said.

"If you're interested only in activity in the back booth, you don't need to do much. When the laptop's on, so is the VCR that the camera sends wireless signals to. Whatever the lens is focused on, you get on tape, imprinted with the date and time the activity occurred."

Linc studied the monitor. The real-time view of The Hideaway's back booth showed it was currently vacant, the small Reserved sign displayed on the table's edge. "Crawford, I'm impressed. The quality of that picture is perfect."

"Latest technology—it's as good as standing in the spot you're watching." Crawford fingered a toggle switch. "If you want to check what's going on in other booths, use this. Puts the camera planted inside the juke in scan mode."

"Sounds simple."

"As pie," Crawford agreed, continuing to work the toggle switch. "Well, well, there's your partner, snuggled in a booth with some cowboy." Crawford crooked a brow. "He looks at Carrie like he's planning on carrying her off into the sunset. Man's got it bad, I'd say."

"Understatement," Linc concurred, making a concerted effort not to scowl. "His name's West Williams. He hit on her the first night and hasn't let up."

"The way she looks, do you blame him?"

"No." Linc kept his gaze locked on Carrie's image. Tonight she was decked out in a slinky, off-the-shoulder white sweater and jeans that fit like a second skin. Her hair was a mass of fiery waves, her blue eyes bright and alluring.

Almost as alluring as they'd looked yesterday in the stairwell when he had his mouth an inch from hers.

That gnawing memory had him easing out a breath. He shifted his gaze out the windshield and studied the packed-to-the-brim parking lot while picturing how Carrie had looked with her face tilted upward, her full, sensuous mouth his for the taking. He had wanted to kiss her badly. Ached to have her warm, erotic taste swirl through his system again. And he damn well would have had his mouth *and* his hands on her if Quintana hadn't walked through the door.

In retrospect Linc figured the lieutenant had done him a favor. Because Linc knew without a doubt, kissing Carrie McCall twice in one lifetime would have been a mistake. A huge one.

Hadn't he already spent a few sleepless nights hammering a reminder into his brain that he did not intend to repeat the kiss they'd shared behind The Hideaway? *That* kiss had been business. An act. A necessary response to the bouncer's sudden appearance. Their cover had been threatened, they'd had no choice.

If he'd kissed his partner yesterday it would have had nothing to do with duty and everything to do with emotion. That was a place he did not want to go with the luscious, compelling Carrie McCall. Nor with any other woman. Never again.

He needed no reminder of how heady it could be to find a woman who made lightning strike and thunder roll. How seductive. *Enticing.* And how devastating when she was gone.

No, Linc thought, cementing his determination. Never again. His new partner might keep him awake at night with longings for things he had put behind him, but that's where he intended for them to stay. Behind him.

"A waitress just served Carrie and the cowboy a beer," Wade commented. "Carrie sure is showing an interest in the bracelet that waitress is wearing."

Linc checked the monitor. The bracelet was a silver cuff inset with a piece of green turquoise the size of a tequila glass. His cop's sixth sense spiked when he noted Carrie gazing at the piece of jewelry with acute interest.

"Crawford, can you zoom in on the bracelet?"

"No problem." The laptop's keys clicked softly as the Vice cop typed commands to the hidden surveillance camera. "The way Carrie just got that waitress to angle her wrist toward the juke makes me think your partner's hoping we've got the camera on."

"That's exactly what she's doing," Linc said. It occurred to him he knew her so well now he could read the intent in her eyes as she gestured toward the bracelet while talking to the waitress. "Carrie knows I slipped outside to meet you so we could test the camera," Linc added. "She wants us to get that bracelet on tape."

"Mission accomplished," Crawford said. "Okay, the waitress just moved off, and it looks like Carrie's saying happy trails to Roy Rogers. Or trying to, anyway. Dude isn't exactly excited about her leaving."

Linc watched the screen, his jaw going tight when Williams dropped a kiss on her cheek. With breezy laugh, she slid out of the booth, gave Williams a wave, then stepped out of sight of the camera's probing eye.

"Chances are she's on her way here to tell us what's going on with the bracelet," Linc commented.

He turned his head and focused on The Hideaway's front door and waited. Minutes later Carrie appeared on the now vacant porch, wearing the pale-olive trench coat that had felt as soft as warm butter when Linc had slipped it off her shoulders after they'd arrived there this evening. She moved gracefully down the stairs, stepping through bright pools of light that dotted the parking lot. Linc lost sight of her momentarily as she threaded her way through the sea of haphazardly parked vehicles.

The instant she pulled open the SUV's passenger door and climbed in the need tethered tight inside him strained hard at the rich, sensual scent of her. Fisting his hand against his jeaned thigh, he suspected that, for him, her presence would forever be the equivalent of waving a shot of whiskey under an alcoholic's nose. She lured him. *Tempted.* Still, resisting her—resisting everything he knew a woman like her could bring to his life—was necessary. He couldn't risk again. Would never survive another loss.

Carrie closed the door behind her and swiveled toward the back seat. "Is the camera working?"

Crawford scowled. "Another person of little faith."

"Don't get that ego of yours bruised, Wade. I'm just

hoping everything was on-line in time for you to catch my conversation with the waitress.''

"We saw it," Linc said. "What's with the bracelet?"

She swept him a look under her lashes. "Does anything get past you, Reilly?"

"On occasion. Tell me about the bracelet."

"It's genuine. Solid silver with a green turquoise stone."

"Which, at least on the monitor, looks big enough to choke a goat," Linc added.

"It looks that way in person, too," Carrie said. "The waitress's name is Yolanda. When I asked where she got the bracelet, she turned coy, said she has a generous boyfriend. After she walked away, West told me she doesn't have a boyfriend, that she bought the bracelet herself from a guy named Howie."

"I'll take a wild guess," Linc said, resting his wrist over the top of the steering wheel. "Howard Klinger, a.k.a. Howie Kling is the seller."

"I give," Crawford said. "Who's Klinger? Kling?"

"An ex-con who shows up here every night," Linc explained. "He disappears after he gets inside the front door. Which means he's not coming here to bask in The Hideaway's ambiance."

"He dealing in stolen jewelry?" Crawford asked.

"After seeing that bracelet, I'd bet on it," Carrie said. "He has priors for larceny. Was nabbed on a residential burglary charge, which got reduced to possession of stolen property. Our first night here, Linc and I spotted Klinger in the parking lot, but we didn't see him inside. We had the guys in Intelligence ask around about him. Word on the street is that Klinger's running a fencing operation out of the back of some bar."

Crawford adjusted the toggle switch on the computer. "Doesn't take Sherlock Holmes to figure out *which* bar."

"I think we've got that covered," Linc said.

"Wade, can you print a picture of Yolanda's bracelet?" Carrie asked. "If we get a hit on it as stolen, we can use her to prove Klinger's selling hot property. Then hopefully tie him to the theft of the bracelet."

"I can get you as many prints of that bracelet as you want." Crawford wiggled his brows. "Maybe you'd like to come to my place and see my other prints?"

"Settle down, bayou boy." Carrie's husky tone kick-started desire clawing in Linc's gut. Had he ever felt this searing physical hunger for a woman before? Even Kim? He couldn't remember.

"That okay with you, Reilly?"

He looked at Carrie. "Sorry, my mind was somewhere else."

"I've danced my feet off," she repeated, then diverted her gaze out the windshield. "I'm going home."

A warning blipped in Linc's brain. It was the same alarm he'd heard yesterday in the stairwell when she failed to maintain eye contact after he'd told her he didn't want her to have misgivings about him. As a cop he had witnessed the same behavior countless times—a suspect refusing to make either eye contact or unable to sustain it because he or she had something to hide.

"You feeling all right?" he asked.

"Fine." Her eyes flicked to his face, then shifted.

Blip. "Go home and get some sleep," he said quietly.

Did she have something dark and deep on her mind? he wondered. Or was his innate cop paranoia working in overdrive? That was possible, he reasoned—she *had* spent most of the night on The Hideaway's dance floor. Still, that didn't explain her reaction in the stairwell. Didn't explain why she couldn't look him in the eye tonight.

"I'll run a trace on the bracelet tomorrow," she added.

He nodded. "See you at the office."

After saying good-night, she pushed open the door and slid out. A gust of cold air swept inside the SUV when she closed the door behind her.

Linc tracked her progress across the lot, wondering about her now in more than just the male-female sense. She was no longer simply a woman for whom he felt gut-searing attraction. She was a puzzle that begged to be solved.

Crawford whistled softly. "McCall's got a body a man could spend his entire life dreamin' about. I'm giving the lady a call."

Jaw set, Linc watched Carrie slide inside the Corvette. Whether she had secrets or not, whether he needed to be smart or not, the idea of another man putting his hands on her scraped him raw.

"Leave her be while she's working this operation," he said, sending the Vice cop a searing look. "I don't want my partner distracted."

"You know, Reilly, that's the same song Alex Blade gave me when I told him I planned to call Carrie's sister. Morgan and Blade are engaged now." Crawford closed the lid on the laptop. "I'm thinkin' history is about to repeat itself."

"You're way off the mark," Linc returned, amazed at how angry he sounded.

"Uh-huh. Well, something tells me that if I've got a yen to date a McCall, I'd have less chance of runnin' into some cop's fist if I focus my sights on Grace."

"Smart thinking," Linc muttered.

For the second time that night, Carrie climbed into the passenger seat of an idling vehicle. For this meeting, Internal Affairs Captain Patricia Scott had chosen the shadowy edge of a library parking lot not far from the house Carrie shared with her sisters.

"I think you've targeted the wrong cop," Carrie said before she even shut the van's passenger door.

"Is that so?" As always, the IA commander wore her salt-and-pepper hair twisted into a tight topknot, which in the dim light made her fine-boned face seem gaunt. Tonight she'd bundled her lean frame into a black, bulky coat.

"That's so." Carrie gave a little shiver now that she was out of the biting wind. "I don't think Reilly is the Avenger."

"Do you have evidence to back that up?"

"Not the type you're thinking about." Carrie paused. She knew what she was about to say wouldn't hold weight in the investigative process, but she wanted her opinion on record. "Reilly doesn't feel right for it, Captain."

"That your women's intuition talking?"

"Cop instinct." Carrie narrowed her eyes. "I would have expected a comment like that from a man, not a woman who's been on the force twenty-five years."

"You're misreading me, Sergeant. I trust my female intuition far more than my cop instinct when it comes to anything about men." Scott raised a brow. "I bet you're damn good at reading men yourself."

"That I am." So good, Carrie added silently, she had felt her insides go cold less than a half hour ago when she'd looked up after telling Linc she was going home and saw that his gaze had focused on her like a laser. A finger of fear had pressed against her heart at the sense he was looking *into* her instead of *at* her. She could tell herself there was no way he could know she was IA. Still, there had been a reason his eyes had locked on her with bone-chilling intensity.

God, had she given herself away? Or was the mounting unease she felt over her assignment making her paranoid?

Either way, she knew she'd be handling the situation better if she didn't feel so damn guilty about deceiving Linc!

Closing her eyes, she reminded herself it was pointless to let what she was doing eat at her. She was simply following orders: take down a cop who'd turned himself into a one-man death squad. Fine, she would do that. What she would not do was railroad the *wrong* cop.

"It's not just my instincts or intuition that makes me think Reilly's innocent," she stated. "There's more."

"You've got my undivided attention, Sergeant McCall."

"You have two other detectives in the SEU who bear a good, long look for the Avenger murders. Tom Nelson is one."

"Because he was accused of planting evidence in the apartment of a serial rapist?"

"Exactly."

"We looked at the details surrounding the accusation. Nothing was never proved."

"Or disproved, right?"

"Correct."

"What if it's true? A cop who'd do that might consider it a small step from setting up criminals to putting a bullet in their heads."

"Do you think Nelson has motive to set Reilly up?"

"No, he seems to genuinely care about Linc. But we don't know for sure the fact Linc has personally handled five of the murder victims has anything to do with how the Avenger chooses who's going to die. That could just be a fluke. All we know for sure is that all the dead scum have SEU files."

"You said there are two detectives who bear watching. Who's the second?"

"Don Gaines. How hard a look has IA given him?"

"As hard a one as we gave Reilly before we put him at the top of our suspect list."

"Look again. Gaines had a relationship with Kimberly Reilly before she and Linc got married. Gaines loved her, *still* loves her and he hates Linc for stealing her away. Gaines cornered me and claimed her death is Linc's fault. When I pointed out he wasn't near the crime scene, it made no difference. Gaines insisted Kim was dead because Linc reneged on his promise to drive her out of town that day."

"Why does that make you think Gaines is the Avenger?"

"Because framing Linc for seven murders would get Gaines big-time payback for Linc winning her in the first place, not to mention her death. Because when she died, that ended Gaines's hope the woman he considered the love of his life would someday dump her husband and run back to him."

Carrie raised a palm. "Think about it, Captain. Gaines has access to every SEU file. All he had to do was handpick his intended victims, making sure the majority had been handled by Linc. The way Kim Reilly died gives Linc a built-in motive for going after scum who have beaten the system. Gaines is no idiot—he knew someone would eventually pick up on the pattern of the killings, and that Linc would get looked at hard for them. For all we know, Gaines is who tipped off the unit's captain about the pattern in the first place."

Scott lifted a shoulder. "You've apparently done a lot of thinking about this scenario."

The nonchalance in the woman's voice had Carrie setting her teeth. "It's our job to think, isn't it? Our job to root out a bad cop, not persecute a good one? Just because Linc *seems* like a good choice for the Avenger doesn't mean he is."

"I agree. It's also our job to consider all the evidence.

Taking into consideration what you just said, you're not going to like hearing the information I received this afternoon.''

Tension balled in Carrie's stomach. "What?"

"Since the latest Avenger murder occurred out of town, we ran a trace on credit card usage of all SEU detectives during last weekend."

"I take it Linc used his credit card somewhere other than here?"

"Yes. On Saturday night at a restaurant in Claremore a little after eight o'clock. Arlee Dell was gunned down in Tulsa about eleven. It's a twenty-minute drive from Claremore to Tulsa, so Reilly would have had plenty of time to eat dinner, drive to Tulsa and find Dell. Then take him out."

"Gaines told me that Kim's family lives in Claremore. She was going to a reunion there when she was killed. Was Linc in Claremore with his in-laws?"

Scott nodded. "A waiter at the restaurant said Reilly ate dinner with an older man and woman. My guess is he took his former in-laws to dinner before he headed for Tulsa."

"Did he use his credit card in Tulsa, too?"

"No, just Claremore."

"Then you don't know for sure Linc went to Tulsa?"

"I have no proof of that. Yet."

A sick feeling joined the knots of tension in Carrie's stomach. "Look, Gaines dated Kim, so he maybe went with her to Claremore to meet her parents. Maybe he even talked to them last week. They could have mentioned Linc was coming to see them. Knowing that would tighten the noose he'd already put around Linc's neck, Gaines went to Tulsa—"

"And murdered Arlee Dell."

"It's possible."

''In our line of work, anything's possible. I just don't think the scenario you outlined with Gaines is *probable*.''

''Linc did a stint in Homicide. A former Homicide cop wouldn't use his credit card two hours before he planned to murder someone in the general vicinity.''

''In this case, Reilly's in-laws could testify he was in Claremore, so why shouldn't he charge dinner? His in-laws can present undeniable proof he was twenty minutes away from the crime scene.''

''No.'' Carrie shook her head. ''The Avenger doesn't leave loose ends hanging. He's capped do-wrongs for nearly two years and hasn't left a trace of himself. Nothing. He wouldn't start now. If Linc had committed that murder, he would have bypassed the in-laws and visited them another weekend.''

''You and I could sit here all night and try to figure out which of our brother cops has crossed the line. Debate why we're even looking to stop a cop who's killing bad guys and making life safer for the law-abiding, decent ones.''

Carrie rubbed the bridge of her nose. ''In the academy, they hammer into our heads that we're supposed to work for the victims. Problem is, the victims we're working for now have hurt lots of innocent people. Ninety-nine percent of the population is better off because those seven men are dead. There are a lot of gray areas here, Captain.''

''The people with the badges are supposed to be the good guys. Period. The cop we're after has the idea he can kill and hide behind his badge. He can't. We have to find out who he is and stop him.''

Scott fished a manila envelope from beneath the driver's seat and handed it to Carrie. ''Inside is the key to Reilly's house made from your clay mold. And the alarm code off your recorder. There's also a miniature camera in there. Remember, when you conduct the search, if you find any evidence that points to Reilly being the Avenger, you're to photograph it but otherwise leave it alone.''

''I remember. I have no idea when I'm going to get a chance to search the house. Linc doesn't volunteer his schedule. He's spent a few nights at the motel where his undercover persona has a room, but he doesn't tell me ahead of time when he plans to stay there.''

Scott gave her an even look. ''I bet you can figure a way to get that information.''

Dread built in Carrie's chest at the thought of what she had to do. ''Tell me something, Captain. After I sneak into Linc's home and search through everything he owns, how the hell am I supposed to look him in the face?''

''You keep in mind that if Reilly is the killer, he's done this to himself. Ruined himself. None of that is your doing.''

Carrie shivered against a chill that had nothing to do with the frigid wind hammering against the van's windows. It had everything to do with the fact she was spying on another cop and trying to find something rotten. A cop for whom, despite her best intentions, she was fast developing feelings.

The thought of how deep those feelings already went, just the thought, was like a fist clamping around her heart. Caring for Linc wasn't what she wanted, and yet, she couldn't seem to stop it from happening. Even when he wasn't anywhere near, he kept filling her mind, crowding her senses.

The setup of her working with Linc was all pretense, but her response to him wasn't. Every day her control over her feelings faded as the strength of her need for him grew. She had no idea how to handle that. No idea what she would do if her investigation proved him guilty of seven murders—

What in the name of heaven was she supposed to do?

Chapter 7

Carrie's dread over the prospect of searching Linc's house spiked two nights later at The Hideaway when he mentioned he planned to spend the night in his room at the Drop Inn.

Strung tight with tension, she forced her mind on business through the remainder of the evening. Doing so had been somewhat easy since Zack, the bartender whose trust she'd worked to gain, had at last set her up on a video poker game that paid off in something other than additional game points. Carrie's delighted squeal over winning had prompted a smiling Zack to award her an unopened bottle of whiskey. Problem was, the bottle was minus the state liquor tax seal. She'd sent Zack an air kiss while mentally adding the liquor violation and illegal gambling charges to the growing list of offenses she and Linc had observed.

Now, a half hour after she and Linc had called it a night and driven away from the Hideaway, Carrie walked out of a bustling convenience store, popping antacid tablets like they were candy. Although urgency pulsed through her to get the search of Linc's house over with, she had to proceed with caution. She knew it would have taken him fifteen minutes to drive from The Hideaway to the Drop Inn. She planned to drive by the motel to make sure his SUV was parked in the lot. Only after making visual confirmation would she head to his house and conduct her search.

The damn search that had her stomach churning pure acid!

She didn't want to believe Linc was the Avenger. Didn't want to think about what would happen if she found evidence tying a man for whom she had such confused, unsettled feelings to seven murders. But what if she *did* find evidence? Could she sit in the witness stand and coolly gaze across a courtroom at Linc while she testified against him?

No, she thought. It can't be him. It can't be.

She popped another antacid tablet into her mouth, then shoved the roll into the pocket of her trench coat. The instant she reached to slide the key into the Corvette's door lock, a hand settled on her wrist.

She whirled. A pair of friendly dark eyes and the flash of a grin stopped her from going for the gun in her boot.

"Hey, red," West Williams drawled. "Did you forget you promised me a dance before you left The Hideaway?"

"Hello, yourself, cowboy." Clamping down on a curse, Carrie spotted West's battered orange pickup truck parked at one of the convenience store's gas pumps. She truly liked West and his polite ways. And the fact he seemed to have a general knowledge of—but not be directly involved in—some behind-the-scenes activity at The Hideaway was a plus. One made even bigger since the more time she spent with him, the freer others at the bar talked about those activities in her presence. But tonight, with tension clawing at her insides, she wanted to be left alone to scarf down antacids and get the search of Linc's house over with.

"Sorry, West." She unlocked the Corvette's door, then pulled it open. "In all the excitement over my video poker win, I forgot the dance I promised you."

Standing in the wedge between the car and open door, she smiled up at him. He was dressed in jeans, a work shirt and scuffed cowboy boots. As a concession to the freezing wind he'd pulled up the collar of his sheepskin coat, but hadn't bothered buttoning it. With his thick, dark hair, amiable brown eyes and easy laugh, Carrie had to admit he made a compelling package.

She angled her head. "How about I make it up to you tomorrow night? I promise to wear my dancing shoes."

"I'll hold you to that, red." When he stepped into the wedge with her, Carrie realized the mistake she'd made letting herself get trapped. His muscled body was a formidable barrier to her moving even an inch in any direction.

He settled his hands on either side of her waist and gave her an intimate smile. "In fact, I'd like to hold you in a lot of different ways. I figure you know that."

She slapped her palms against his chest. "I'm flattered." Even through her leather gloves his chest felt like solid stone. "But I'm Linc's girl. I've been honest with you about that."

"I know that's what you say. But the two of you haven't spent much time together the past couple of nights. He's mostly at a pool table. You're dancing or playing the videos. Hell, you hardly even *looked* at each other tonight. Makes me think you and old Linc aren't as serious as you were when you started coming to The Hideaway." West gave her a crooked grin. "I plan on taking advantage of his being an idiot."

Dammit, Carrie thought. The agreement she and Linc had made to step back from the attraction they both felt had clearly affected the way they now interacted even while undercover. She hadn't realized the invisible wall they'd built between them was so obvious to those watching, and she bet Linc didn't, either.

When West nuzzled her throat, Carrie held back the urge to deliver a punch. After all, he wasn't one of The Hideaway's infamous regulars; he didn't even have a traffic ticket to his name, much less a criminal record. He was just a friendly, twenty-one-year-old man who worked on the assembly line at the nearby automobile manufacturing plant. A young man with a crush on a woman who possessed the innate ability to steer men where she wanted them to go. A woman who'd done her best to steer him into helping her ferret out information.

Acknowledging she'd used West since her first night at The Hideaway delivered a sharp stab to Carrie's conscience. Great, just great, she thought. With the guilt she was already dealing with over investigating her partner, the last thing she needed was a lovesick cowboy whose ego she had no desire to crush.

"You're driving me crazy, red," he murmured against her neck. "Come home with me. Let me make love to you. I'll show you how good it can be with a man who really cares about you."

"No." She increased the pressure on his chest until he eased back a step. "We can't do this." Hoping to take the edge off the disappointment in his eyes, she added, "If it wasn't for Linc, you bet I'd jump at your offer. But I gave him my word to be true as long as we're together."

"He'll never care about you the way I do." As he spoke, West dug into the pocket of his coat, then held out his palm. "I was planning on giving you this after we danced tonight."

The breath froze in Carrie's lungs as she stared down at the wide silver bracelet set with dark blue stones. "West, I—"

He snagged her hand. "The stones are lapis cabo...cabo somethings," he said, sliding the cuff onto her wrist. "The silver's sterling."

The bracelet was heavy and she knew instinctively it was the real thing. Those instincts gave her a good idea where he'd obtained it. The thought that West had just slapped a piece of stolen jewelry around her wrist added to the sick feeling in her roiling stomach. "This must have cost you a week's pay."

"Nah. Howie cut me a deal."

"Howie," Carrie repeated, confirming her suspicions.

"Yeah. You made such a fuss the other night over Yolanda's turquoise bracelet that I asked her to find out if Howie had something close to it."

Carrie nodded. As she had done with the turquoise bracelet, she would run this one to see if it was stolen. On the off chance that it wasn't, she would return it to West.

"It's beautiful," she said, the woman in her meaning it. It was the cop who added, "If Howie has other jewelry, I sure would like to look at it. I've got a real weakness for baubles."

West shrugged. "I can probably sweet talk Yolanda into setting up a time for you to get with him."

"Just tell me when and where."

"Sure." West cupped a hand against her cheek. "Carrie, I gave you the bracelet to show you how much I care. You can't say the same about Linc. If he had real feelings for you, he wouldn't drive off from The Hideaway every night and hope you got home safe. He'd take the time to follow you. Like me."

His comment narrowed her eyes. "Wait a minute. Isn't that your pickup parked over by the pumps?"

"That's right. What about it?"

"I thought you were here because you needed gas. That it was just a fluke we ran into each other."

"Nah. There just wasn't anyplace else to park when I followed your car into the lot."

"You *followed* me from The Hideaway?"

"Yeah."

Hell, she'd been so engrossed in her own jittery thoughts about searching Linc's house she hadn't noticed she'd snagged a tail. What if she hadn't stopped here? What if she'd driven directly to Linc's house? West wouldn't automatically know a cop lived there, but he might have gotten curious. Maybe started asking questions and found out Linc lived there, instead of in the room at the Drop Inn like he claimed.

"I'm following you home tonight," West added. "Just to make sure you get there safe."

Another thought intensified the acid burn in Carrie's stomach. "West, I need you to tell me the truth," she began evenly. "Have you followed me home before?" If he had, her and Linc's cover might not be totally blown, but enough so they'd have to end their participation in the operation.

"No," West answered. "But now that it looks like you and Linc are on the outs, I'm going to escort you home every night."

"No. I don't need a bodyguard. Don't *want* one."

"You've got one, red," he countered. "While you're driving, think about what man it is who cares most about you. The one in the car behind yours or the one who isn't around."

One look at the stubborn determination in West's eyes and Carrie knew she would get nowhere arguing. She needed to expend her energy on figuring out how to get rid of her self-proclaimed protector. Because with him on her tail, she couldn't drive to Linc's house and conduct her search. Nor could she go to the home she shared with her sisters. And she for damn sure couldn't traipse into the building that housed all of OCPD's undercover units!

While clouds darted beneath the moon and stars overhead, she considered using evasive driving tactics to lose West once they got out in traffic. But doing so might clue him in that she had training best not put on display by a cop working undercover.

"You ready to go?" he asked.

Taking everything into consideration, the only way to keep her cover intact was to go to Linc's room at the Drop Inn. "West, I have to warn you. I'm on my way to see Linc."

A shadow dimmed his eyes. "Doesn't matter." He skimmed his knuckles down her cheek. "I'm following you."

Damn snakes, Linc thought as he sipped scotch and studied the photos spread on the motel room's scarred table. He had lost count of how many snake tattoos he'd looked at in the two years since Kim's death. Still, none were a match for the portion of the tattoo on the suspect's forearm captured on the gas station's grainy surveillance tape.

With fatigue pressing down on him, Linc mentally replayed the tape. He saw the panicked desperation in the clerk's eyes. His lunge for the suspect's automatic. The portion of the suspect's tattoo that appeared to coil as his muscles tensed during the struggle. The gun's muzzle flash just as Kim walked in the door. Her horrified awareness when she whirled and fled. The killer bolting after her.

Linc clenched his fingers on his glass. Rage, black and

vicious, grabbed him by the throat at the thought of what
she had endured during the two days the bastard kept her
alive. Hand unsteady, he drained his glass and barely prevented himself from heaving it against the wall. Not for
the first time he cursed fate for preventing the camera from
getting a shot of the killer's entire forearm. Usually, a tattoo was a slam-bang identifier, especially one on tape. A
partial tattoo was a different matter.

Still, since the scum had worn a ski mask, the section
of the tattoo that *looked* like a snake's tail was all Linc
had to go on. That, and the fact his snitch had sworn he'd
spotted the pool player with a matching tattoo at The Hideaway.

Refilling his glass, Linc throttled back his anger and
centered himself mentally. He couldn't bring Kim back.
Couldn't make up for his failing to protect his wife. The
one thing he could change—*would* change—was that the
murdering rapist scum was still free. Still dragging in air.

A sharp rap on the door brought Linc's chin up. It was
past midnight and he wasn't expecting company. He swept
the photos into a report-jammed file folder, then rose and
snagged his Glock off the bed. When he jacked a round
into the chamber, the harsh, ratcheting noise bounced off
the room's faded yellow walls.

Because the fleabag motel didn't have doors with peep-
holes, he moved to the window, the automatic pressed
against his thigh. When he pushed back one panel of the
lime-green curtain and glimpsed Carrie, alarm shot through
him. No way had his partner stopped by just to chat.

He crossed to the door and pulled it open. She swept in,
bringing with her a gust of frigid air and the faint scent of
smoke from The Hideaway.

"What's wrong, McCall?" He did a quick scan of the
parking lot before closing the door behind her and resetting
the lock.

"I've got a problem." Her gaze flicked to his hand. "I think it's solvable without your having to shoot anyone."

Shrugging, he laid the Glock on the cigarette-pock-marked chest of drawers. "In this neighborhood, it's best to be prepared." Despite her trench coat, he could see she held her shoulders as stiff as a knife blade.

"What's going on?" he asked.

"In two words—West Williams."

"Your cowboy pal."

"Who has decided to turn up the heat on our relationship."

Linc arched a brow. "I thought your relationship involved only dancing."

"So did I. Until he followed me to a convenience store." She angled her chin. "In all fairness, I've laid on the flirting heavy since we realized West knows people who have a hand in the illegal stuff going on at The Hideaway. West apparently took all that attention to heart." Turning, she stepped to the window and peeked around the curtain Linc had left open. "Dammit, I've got to figure out a way to get rid of him."

Linc moved behind her, careful to stay out of sight of anyone outside. "He followed you here?"

"Yes." She shifted so he could see. "The orange pickup."

Linc spotted the truck parked at an angle to the room. The motel's road sign gave off enough illumination that he could make out Williams's broad-shouldered silhouette in the driver's seat.

Standing there, Link again caught the faint whiff of smoke that clung to Carrie's clothing. Now, though, it mingled with her smoldering perfume. *Be smart, Reilly,* he cautioned when he felt his blood stir.

He turned, saw she was staring at the thick file folder

on the table. "I've been catching up on paperwork," he said.

Her gaze lifted slowly. "Need some help?"

Tonight her eyes were shadowed in shades of sultry violet and lined with dark kohl. Eyes so expressive an artist would paint them. Eyes, he reminded himself, that sometimes averted from his when she couldn't quite look him in the face.

"Thanks for the offer, but it's an old case." He slid his thumbs into the back pockets of his jeans. "Exactly why did Williams follow you here?"

"He decided you and I are on the skids, relationship-wise."

"What gave him that idea?"

"We did." She pulled off her leather gloves, jammed them into her coat pockets. "West pointed out that when we're at The Hideaway, we don't spend a lot of time together."

"That's part of our ops plan," Linc pointed out. "We split up so we can observe as many violations as possible each night."

"That's not all. West said that lately when you and I *are* together, we barely look at each other. Like tonight when we sat at the bar." Her eyes stayed level on his. "It's obvious to him something between us has changed."

"Yeah." Since that day in the stairwell, he and Carrie had apparently done a damn fine job of keeping their agreement to back away from each other. "The department should hire your cowboy pal. He's hell at reading people."

"*Too* good."

Linc rechecked the parking lot. "He's still there. You might as well get comfortable."

"Great." Giving her head a disgusted shake, she unbelted her coat and shrugged it off. Just as it had a few hours ago at The Hideaway, Linc's blood pumped harder at the sight of her snug red sweater and thigh-baring denim skirt. Her glossy black boots had heels sharp enough to pierce the room's cheap carpet.

"I'm stuck here until he leaves." She tossed the coat on the bed. "What if he sits out there all night?"

Linc's gaze ranged across the bed. He had a vision of himself peeling off that sweater, the skirt. An image of her sprawled naked on the flowered spread, her flesh slicked with sweat. He bit off a curse when he felt a slash of lust, then something deeper and stronger than he'd expected. Something he had no desire or intention of analyzing.

He scrubbed his fingers over his jaw. "You've got one persistent cowboy on your hands."

"You should have seen his face when he said he plans to follow me every night when I leave The Hideaway." She plopped down in the chair at the table. "He means it, Reilly. With him on my tail, I can't go home. I sure can't drop by the office."

Linc furrowed a brow. "You think he's a stalker in the making?"

"I don't think so." She stood, paced a few steps, then circled back to where he stood. "He's just a sweet guy with the hots for a woman he considers a defenseless damsel."

Linc slicked his gaze down the long, slim length of her thighs. "If he knew about the automatic in your boot, he'd think again."

"But he doesn't know. *Can't* know. That's another reason he said he can tell 'old Linc' doesn't care about me. If you cared, you'd follow me home every night to make sure I stayed safe."

"*Old* Linc?"

Her mouth twitched. "His words, not mine."

Linc swallowed a snarl. "You'll recall from our ops plan my undercover persona has a hair-trigger temper."

As he spoke, he grabbed his bomber jacket. "That if anybody touches my woman, I believe in big-time payback."

Carrie rolled her eyes. "Cool your jets, Reilly. I didn't come here so you could hammer the guy because he has a crush."

"Our operation doesn't need some lovesick cowboy screwing things up."

"I agree." She settled a restraining hand on his arm. "The problem is, the cowboy might be our ticket to bigger things."

Linc fought the urge to jerk on his jacket and head out to face off with Williams. Irrational as he knew it was, the fact the guy had decided to move in on territory that neither of them had claim to annoyed the hell out of him. "Yeah? How?"

"Look at this bracelet." She held up her left wrist. "West gave it to me during the stop at the convenience store. I'll book it into the property room tomorrow and run it for stolen."

Linc circled his fingers around her wrist and studied the bracelet. Even to his untrained eye the silver cuff and blue stones looked genuine. "Any particular reason Williams gave this to you tonight?"

"He wanted me to go home with him. To show me how good it can be with a man who cares."

Linc settled his gaze on her glossed mouth while his thumb ran over the pulse point in her wrist. "Unlike *old* Linc," he said quietly. "Who isn't attracted to you." Beneath his thumb, he felt her pulse jump. "To whom you're not attracted."

"That's…what you and I agreed."

"Not quite. We agreed we were attracted but we wouldn't act on that attraction."

"Whatever." She stepped back, forcing him to drop his hand. "West bought the bracelet from Howie. When I mentioned I had a weakness for baubles, he said he could probably help set up a time for me to get with Howie.''

''So, if I go after Williams for messing with you, he might change his mind about making that introduction.''

''Right. If Howie is fencing stolen goods out of the bar's back door, he's too big a fish for us to let slide off the hook.''

''Agreed.'' Resigned, Linc tossed his jacket onto the table. ''After our brush with Quintana in the stairwell, I don't want to be the one to tell him we screwed up this assignment because some cowboy has a crush on you.''

''Neither do I.''

Linc rechecked the parking lot. ''Pickup's still there.''

''I told West I was coming to see you. Even that didn't dissuade him.'' She checked her watch. ''It's almost one o'clock.''

''Seems to me if your paying me a visit was going to make him back off, he'd have left by now. If you want him gone, you'll have to give him some incentive.''

''Of course I want him gone. Do you know how to make that happen without beating him?''

''Yes.'' The cop in Linc knew how to protect their cover. The man in him heard a siren blare at the prospect of going through with his plan. That was one drawback of working undercover—sometimes what needed to be done was damn dangerous. In this case the danger didn't come from an external source. It was his own emotions presenting the threat. Emotions that blurred the line between the cop and the man who yearned for the woman standing inches away. The man who would have to keep reminding himself he had no intention of risking his heart again. No desire for their make-believe relationship to become real.

''Look, McCall, before I tell you my idea of how to get rid of your paramour, let me run this down from a male point of view.'' Leaning against the table, Linc crossed his arms over his chest. "Bottom line is, a woman who looks like you is a heady cocktail for a thirsty man."

He paused, taking in her trim, sleek body poured into the red sweater and denim skirt, her fiery hair an untamed fall across her shoulders, her sultry blue eyes. How the hell could he fault Williams when the sight of her left his own throat dry?

"And?" she prodded.

"The cowboy freezing his butt off in that pickup has one hell of a thirst," Linc continued. "He wants you, McCall. Now he's picked up on the fact you and I have backed off from each other. He thinks that means I no longer care about you. That's why he made his move tonight. Hell, he's probably convinced you're in here breaking things off with me. That if he waits long enough you'll run out, jump into his truck and go home with him."

"What a mess." Jabbing a hand beneath her hair she rubbed the back of her neck. "Okay, Reilly, what's your plan?"

"We have to show him how wrong he is."

Her chin slowly lifted. "*Show* him?"

"We have to be convincing. If we aren't, Williams could do something that might force us to blow our cover." Linc nodded toward the bathroom. "Reach in there and turn on the light."

Frowning, she did so. "What have you got in mind?"

He flipped off the overhead light. The illumination from the low-wattage bulb in the bathroom provided the perfect backlighting. "Here's the deal. We haven't closed the curtain, so he probably thinks we've been talking since you got here. Which happens to be right. The light just went off, a sign that we're done talking. There's a different mood between us now. You and I *show* him that mood by edging in front of the window and giving Williams a performance that convinces him our relationship just got back on track. We need to sell the guy on the fact he doesn't have a chance in hell of getting his hands on you.''

''In other words, you and I make out?'' She shook her head. ''I didn't show up here so you and I could engage in another lip-lock session.''

''No, you showed up here because you need your partner's help. That's what partners do, McCall. They help each other. Back each other up.''

''I've been a cop over five years, Reilly. You don't have to explain the concept of partners to me.''

Because his pride leaped up, Linc added, ''Well then, let me explain that I'm looking forward to our engaging in another lip-lock session with the same enthusiasm as you. Unfortunately, our doing that is the best idea I can come up with. You have a better one, McCall, toss it out. Just keep in mind if the cowboy keeps coming at you, following you, maybe even checking on you, he's bound to see or hear or dig up something he shouldn't. That happens, our operation's in jeopardy. If Quintana doesn't put our heads on a chopping block, the mayor will.''

She tossed her hands up. ''Could this assignment get any more complicated?''

Linc thought about his own hidden agenda for wanting to keep their operation on track. The Hideaway was his sole tie to his wife's killer. Now some lovelorn cowboy threatened to blow things. ''Each day I ask myself that same question,'' he said dryly.

Carrie's mouth softened. ''I don't mean to sound like I think you're some sort of pervert lech. I don't. You're trying to help. I understand that.''

''All in the line of duty.''

Her fingers went to her wrist, twisted the silver cuff. After a moment she shrugged. ''It's not like we haven't done this before for the sake of the job, is it? We fooled the bouncer at The Hideaway. We can fool West.''

"That's the plan."

Blowing out a breath, she stepped to him. "Okay, let's give the poor guy a show he won't forget."

"Yeah, let's." Linc curled his hand around the back of her neck and eased her with him into view of the window. In the soft light cast from behind, her hair darkened to burnished mahogany. Her skin glowed gold. And her eyes... Despite the bravado in her manner, in her voice, he could read the uneasiness there as clearly as he could see their color. Two cops, he thought, doing what it took to get the job done.

With his free hand, he traced her shoulder, his palm drifting upward to cup the side of her throat. His lips brushed her temple, as soft as a whisper, then nibbled on her earlobe.

"I..." Pulling back, she shuddered as puzzlement slid over her face. "Look, the deal is you're going to kiss me."

"You're right, I am." He framed her face with his hands then dipped his head to toy with her lips. Slowly. Gently.

"Not like this." Her fingers locked around his wrists. "Like you kissed me before."

"No." His lips roamed over her cheek, then traced a path to her jaw. "Think about it," he murmured. "If this was like before, all Williams would see was the heat. The speed. A fast ride."

Her lashes fluttered when his mouth moved to her throat. "Isn't...that the idea?" she asked, her voice a hoarse whisper.

He could hear the unsteadiness in her breath, feel it coming slow and heavy through her lips. He did not want to acknowledge that his own breathing had deepened, roughened. This was an *act*, a part of their job. The success of their current operation might hinge on their performance over the next minutes.

"You can buy heat, speed and a fast ride on a street

corner,'' he continued, his mouth hovering an inch over hers. ''In those back rooms at The Hideaway.'' He slid his hands in one long, possessive stroke down the sides of her body. Then up. ''The cowboy doesn't believe we care about each other. That's what we have to show him. What he needs to see.'' His arms slipped around her while his teeth nipped her jaw. ''The caring. The emotion.''

Her hands slid up his arms, her fingers curving around his neck. ''Makes…sense,'' she breathed.

Wrapped in woman, Linc felt his blood heat and reason slip against the pull of need. In one hammer beat of his heart he realized he had made a very big mistake. Holding her had led to wanting her. Needing her would be a breath away.

He had vowed to never again care enough about a woman to want. *To need.* He knew too well the high price a man could pay for loving a woman. For failing her. For letting her die because he put his job first.

He felt the familiar stab of pain through his heart and knew he should step away. *Now.* Hope the cowboy had bought their act. Figure out some other way to deal with the situation if he hadn't.

Carrie melted against him, dangerously warm, dangerously soft. Her surrender hit him with the force of a bare-fisted punch. In that one shimmering moment he realized he could not be just a cop, intent on getting rid of a tail. He was foremost a man, holding a woman who had begun to touch something inside him.

He damned himself even as he speared a hand into her hair and pressed his lips to her throat. Her taste, her very essence, seeped into him, pore by pore.

When a beam of light lasered through the dim room, it took an instant for his brain to click back. Lifting his head, he glanced out the window in time to see the taillights of Williams's pickup disappear into the night.

"Reilly?"

Carrie's raspy whisper pulled his gaze from the window. She gazed up at him, her face flushed, her eyes huge. Against his chest he felt her breasts heaving, her body shuddering.

"The cowboy's gone," he said quietly.

Rising on her toes, she nipped her teeth into his bottom lip. "Do something for me?"

His hand fisted in her hair as need rolled through him. His blood was raging now, the taste of her hot on his tongue. "What?"

"Close the curtain."

When she tugged his mouth down on hers, Linc felt his control snap, echoing like the violent crack of a gunshot.

Chapter 8

Carrie had felt certain she'd known what Linc's plan to get rid of West Williams entailed. So in the seconds before stepping into her partner's arms, she'd prepared herself to deal with much the same emotional onslaught she'd felt during the searing kiss they'd shared behind The Hideaway.

She had expected her blood to heat.

Predicted her legs would turn jittery, her knees weak.

Acknowledged she could do nothing to prevent Linc's kiss from knocking her somewhat off balance.

Logic, however, had told her tonight's performance would be less bone rattling this time around. That the experience would be much the same as taking repeat rides on a roller coaster; after the first trip, the ones that followed simply didn't pack the same punch.

Nothing could have prepared her for this foray into tenderness. The lightness of Linc's touch had sparked bolts of heated sensation beneath her skin that made her muscles quiver. His slow, gentle, tormenting kisses had stolen her breath. She'd been aware of every pulse point in her body coming alive, of the long, quiet pull from deep inside her. Aware, too, of her control and common sense slipping away, yet she didn't give a damn.

Nothing mattered but this man who had slowly, achingly transformed her into a volcano waiting to erupt, a storm ready to blow.

Now, with her fingers shoved into his hair and his mouth hard on hers, she had a vague awareness of Linc jerking the curtain closed seconds before they tumbled onto the bed.

As they sank into the sagging mattress, his touch went from heated, lazy discovery to hot, hard and seeking. She, too, was desperate to feast, and so she did, parting her lips to take his tongue into her mouth while her fingers fought open the buttons on his shirt. She spread her palms flat on his chest, reveling in the feel of hard muscle and crisp dark hair.

With a savage groan rising in his throat, he gripped her sweater and jerked it up, their ravenous mouths parting only when he pulled the garment over her head. An instant later her bra followed her sweater into space.

He swore softly, his breath jagged as he filled his hands with her breasts. "You're gorgeous, Carrie," he murmured, brushing a kiss against the hollow beneath her collarbone.

"So are you." In the buttery wash of light his flesh looked golden as she slicked her hands over his chest, down the hard planes of his stomach to the waistband of his jeans. The change in his eyes, the deepening, the darkening as desire grew ignited little licks of fire inside her belly.

"I could eat you alive," he said, then closed his mouth on one nipple and suckled.

Arousal clouded her mind, while pleasure zinged through her body. She curved her hand around the back of his neck, urging him to increase the pressure of his mouth.

A moan vibrated up her throat while need washed over her. Her skin was going hot, then cold, shivering and sweating under his touch. What was it about this man, *this one man,* that made her world tilt? she wondered hazily. This one man who was so wrong for her, yet showing her all the right moves.

So wrong for her. Even as he fed on her, reason broke through desire, bringing a sharp clarity about what was happening. It wasn't just because she had ignored her iron-clad rule to never again get involved with another cop that made Linc Reilly so wrong for her. He was a suspect in seven murders, *her* suspect. And if she didn't do something in the next minute or two, the man she was investigating would not just be on top of her but *inside* her.

"No." She gripped his shoulders, intending to push him away, but her hands were trembling so badly all she could manage was a futile nudge. "Linc, no."

He raised his head; a sensual, feral gleam glinted in his eyes. "Am I hurting you?"

"No." When she attempted to roll away, he tightened his grip, holding her in his control.

"What's wrong?"

"We can't do this." The sense of power, of danger about him sent a dart of panic through her system. "Linc, we can't—"

"We sure as hell can."

One of his hands was cupped around her breast, his other beneath her skirt, his palm pressed against the inside of her thigh. She could swear she felt the separate heat from each of his fingers branding her flesh. He couldn't know, would never know how desperately she wanted to feel those hands move over every inch of her body.

"*I* can't," she amended, hating the thready emotion in her voice, but unable to control it. She sank her nails into his shoulders. "I can't work with you and be involved like this."

His eyes slitted. "Don't you think it's a little late in the game to figure that out?"

"Yes. This is my fault." She squirmed hard enough that he let her go. "I should never have let things get this far." Since the mattress had the same qualities as a hammock, it took added effort to scoot to the edge of the bed. When she shot to her feet she was appalled to feel herself sway in her spiky-heeled boots. Only then did she realize she hadn't even taken her gun out of her boot before she jumped into bed.

Linc surged off the mattress, clamped a hand on her arm. "Steady."

"I'm okay." Just the feel of his hand on her flesh made her throat ache and her body yearn. "I am."

His mouth thinned. "Glad to hear one of us is." His voice was clipped, edged with the same frustration swirling in his eyes.

"I'm sorry." Turning away, she dragged in air while the emotion welling inside her filled her chest to bursting. She had never, *never* been as reckless, as thoughtless as she had just been. Along with that knowledge came a sense of mortification. If she could melt into the cheap carpet, she would.

"I...just need to go," she said, pulling from his hold. She swept up her sweater, jerked it on. Her response to Linc had been lust, she told herself. He had turned her on, and she'd responded. Period.

She pressed a hand to her stomach. If lust were all she was dealing with, why did her insides feel as if she were ripping apart? It wasn't simply lust, she knew. She hadn't almost just had sex. She had been close to *making love*. Her breathing shallowed when she realized she had never before wanted a man with such ferocity and primal greed as she wanted Linc.

"You want to tell me why the hell you suddenly feel the urge to run from me?" he asked, anger vibrating beneath his words.

"I'm sorry," she repeated, her voice a shaky whisper. Struggling to regain her emotional balance, she forced herself to meet his gaze. The hard set to his mouth, the storm in his eyes and the muscle clenched in the side of his jaw were the last things that would help her find any sense of calm.

Looking away, she spotted her coat, which had fallen off the bed into a heap. She jerked it up, dumped the pockets in the process. Crouching, she gathered up her gloves, car keys and the half-consumed roll of antacids.

"Having a problem with your stomach?" he asked as she swept up the roll.

"Not really." She snagged her bra off the chair then rose. "They're more like candy than anything." She'd tried for a dismissive tone, but her voice shook with the same intensity as her hands.

He moved to the table, grabbed the glass that sat beside a bottle of scotch and took a drink. "Candy for a person whose nerves are on edge." His eyes locked with hers over the rim of the glass. "For someone under stress."

She stuffed everything except her car keys into one coat pocket. "Working undercover like we're doing can get to a person. I guess you know that."

He took another long swallow. "So, working undercover does a job on your nerves?"

"Yes." Her unease intensified. He was watching her

just a bit too closely. "Linc, doesn't all the pretense get to you? Don't you ever feel unsettled?"

"We're talking about you right now. Are jittery nerves the reason you can't keep your gaze locked with mine?"

Her hand tightened on her key ring. "I'm feeling a little embarrassed right now."

"I mean all the other times when you can't look me in the eye. If a suspect does that, I know he's either lying or withholding information." He gestured the glass toward the bed. "Now this. You're gung-ho one second, the next you're in a panic to get away from me. I felt you stiffen—it was like some thought caught up with you just in time for you to pull back. Why don't you just level with me? Tell me what's going on?"

Oh, God. Her palms began to sweat, and her lungs needed more oxygen than was in the entire room. "What's going on is I can't be intimate with you and work with you. I'm sure you'll agree our mutual attraction has already caused a problem for us where West Williams is concerned."

He set the glass on the table. His long, tapered fingers drew her gaze as he began buttoning the shirt she had nearly ripped open. "Keep going."

"There's nothing else. It's the job." She started to pull on her coat, had both arms in the sleeves when he moved in with lightning speed, clamping his hands on her shoulders. "Hey—"

With her arms caught behind her in the coat, she was essentially helpless as he propelled her back against the wall and held her there.

She could have him flat on the floor in a heartbeat—so she told herself. Yet she remained motionless, her heart thudding against her ribs as she glared up at him. "What the hell do you think you're doing?"

"Trying to get a straight answer out of you," he retorted. "I've been a cop a long time. I *know* when some-one's holding back on me. Some thought, some *something* hit you and you backed off. You're carrying around extra weight, lady. We both know it."

With her insides in turmoil she forced a cool smile. "Reilly, don't you know it's not smart to tell a woman she's carrying around extra weight?"

His tawny-gold eyes narrowed. "Sidestep the subject all you want, McCall, but I know what I know."

"Wrong." Shoving out of his grasp, she jerked up her coat. "In this case you're way off base," she countered, even as she silently acknowledged he'd read her like a book.

Hands unsteady, she cinched her coat's belt around her waist while her gaze returned to the scarred table. She focused on the thick file folder beside the scotch bottle. If she looked inside the folder would she find notes on all the Avenger's victims? Maybe a list of career criminals slated for a head shot? If so, the search she still intended to conduct of his house tonight would be wasted effort.

Searching Linc's house. She had almost slept with the man, and here she was, planning on rummaging through his home. Guilt over what faced her weighed like a stone on her heart. The heart that even now did a long, unsteady cartwheel at the memory of the feel of his hands on her flesh. The same heart that couldn't quite accept he was the killer she sought.

"Linc..." A wave of emotion closed her throat. She'd been born knowing a lot about the male species, but she was totally unsure how to deal with this grim-eyed man who demanded answers she couldn't give. Most answers, she amended. After what had just happened between them, he deserved to hear the part of the truth she could tell him.

"You got something to say, McCall?"

"Yes." She met his turbulent gaze. "This isn't easy to

talk about, so bear with me. Do you remember a cop named Parker Jackson? He quit the department nearly two years ago.''

"I knew of him," Linc said. "He lost his job because he got too rough with a suspect, right?''

"Good memory.'' A drag of old pain had Carrie wrapping her arms around her waist. "Park and I weren't partners but we both worked the same shift out of the Hefner briefing station. He'd been divorced a couple of months when we got involved. There were rumors we were messing around with each other prior to that. We weren't. And when we did start seeing each other we agreed to keep the job separate from our personal lives.''

"I guess you're telling me this because that's not what happened?''

"No. I knew Park felt protective of me. That he needed to look out for me on the job. That's the last thing I wanted. He swore he could handle my working the streets, and I believed him. Then one night I was on patrol and saw this juvie stumbling along the sidewalk. I had the window down and even from inside the car I could smell the beer on him. I pulled over, radioed dispatch. Park was in the area, so he advised dispatch he would back me on the call.''

"Standard procedure,'' Linc commented.

"The instant I confronted the drunk kid he started mouthing off, calling me every name in the book. I'd heard it all before and it just rolled off. I had one of his wrists cuffed when he suddenly decided to resist. He was tall and hefty, and when he wheeled around and shoved me backward I lost my footing. I kept my grip on the cuffs so when I went down he did, too, on top of me. I hit my temple on the curb and it started bleeding. The cut wasn't bad, but I could barely see for all the blood.''

"Let me guess. Jackson took it personal that the kid hurt a woman he cared about."

"Park went nuts. Before I could get back on my feet he grabbed the kid and slammed him face down. Instead of cuffing him, he stomped on his arm. Broke it." Carrie paused. Even after nearly two years she could still hear the sickening sound of bone snapping.

"If it had been any other cop hurt but you, Jackson would have just cuffed the kid," Linc ventured. "Instead, his feelings for you caused him to lose control."

Carrie nodded. "The juvie's lawyer agreed not to sue if his client walked on the public-drunk, resisting-arrest and assault-on-a-police-officer charges. The city covered the kid's medical expenses."

"And Jackson agreed to quit the job to avoid facing an aggravated assault charge. A felony."

"He could have gone to prison. Because of me."

"No," Linc said, giving her a pointed look. "He was responsible for his own actions. Every cop is."

"Say that all you want, but if I hadn't been involved with him he would probably still be on the job," she countered. "Still have a pension in his future."

"What happened after he quit?"

"We tried to make a go of our relationship." She felt the ripple of regret that always accompanied thoughts of the man for whom she'd begun to care deeply and had contemplated a future with. "At first Park seemed to accept things. He got a job and studied to get his real estate license. But as time passed he got bitter. His having to see me in uniform just reminded him of what he'd lost because of me." She dragged in a breath. "He wasn't the only one having problems. It got to the point that every time I looked at him I heard that kid's arm break. Our relationship ended by mutual agreement."

Linc stepped toward her. "Sounds like you both lost something."

"We did. For a while tonight I forgot about that. Forgot I swore I would never get involved with another cop I worked with." Her gaze shifted toward the window, to the cheap curtain Linc had closed at her bidding. "When you told me West drove away, you expected me to step back. I should have. But I didn't and we wound up on that bed because I…" She pressed her fingertips against her eyes.

"Because you what?"

"Because I *wanted* to be there with you. *Still* want to be there." She shook her head. "You're angry because you feel like I intentionally led you on. I didn't. What I did do is suddenly remember how bad things can turn when cops who work together get involved." She raised a hand, let it fall. "Linc, I can't be your partner and your lover. I can't do both and keep a clear head. That day on the stairwell we agreed to back off. To be smart." She attempted a smile but it wouldn't gel. "Your part of tonight's plan *was* smart—West went away. *I* turned things into a fiasco by dragging you into bed. Now we've got even more problems to deal with. This is all on me and I was wrong. I'm sorry."

He watched her for the space of a dozen heartbeats, his eyes unreadable. "Smart," he murmured. "I haven't wanted to put my hands on a woman since… Then you came along."

His words had her heart doing something that felt like a skip. She said nothing. She trusted neither her voice nor the tangle of emotions knotting together inside her.

"You weren't the only one on that bed, Carrie. I could have backed off." Turning, he grabbed his jacket. "We *both* broke our agreement, so we both make sure that doesn't happen again. From now on, we stay smart. Keep our minds on the job. Deal?"

"Deal." Feeling a measure of relief, she watched him shrug into his jacket. "Going somewhere?"

"I'm following you home."

"There's no need—"

"I suspect your cowboy got our message, but I want to make sure. For all we know he's parked down the street, waiting for you to drive away so he can start tailing you again."

"I live all the way across town. It's ridiculous for you to drive there, then come back here."

"You're right." He holstered his Glock, clipped it onto his waistband beneath his jacket. "I'll sleep at home tonight."

She felt an almost crazy relief knowing her search of his house had just been postponed. With her emotions in upheaval, she needed time to level. To think. "That's probably smart."

His mouth lifted in a sardonic curve. "It's what we just agreed." He snagged the file off the table. "Speaking of chart, we also need to make sure your cowboy pal believes I've put the shine back on our relationship. From now on, we'll meet at the office and ride together to and from the Hideaway. And we'll start spending more time together while we're there. All that should keep Williams at bay."

"Fine." Carrie fisted her hands at the thought of spending even more time with Linc, but what he said made sense.

"You ready to get out of here?"

She looked at the bed. The same sort of panic she'd felt as a green rookie answering her first shots-fired call settled inside her at the thought of how effortlessly she had turned her back on caution and self-control. She had screwed up royally by allowing herself to get swept away by passion. There was no changing what had happened, but she *could* control future events. She had to block her feelings for Linc—whatever the heck they were. Build a wall around herself that emotion couldn't penetrate. That way she could get back on course, deal objectively with the demands and pressures of the job. Follow orders. *Do her duty.*

"I'm more than ready to get out of here," she answered quietly.

Chapter 9

he morning air delivered a chill that cut to the bone and
ved with Linc on his way up the stairs to the Selective
orcement Unit's third-floor office.

he instant he stepped into the squad room, Evelyn
bes's brows slid together while her fingers continued
ing her computer's keyboard. "Either I'm in a time
p or you're here on your day off." The SEU's secretary
a slim, attractive brunette in her midthirties, efficient
discreet in her work. Linc concurred with the unoffi-
survey that had pegged her as the civilian employee
the best legs in the department.

Relax, Ev, you haven't stumbled into some parallel
rse." He snagged a piece of caramel out of the bowl
ept perpetually filled on her desk. "I've got paper-
to catch up on."

ping the caramel into his mouth, he headed to the
maker behind her desk. Since the brew in the pot
led mud he asked, "How long has this been sitting

"Coffee's so fresh you'll have to slap it," Evelyn answered without missing a beat on the keyboard. "It looks strong because that's how I made it. Sammy has colic, so I was up most of the night. Consuming nuclear-strength doses of caffeine is the only way I'll manage to stay awake all day."

"Whatever works," Linc commented. He retrieved an empty mug, noting the air in the squad room still carried the scent of the pine cleaner the janitorial service swabbed the tile floor with every night.

"Must be one tall stack of paper to lure you in on your day off," Evelyn ventured.

He shrugged. "Call me dedicated." Although he had several minor repair jobs to do around the house, he had not wanted to spend the day with only Kim's glowering Siamese for company.

Evelyn's phone rang. While she snatched up the receiver, Linc filled the mug. Cognizant of the routine background noise of murmuring voices and keyboards clicking, he swept his gaze over the squad room where Tom Nelson and a couple of other detectives sat working at their desks. Despite his best intention not to, Linc shifted his attention to Carrie's neat, orderly desk on which she had yet to add even one personal item. No plant, no framed photo of her close-knit cop family, not even a paperweight. Atypical for a woman who liked to accessorize, he thought, then chided himself for wishing the desk's occupant would appear. He knew she wouldn't show until late tomorrow evening when it was time for them to leave for The Hideaway.

And when she did strut into the squad room, he predicted she would treat him with the same crisp, ruthlessly all-business manner she'd adopted since their encounter three nights ago at the Drop Inn.

His partner, it seemed, was having no problem sticking to their renewed agreement to turn their backs on the attraction they felt for each other and be smart. Since then, she had put up about a hundred walls and turned as cool as the late-November weather. It was as if the woman whose body had heated and shuddered beneath his touch had disappeared. Now, she was solely a cop, intent on completing an assignment.

Despite the walls, she continued to do a damn good job of acting while they were at The Hideaway. There, she treated him with sassy, open seductiveness while she cuddled against him at the bar. And when they danced, she twined her arms around his neck and moved against him in a sultry, sexy sway that tightened his gut. Anyone watching saw a man and woman deep in the throes of lust and passion. But the instant he and Carrie drove out of sight of the bar, the walls went up, and the woman who had rolled with him across the motel's sagging mattress no longer existed.

Which was how things had to be, he acknowledged.

Considering Carrie's past with Parker Jackson, Linc understood why she'd sworn off getting involved with another co-worker. Further, he agreed their operating within professional boundaries was the only way they could effectively do their jobs.

Even so, he had a very different reason for having shored up his own defenses.

During the erotic, seductive hover of time he'd held Carrie, he had forgotten there was no room in his life for a woman. Any woman. His wife had died because *he* had put her at risk. The weight of Kim's murder sat on his conscience, an unrelenting, sick heaviness that he would never shed. Had no right to shed. He would never again risk, never again put himself in the position to hurt or be hurt.

Still, he conceded, his resolving to keep his hands off Carrie had been the easy part. Too bad his grip on restraint didn't prevent his mind from continually replaying how she had looked lying in his arms, a wash of gold light against her flesh, her eyes dark and smoky, her hair a tumble of flame around her face. No matter how he tried to erase the image, it clung in his mind. He knew he would remember that vision of her for the rest of his life. Just as he would never forget the panic that had flashed in her eyes and the feel of her muscles going stiff beneath his touch.

Deception was an art, he thought, his eyes narrowing on her neat desk. One he had perfected during his years working undercover. He'd learned the trick to successful deceit was to get as close as possible to the truth. Instinct told him his partner had been about a solar system away from the truth when she'd claimed she had no reason *not* to look him in the eye.

He couldn't have the woman, he accepted that. What he could have was Carrie McCall's secret. He was patient. He knew how to wait, to choose his time and his place. He would find out whatever it was she was keeping from him. Eventually.

"Hey, Detective Dedicated," Evelyn said as she hung up her phone. "Your presence is requested."

Linc took his first sip of coffee. "By whom and where?"

"Quintana. His office." Evelyn's dark hair swung against one cheek when she dipped her head. "He just got back from a meeting downtown. Now he wants to see you. Better you than me, since he sounds like a rabid dog looking for a leg to rip off."

"Thanks for the warning."

Through the glass pane that looked out on the squad room, Linc spotted the lieutenant at his desk, snatching up his phone. To give Quintana time to deal with whoever was on the other end of the call, Linc swung by his desk and shrugged out of his leather bomber jacket.

Across the aisle, Tom Nelson, looking as scruffy as ever in a wrinkled shirt and ratty jeans, had his own phone plastered to his ear. Light from the overhead fixtures glinted off the gold badge hanging from a chain around his neck as he furiously jotted notes across a legal pad. The detective gave Linc a vague nod and continued writing.

Still on the phone, Quintana glanced up just as Linc reached his office. Rolling his eyes toward the ceiling, the lieutenant waved him in. Linc settled into a chair, noting that Quintana's dark suit, starched white shirt and striped tie looked as immaculate as always. His black hair, fading to gray at the temples, was cropped close, a leftover from his days as a Navy SEAL. Although he'd spent the past twelve years behind a desk, John Quintana appeared to be as fit and tough as when he rode the streets.

"You want to make excuses?" Quintana barked into the phone. "Fine, make all you want, but not to me. Bottom line is I need those figures on my desk before five o'clock." He ended the call by slamming down the receiver.

Raising a brow, Linc sipped his coffee. "Your morning going well, Lieu?"

Quintana cursed. "You ever think about taking a supervisor's job, Reilly, think again. A month ago I turned in this unit's budget for next year. I go to a meeting downtown this morning and get told by some idiot bean counter I have to cut expenses another five percent. *Five percent!* Want to guess what I'll be working on Thanksgiving break?"

"I think I've got that figured out." Linc stared into his coffee while his gut knotted. Kim's body had been found on Thanksgiving Day. The closer it got to the second anniversary of her murder, the harder it was to accept that he had failed to track down her killer. Failed to even pick up a whiff of his scent, despite an informant who'd sworn he'd spotted the tattooed bastard at The Hideaway.

"Enough about the damn budget." Blowing out a breath, Quintana smoothed a hand over his dark hair and focused on Linc. "Isn't this McCall's and your day off?"

"Yes. I came in to catch up on paperwork."

"If you hadn't I would be calling you about right now."

"What's up?"

"I ran into Chief Berry downtown. He's got a meeting with the mayor this afternoon. Berry wants to brief His Honor on the status of The Hideaway investigation, which means I've got to brief the chief. Last time I talked to you and McCall you had the video-gambling and illegal-distribution-of-liquor charges locked in. What else can you add?"

"Since we last briefed you, McCall and I have witnessed a couple of liquor sales to minors," Linc began. "The illegal gambling we now know about includes not just the video games, but football, horse racing and shooting dice."

"Good. What about the working girls?"

Linc set his mug on the edge of Quintana's desk. "I've written up soliciting charges on five of The Hideaway's female employees. Another one hit me up last night while I played pool. I'll do the paperwork on her today."

"How they running things?"

"Using a whiskey and champagne hustle." Linc propped one booted foot on his opposite knee. "To start, each hooker requires her *date* to order three drinks from the bar, ten bucks per drink. The john is then primed with enough booze so he agrees to buy the required bottle of champagne. The stuff they serve is cheap, but he's charged

$125. Only after that does the hooker take him into one of the small rooms in the rear of the bar.''

"Let me guess," Quintana said. "After they're in the room, the horny schmucks get told there's an additional charge for sex.''

"Exactly," Linc said.

"Okay. What's the status on the back booth?''

"McCall and I are sure it's a distribution point for drugs. We just haven't been able to get anybody to bite yet when we ask about making a buy for ourselves. We think we've built up enough trust with one of the bartenders and a couple of waitresses that we'll get to start making purchases soon. The more buys we make ourselves, the tighter the case we present to the D.A. The camera Crawford planted in the jukebox has netted us plenty of pictures of customers who've done business in that booth. Using those, it should be easy to convince a judge just how much dope gets distributed there every night.''

"What about the guy you suspect is dealing stolen property?''

"Howard Klinger, goes by Howie Kling. McCall has made a connection at The Hideaway who claims he can get her in to buy jewelry from Klinger.''

"How soon will that happen?''

"Hard to say. Her contact hasn't shown up at the bar for three nights running.''

"You think he's made you as cops?''

"Not a chance." Considering the show he and Carrie put on for West Williams's benefit, Linc wasn't surprised the cowboy had gone off to lick his wounds. "It's my bet he'll show up again soon. Meanwhile, McCall has put out the description to law enforcement of both silver bracelets she knows for sure Klinger sold to people. Both pieces of jewelry are distinctive, so we're hoping we get a stolen hit soon.''

Quintana turned a pen end over end. "Thanksgiving is three days from now," he said after a moment. "Doesn't sound like you and McCall will wind things up before then."

"We won't." For the hundredth time, Linc damned the fact he had yet to spot his tattooed quarry. Once law enforcement raided the bar and shut it down, he would lose his sole connection to Kim's killer. Something close to desperation pushed him to buy more time. "We'd be crazy to end the operation before we get something firm on Klinger. It's clear he's operating with full knowledge of The Hideaway's owner, so if we nail Klinger, the big boss man is looking at a conspiracy charge for concealing stolen property. That'll go a long way in stopping him from ever operating a bar in this state again."

"True. I'll make sure the chief points that out to the mayor. It might keep His Honor's impatience in check."

"The more time McCall and I spend at The Hideaway, the more illegal acts we observe."

Quintana set his pen aside. "Speaking of McCall, how are things going between you and your new partner?"

Figuring his boss was referring to the near kiss he'd witnessed in the stairwell, Linc replied, "Sergeant McCall and I are concentrating solely on The Hideaway investigation. On what needs to be done to make you, the chief and the mayor happy."

"Good. And after this operation wraps up? You want to keep her as your partner?"

Linc knew if he said no, Quintana wouldn't ask questions. He would simply shift assignments and pair Carrie and him with new partners. Stepping back, distancing himself from anything that would bring him into contact with her again and again would be the smart thing to do. Linc *knew* that.

Knew, too, there was something inside him that couldn't

totally walk away from her. Not when just the thought of doing so put a quick twist of emptiness in his chest.

"McCall and I make a solid team," he said. "Good working partners. I'd like that to continue."

"All right." Quintana gave him a considering look. "You two have been paired for a couple of weeks. Partners tend to talk. Have you told her your theory that a rogue cop is killing people who commit nasty crimes? And using this unit's files to choose them?"

Today was Quintana's first mention of the killings since Linc confided in him after learning of the murder in Tulsa. "I haven't told McCall. If I am right and the cop figures out someone's on to him, it'll be safer for her not to know."

"Makes sense. Any idea yet on which of your co-workers might be pulling these murders? And maybe setting things up so it looks like you capped those victims, or whatever you'd call them?"

Linc thought about Don Gaines, of how viciously the man hated him for Kim's death. He didn't want to believe his former friend would resort to murder to set him up, but Linc had long since learned that in police work—and in life—one had to expect the unexpected. Still, he had no proof Gaines was pulling the trigger, and he wasn't going to voice his theory until—and if—he got that proof.

"All I know is it isn't me."

"Reilly, you've been under my command for two years. I know how you work. If it *was* you, you wouldn't target the scum you dealt with yourself. Nor would you have shot a guy in Tulsa the same weekend you stayed nearby with your in-laws."

"You're right, I wouldn't." Because Quintana had broached the subject, Linc decided to press on. "When I came to you about the killings, you said you'd take my theory to Captain Vincent."

"I did." Quintana leaned back in his chair. "The boss about had a stroke. He assured me he would take the matter up the chain of command."

"If that's the case, I'm surprised this unit hasn't had a visit from Internal Affairs."

"Actually, I've been in touch with Patricia Scott a couple of times," Quintana said, referred to IA's female captain. "Have you seen the news lately? Watched the video where the so-called 'Good Samaritan' taped two uniform cops using their night sticks on the pimp?"

"Hard to miss it when it's shown on every local channel at least three times a day."

"The mayor, city manager and chief are buried with calls from citizens giving their opinions. IA is handling the initial investigation. Their findings have to be turned over to the Feds soon, so the clock is ticking. Captain Scott said IA is covered up. She'll get one of their people here as soon as she can cut someone loose. In the meantime, she's asked me to get files from this unit together. I'm also taking a hard look at my own people. See if I can figure out what cop is pulling these murders, if one is." Quintana picked up his pen. "You know, Reilly, thugs do get killed on the street by other thugs."

"That's not the case here, Lieu. These homicides are too efficient. Preplanned. There's a pattern that says 'cop.'"

A sharp rap had Linc and Quintana looking toward the door.

"Sorry to interrupt," Tom Nelson said. "There's a Dallas cop on the phone, asking to talk to McCall." As he spoke, Nelson scratched his untrimmed beard. "Says he has information about the jewelry she issued a flyer on."

Quintana looked at Linc. "Take the call. Maybe you just got lucky. Could be this cop has the connection you and McCall need to wrap up your Hideaway investigation."

"Yeah," Linc said as he rose and headed for the door. "Lucky us."

"Come on, Mom," Carrie chided. "We scheduled this spa day to relax and plan Morgan's wedding. It's your turn to let Fritz put his very talented hands on you. *All over you.*"

Because that was what the amazing Fritz had just done to her, Carrie—swaddled in a terry robe—slid bonelessly into the padded salon recliner beside her mother's.

Reaching a freshly manicured hand toward the glass-topped table between the recliners, Carrie retrieved the crystal flute that held her second mimosa of the morning. "It's a huge bonus that Fritz is a gorgeous hunk," she added, her languid voice mixing with the soft music drifting on the scented air.

Despite the green purifying mask that covered her face, Roma McCall's frown shone through like a beacon. "I'm opting for a female masseuse. After all, Fritz is not your father."

"Thank goodness." Blond hair piled on top of her head, Morgan McCall plucked a chocolate-covered strawberry from the table that had been wheeled into the privacy room. With the mud mask on her face almost dry, Morgan could barely open her mouth wide enough to nibble on the ripe fruit. "No way would I be looking forward to stripping down to my birthday suit if Daddy were the man doing the massaging."

"What about Alex?" Grace Fox asked. Her dark hair in a ponytail, Grace's wide-set eyes were teasing as she sidled up to the table beside her sister. "How's he at giving massages?"

"Let me put it this way," Morgan said, her mouth curving. "My fiancé has the best hands in the state."

With aromatherapy candles scenting the warm air and alcohol dimming her defenses, Carrie's thoughts slid to Linc. To the throat-catching thrill of his palms racing across her heated flesh, and the shuddering feel of his fingers pressed against the inside of her thigh. Over the past three days she had held her thoughts in check, refused to think about their encounter in the dimly lit motel room. Now, with her guard down, thoughts of the erotic moments she had spent in his arms settled a lovely liquid tug in her belly.

She took another sip of her drink and eased out a desire-laced breath. "Don't be so sure, Morgan," she murmured. "I know a man who might give Blade a run for his money in the best-hands category."

"Keep going." Grace sniffed the bouquet of yellow roses on the table before popping a purple grape into her mouth. Fresh from a pedicure, she had pieces of pink tissue snaking between her coral-painted toes. "I don't know about Mom and Morgan, but I had no clue you'd started seeing someone. Tell all."

"Yeah, Carrie," Morgan chimed in, then took a sip of champagne. "No fair keeping quiet when you've got a man on the hook. Tell all."

"Girls," Roma cautioned, holding up a hand encased in a fabric heat mitt. "We scheduled this spa day so we can plan Morgan's wedding in between treatments. We haven't gotten much done. Not that they're not interesting topics, but if you start talking men and sex we won't get a lot planned."

"Mom's right." Giving herself a mental shake, Carrie set her mimosa aside. The last thing she needed was to loosen her tongue with even more alcohol and start blathering about Linc. "So, Morgan, tell us what you've decided about our dresses."

"Sleek and sexy." Morgan stabbed a stick of celery into a silver bowl filled with dip. "When we hit the bridal store, Tory goes with us. I want her in the wedding, no matter what happens between her and Bran."

"Any updates on that?" Carrie asked. Several weeks ago the eldest McCall brother shocked the family with news that he and his wife had separated.

Roma let out a weighty sigh. "Tory's out of town so I haven't talked to her. Bran's mood is as dark as a gathering storm. He won't say one word about what happened between them."

Just then, a pink-frocked spa attendant peeked through the door. The woman was a long-stemmed Barbie clone with a body that was apparently no stranger to the StairMaster. "Ladies, Fritz is ready for another massage. Who wants to go next?"

"Morgan, let the man work his magic on you," Roma said.

"If I must." She lifted her crystal flute in a toast before padding out the door in pink slippers that matched her terry robe.

Roma held up her mitt-encased hands. "I think my cuticles are well-done."

The attendant slipped off the mitts, then the plastic and paraffin beneath. She then dabbed a fingertip into the green goo covering Roma's forehead. "The mask needs a few minutes longer, Mrs. McCall. In the meantime, let's move you into a treatment room for your full-body scrub and facial."

The woman turned to Carrie and Grace. "Can I get you ladies anything while you wait for the hairstylist?"

"We're fine," Grace said, then settled into the recliner her mother vacated. The senior McCall sister waited until the door closed then turned to Carrie, interest twinkling in her dark eyes. "So, who's the man with the great hands?"

Carrie raised a shoulder. It had been a year and a half since her relationship with Parker Jackson had ended. She'd had plenty of dates since then, but no man had garnered enough enthusiasm for her to even mention him to her sisters. It was no wonder her ill-advised comment had piqued Grace's curiosity.

"He's no one who's going to make a difference in my life. Grace, I need some advice."

A freshly plucked brow slid up her sister's forehead. "Surely not about men? You're the expert."

After the way she'd handled the situation with Linc, Carrie considered herself an amateur.

"I need advice about the job. You've worked in various units. Conducted tons of investigations. I need to know about handling an investigation the *right* way."

"Is something going on with the bar assignment you and Reilly are working?"

Grace had stopped by the SEU recently when Carrie and Linc were catching up on reports. Linc had given Grace a vague overview of their operation. "I can't give you specifics," Carrie said carefully. "What I need to know is if you ever worked a case where you had something that felt close to tunnel vision? Maybe you got so focused on one piece of evidence or a certain suspect that you ran the risk of missing crucial pieces of the puzzle?"

"Sure I have. It's when you're almost positive something is just so, even when it isn't. That something about the case feels so good it just has to be. Maybe you, your partner, even your boss can build a great logical case out of pure conjecture and everything fits."

"Everything fits," Carrie agreed, thinking of the case IA had built against Linc. "That's how it is with an investigation I'm working. Things fit. But something tells

me I'm looking at the wrong suspect.'' Her heart, she thought. It was her heart that kept telling her Linc was innocent. Both unable and unwilling to ignore the message, she'd spent hours of her off-duty time poring over the files IA had supplied her on the seven murders. Hours studying the background of every detective in the SEU. She'd found nothing that might turn the finger of suspicion away from Linc and on to another cop.

Carrie made a frustrated jab at a stray tendril of hair. ''I *know* I'm misreading a piece of evidence. Definitely missing one. It's like when I was assigned to Patrol, riding the streets. I'd get a feeling something was wrong, and sure enough something was. That's how I feel now.''

''A cop's sixth sense,'' Grace said. ''I bet in the history of law enforcement there have been a zillion cases solved solely because a cop listened to his or her instincts instead of accepting something at face value.''

''I can't accept certain things. I *won't*.''

''Then don't,'' Grace said, her dark eyes alert, measuring. ''Carrie, working investigations isn't so different from operating out of a black-and-white. You trust instinct to guide you. No matter what type of case you've got, you have to start somewhere. Maybe the only starting point is your cop's sixth sense telling you where to dig. So, you dig there and hopefully turn up evidence. If not, you dig somewhere else, and keep at it until you find what you need. Maybe you don't even know you need it right then, but you hold on to it and make sense of it later. The worst thing you can do is jump to conclusions because something sounds so logical it just 'has to be.'''

''Thanks.'' Carrie gripped her sister's hand and squeezed. ''I appreciate the advice.''

''You're welcome.'' Grace tilted her head. ''Something tells me you already knew all that.''

''It just helps to hear another cop say it.'' Carrie studied her sister's elegant, manicured hand, the bare ring finger on which she'd once worn a wide gold band. It was hard to believe Grace had been a widow nearly three years.

"So, speaking of guys with great hands," Carrie began. "Is there anyone on your radar screen?"

"Hardly." Grace shook her head, her ponytail swaying with the movement. "It's impossible to imagine anyone taking Ryan's place."

"That's not how it works, Gracie. You look for a man to build a new life with, not for one to take his place. That would be impossible."

"Let's get back to your man with the great hands. Are you sure things won't turn serious?"

Carrie didn't protest the change of subject, not when she saw the shadow that had settled over her sister's eyes. "Serious isn't even in the same ballpark. It's more a major case of the hots."

"Hots can lead to serious."

"Not this time."

"Why, because the man with the great hands is Linc Reilly?"

Carrie wouldn't have been more surprised if Grace had picked up the vase of yellow roses and dumped it over her head. "Good grief, Grace, how do you *know* that?"

"That day I dropped by the SEU? I could tell."

"Tell *what?*" Carrie tugged her hand from her sister's, rose and began prowling the small room. "Linc and I were writing reports in the interview room. He gave you an overview of our case. That's all that happened."

"It wasn't anything either you or Linc said. It's just a feeling I got when I saw the two of you together. Like there's this chemistry."

"Great." Carrie paced to the table of food, then turned. "Okay, so maybe Linc and I have this chemistry going.

That doesn't mean we have a relationship. Even if we did, it wouldn't go anywhere. It couldn't.''

''Why? Because he's your partner?''

''Considering what happened between Parker Jackson and myself, don't you think that's ample reason?''

''I agree partners shouldn't get involved. But if they do, the problem goes away when one of them transfers to a different unit. I worked in Investigations, Ryan was assigned to Patrol. Our both being cops was never a problem.''

''Yeah, well, you and Ryan got lucky.''

''Yes, we did.'' Grace rose and moved across the room to where Carrie stood. ''And who's to say you haven't? I don't know Linc well, but he has the reputation of being a good, solid cop. And I know a little about what he must have gone through when his wife was murdered. It's obvious you're attracted to each other. If he's ready to move on with you, I think that's great.''

Move on, Carrie thought. There was no way to ''move on'' with a man to whom she lied every time she saw him. Even if Linc wasn't the Avenger, he would eventually find out she was working for IA. He would learn she'd been ordered to get close to him. Investigate him.

Just the prospect of his reaction when the truth came out had panic tightening her chest.

''Carrie?'' Grace took a step toward her. ''What's wrong?''

''Nothing.'' She forced a smile. ''It's nothing.''

''Then why did you just go as pale as snow?''

''The mimosa.'' Carrie turned to the table, snagged a carrot stick she had no taste for. ''Too much champagne so early in the morning. And on an empty stomach.''

''If you say so.''

Carrie was saved from having to respond when the door opened. ''Excuse me, ladies?'' The spa's dark-haired receptionist swayed into the room, looking tall and sleek in a black jumpsuit and ice-pick heels. She had a voice like cream and skin to match. "Which one of you is Sergeant McCall?"

"We both are," Grace said. "Do you want Carrie or Grace?"

"I don't know." The woman's red-glossed bee-stung lips curved. "I'll just have to go back up front and clarify that detail with the handsome gentleman."

"Some guy is *here?*" Carrie asked. "Wanting to see Sergeant McCall?"

"Yes. He showed me his badge and said it was important he speak with you." The woman's gaze flicked from Carrie to Grace, then back to Carrie. "Well, one of you."

"Describe him," Carrie said. "Other than handsome."

"Tall, dark and lean. No wedding ring." She stroked a crimson fingernail down the length of her throat. "He's got the most compelling eyes. Brown and gold, like a cat's. Yum."

"Linc Reilly." Grace sent Carrie a self-satisfied smile. "The man with the great hands."

Chapter 10

Considering the way the smoldering brunette in the black cat suit swayed against his side, Linc was surprised she didn't throw out a hip. Or break an ankle in her stiletto-heeled pumps. Maybe both.

Tightening the arm she'd hooked through his, she led him around a corner then continued down the spa's plush, carpeted corridor. "I got all flustered when I discovered there were two Sergeant McCalls," she breathed.

"Sorry for the confusion," he said. "I didn't think to mention which Sergeant McCall I'm here to see."

"I just bet you're used to getting women all flustered."

He slid her a look and said nothing as they passed an alcove with a pair of pink upholstered chairs. The air in the dim hallway smelled like a flower cart. Classical music seeped from hidden speakers. He figured the spa was top of the line, but he preferred the sweaty, salty scents and muffled grunts that hung in the air at the police gym.

"Here we are." Pausing, his escort pointed a crimson

nail at a closed door. "If you want Grace McCall, she just moved into this room with the hairdresser."

"My business is with Carrie."

"In here." The receptionist swiveled and gripped the knob on a nearby door. She tipped her face up to his. "My name's Monique. Why don't you give me a call when you get off duty?" She twisted the knob and eased open the door. "We could have drinks. Dinner."

"Nice to meet you, Monique."

Her smile dimmed when he declined to take the bait. "If you change your mind, you know where to find me."

"That I do."

Linc stepped into a small room in which the scent of roses and vanilla hung heavy on the air. His gaze swept over matching padded recliners, a gleaming glass table and shelves lined with various-size bottles and pots of lotions and oils. He spotted Carrie at the same time the door closed behind him.

"Good morning, Reilly," she said, nibbling on a celery stick. "Sounds like you just tap-danced your way around a pass."

Barefoot and clad in a pink robe, she stood beside a cloth-covered table loaded with food normally found on a salad bar. Her fiery hair was pinned up; a few tendrils brushed her cheeks and throat. She wore no makeup. He was well aware that the vamp in the cat suit hadn't made his blood run a few beats faster, but the woman standing before him did.

"Some pass." He glanced back at the door. "Monique'll have another date lined up before I manage to get out of this place."

Carrie took another bite of celery. "Speaking of this place, why have you tracked me down on our day off?"

"Sorry about showing up like this. I left a message on

your machine at home. I also tried your cell but got no answer.''

''My phone's in a locker with my clothes and purse.''

Her clothes. His gaze slicked down over the swell of her breasts. He didn't need to fantasize what those curves beneath the robe looked like, felt like. He knew.

''What's on your mind, Reilly?'' she asked, her voice level. Impersonal.

He lifted his gaze. That she regarded him with the same placid coolness she had for the past three days heated his temper. Even recognizing the inane emotion for what it was, he had trouble controlling it. How the hell could the woman stand there, gazing at him as if he'd never had his hands on her?

''I was thinking you look...relaxed,'' he said evenly.

''I am, mainly because I no longer have a spine. I lost it while being slathered, rubbed down and massaged by a gorgeous Viking god.''

Linc hooked a brow. ''They've got a Viking god working in this place?''

''Fritz. The man has magic hands and biceps like bricks. Morgan's with him now. If the walls weren't soundproofed, you'd probably hear her moan in ecstasy.''

''Yeah.'' Linc stabbed his fingers through his hair. He didn't want to think about some muscled bruiser putting his hands all over Carrie. ''Getting back to my knowing how to find you. While we were driving back from The Hideaway last night you mentioned getting together today with your sisters and mother.''

''I remember.'' She laid the celery stick aside.

''When I couldn't get you on the phone, I went downstairs to Special Projects and talked to Alex Blade.''

She blinked. ''You went to work on our day off?''

''Had some things to catch up on,'' he explained.

"Blade didn't know the name of this place, but had an idea of the approximate location."

"That probably didn't help, since there are several spas around here."

"That's what I found out when I checked the yellow pages. I could have called each one, found you and left a message. But the clock's ticking and I wanted to make sure you got word in time."

"Word on what?"

"I was briefing Quintana on our investigation when a call came in for you from a Dallas detective who works in their PD's larceny detail. He saw the information you put out on the two silver bracelets we know Howard Klinger sold at The Hideaway."

"We got a hit?" Excitement stirring in her eyes, Carrie took several steps toward him. Linc realized then that it was her skin, not the air, that carried the scent of vanilla. "The bracelets were stolen there?"

"That's the way it looks. This deal has a couple of knots in it, so it'll take some explaining."

She swept a hand toward the table. "Want something to snack on while you talk?"

"I'll pass." He rested a hand on the back of one of the padded spa chairs. "It's a good bet the jewelry leads back to a guy named Richard Zepeda who lives in Santa Fe," he began. "According to the DPD detective, Zepeda represents several designers who operate galleries in Santa Fe. Zepeda takes cross-country sales trips, making calls on upscale boutiques and taking orders for custom-made pieces of jewelry. A couple of those boutiques are in Dallas. About six months ago, Zepeda was there, calling on customers. He stopped to eat lunch at some restaurant. When he came out, the trunk of his car had been popped, and his case of samples was gone."

Linc crossed his arms over his chest. "One of the knots

I mentioned is that Zepeda had everything in his case. Pieces of jewelry, catalogues with pictures of the jewelry, order forms. He didn't have any pictures to leave with the Dallas cop. Zepeda promised to mail pictures of what was stolen, but never did.''

''So that's why the Dallas cop isn't sure the jewelry on my flyer is Zepeda's?''

''Right. He's pretty sure it is, though, because he went into a couple of boutiques that sell custom merchandise from the clients Zepeda represents. The cop said the jewelry on our flyer has the same look. He gave me a phone number for Zepeda. I called Santa Fe and talked to his wife. She's not involved in her husband's business so she has no idea what was in his case.''

''Where's Zepeda?''

''There's another knot. He's flying home from the East Coast today, which means he has to make about three connecting flights. Because he's flying, his cell phone is off. His wife says anytime he has a long enough layover, he calls her. If not, he'll wait and call from the next stop. As soon as she talks to him she'll give him our number and tell him to call our office.''

''And there's no telling when that will be?''

''No.'' Linc checked his watch. ''His first layover is about an hour from now. I want to be back at the office in case he calls then. I've got everything covered, so you don't need to be there. But, since you developed the jewelry lead, I wanted to give you a chance to work it.'' He glanced at the food on the table, the bottle of champagne stabbing out of a frost-coated silver ice bucket. ''I don't want you to leave and get on the wrong side of your sisters or your mom.''

Carrie arched a brow. ''You're talking about two other cops and a woman married to a cop. In my family, duty carries a big whip. No one's going to get upset if the job calls.''

He slid his fingers into the back pockets of his jeans. ''Does that mean you're up for spending part of your day off at the office?''

''Like you said, Reilly, the jewelry's my lead. I want to work it.''

She crossed to a rose-toned granite counter that held an assortment of combs and brushes. As she moved, the length of one of her long, slim legs shifted in and out of his view, but never out of his consciousness.

Linc set his jaw against need that he forcibly balanced with caution. He did not want a relationship with this woman. *Any woman.* Too bad his glands weren't getting that message.

''I've got an errand to run,'' he said, figuring he'd be smart to put as much distance as possible between himself and her sensual vanilla scent. ''How about I meet you at the office?''

''Won't work.'' Meeting his gaze in the mirror, she plucked pins out of her hair. ''I rode here with Grace so I need to hitch a ride with you.'' Her mouth curved. ''Chauffeuring me is the least you can do after dragging me away from ice-cold champagne and Fritz, the Viking god.''

''Yeah, Fritz.''

He watched her hair cascade across her shoulders, her breasts, watched her work a brush through the long, thick strands. Each coil gleamed like wildfire. He'd had that thick, silky hair wrapped around his fingers, could still feel it against his palms. God save him, what he wanted from her this instant—this very instant—had nothing to do with duty.

Hoping a few blasts of icy November wind would cool

him off, he turned toward the door. "I'll wait in my car."

"Linc?"

Pausing with his hand on the doorknob, he glanced across his shoulder. "What?"

When her gaze again met his in the mirror, the coolness was gone, replaced by sharp assessment. "Thanks."

"For?"

"Going to all the trouble of coming here. Including me in on this. You could have dealt with Zepeda, then told me about it when I showed up for work tomorrow night. That would have been the easiest thing for you."

"The jewelry's your lead."

"Yes." She turned to face him, the hairbrush cradled in one of her palms. "That's one thing I've noticed about you, Reilly."

"What?"

"You're fair. You don't cheat at pool. You tip above the limit for good service and you don't run over people. You pay attention to the rules. There's a sense of fairness about you. A strong one."

He shrugged, uneasy with her scrutiny. "I try to do what's right."

"That means something," she said quietly.

He waited, sensing she had more to say. When she remained silent, he narrowed his eyes. "What's your point, McCall?"

"No point." She did nothing more than ease out a breath, but he felt her retreat as if taking a step back toward whatever secret she harbored. "Just making an observation."

"Yeah." Her secret was still secret, and his determination to unravel it was stronger than ever. "I'll see you outside."

"Give me five minutes."

He swung open the door, tormenting himself with one last glimpse of her before he closed it behind him with a snap.

Hours later Carrie savored the last bite of a foot-long chili cheese dog. "Nice of you to spring for dinner, Reilly."

"Don't mention it." With one shoulder propped against the driver's door of his idling, impeccably clean Cadillac Allanté, he nabbed a French fry from the cardboard carrier wedged on the console. "Springing for your chili dog, fries and shake didn't exactly put a hole in my budget. And it's the least I can do after I dragged you away from Fritz the Viking god."

"That was pretty cruel." Carrie glanced at the clock on the dash and did the math. Nearly seven hours had passed since they'd left the spa. What had been a gray, blustery day with a steady drizzle had transformed into a freezing evening with air as brittle as glass.

"You also dragged me into a good chunk of overtime," she said before polishing off her own French fries. "Since I'm about to start my Christmas shopping, the extra money will come in handy." She gathered up napkins, unused salt and ketchup packages, then stuffed everything into the sack their food had come in. "Working on our day off was productive in another way. We know for sure the silver bracelet the waitress at The Hideaway showed me was stolen in Dallas. Same goes for the bracelet West gave me the other night."

"Both sold by Howard Klinger, aka Howie Kling," Linc said, setting his shake in the cup holder. "And we now have pictures of twenty more pieces of jewelry that were in Zepeda's sample case when it was boosted from the trunk of his car."

Carrie pulled on the leather gloves she'd taken off while

eating. "I guess the next step is for me to memorize those pictures," she said, flexing her fingers into the snug fit.

"Right. The more entrenched those pieces of jewelry are in your mind, the better chance you'll have of spotting the actual item when you get in to see Klinger's inventory."

"*If* I get in," Carrie amended. "West Williams has yet to make a return appearance at The Hideaway."

"He'll be back," Linc said, the certainty in his voice matching the look in his eyes. "Despite the show you and I gave him in my motel room, the guy has the hots for you. He won't be able to stay away much longer."

At the mention of what had transpired between her and Linc, Carrie shifted her gaze out the windshield to the drive-in's paint-chipped building. She could have sworn the faded, handmade sign in the window that advertised Giant Gulp Shakes was the same one that hung there during her teen years. The hole-in-the-wall drive-in hadn't changed much since she'd spent hours here with an uncountable procession of dates. Sitting in souped-up cars parked beneath the rust-spotted metal awning, she had shared a heck of a lot of kisses with those dates. Now, here she was, back under the rusty awning with a man who made her hunger for a lot more than his kiss.

Through the conscious effort of will she'd adopted when they left his motel room, she had managed to act cool and controlled around Linc. Contained. On the inside, however, she felt off balance, as if the tide of unease that had been with her since then rode a little higher each hour she spent in his presence. No matter how strong her will, she knew her feelings for him were deeper than she wanted to admit.

Wouldn't admit. Didn't *dare* admit. Not when those feelings centered on a man she'd been ordered to investigate.

Carrie rubbed at a dull pain in the center of her forehead. Her brain told her Linc could be the Avenger. Her boss in IA swore he was. Why, then, did her heart refuse to budge?

She wished she could call Captain Scott and request a transfer off the case, but knew doing so would get her nowhere. A police department was not a democracy, the troops worked where and when they were told. She would be assigned to the SEU, working as Linc's partner for however long the powers that be wanted her there.

"Got a headache, McCall?"

"A twinge." She stuffed her shake cup into the sack with the rest of their trash. "Probably caused by the gazillion fat grams I just scarfed down."

"You chose this place," Linc reminded her.

"Couldn't help it. When we drove by, I felt this sentimental urge to revisit my past." Shifting her thoughts back to business, she said, "You know, Reilly, we've already got enough violations to shut down The Hideaway for good. Nabbing Klinger on stolen-property charges is just icing on the cake."

"It's icing I want."

"So do I. If you're right about West showing back up soon, it's possible he can get me in to look at what Klinger's selling within the next few days. After that we can get with Quintana and plan the raid."

Linc gave her the flat look all cops mastered early on in their career. "You forgetting about that back booth, McCall? Just because we suspect there's a lot of drugs getting distributed there doesn't mean anything. We need proof."

"Yes, I recall that booth," she said levelly, then narrowed her eyes. Linc's voice had gone rock hard at her mention of planning the raid. "But you and I talked about that. We both think we've built up enough trust that the next time we ask about making a buy, we should get an invitation to conduct business in that booth. Once that goes down, we've got them firm on drug charges. This time next week The Hideaway could be a memory.''

Linc shifted his gaze out the windshield. Carrie studied his rigid profile and felt a twinge at the back of her neck. Something was off about the raid, but she had no idea what.

''Is The Hideaway your favorite social spot now, Reilly? Do you like playing pool so much with bikers and other lowlifes you can't bear the thought of shutting the place down?''

''Can't pull anything over on you, McCall,'' he said, giving her a sardonic look. ''In fact, I'm so charmed by the atmosphere I've encountered during this assignment, I can barely quell my enthusiasm over spending more time in my suite at the Drop Inn.''

''Are you staying there tonight?'' Carrie asked, careful to keep her voice casual.

''Figure I ought to make an appearance.'' He cocked a brow. ''Why the interest? You thinking of paying me a return visit?''

''If you hear a knock on the door, Reilly, chamber a round into your Glock because it won't be me wanting in.'' *Tonight,* she decided. She would search his house tonight.

Between one heartbeat and the next, it hit her, as she rubbed a gloved finger against her temple, that the purpose of her impending search had transformed over time, just as her feelings for him had. Her intent was no longer to find proof Linc was the Avenger. Now her goal was to unearth something that might point to his innocence.

''Is your headache worse?'' he asked.

''A little.'' She dropped her hand. ''I'll take a couple of aspirin as soon as you drop me off at home.''

''If you want some now I can pull in at the Quik Pik.''

Carrie glanced at the mom-and-pop convenience store that had huddled on the block for years next to the drive-in. The structure's windows were obliterated with signs displaying the price of beer, cigarettes and dog food. The widely spaced lights mounted on the store's roof did little to illuminate the parking lot where a lone pickup sat.

"Thanks, but I can…"

Her senses went on alert when a woman, clad in jeans and a white parka, staggered out from behind the convenience store in a lumbering run. Seconds later a man charged around the corner. A burly, menacing figure in a billowing black coat, he chased his prey toward the store's entrance. When he slashed his arm upward, light glinted off the knife gripped in his hand.

"Linc, he's got a knife."

"Yeah." He tossed his cell phone her way. "Call it in," he said, then shoved open the Allanté's door and broke into a run.

Carrie had her automatic and handcuffs out of her purse and was out of the car in seconds. Dashing on Linc's heels, she stabbed 911 into the phone. Identifying herself, she barked their location and situation to the dispatcher.

"Police, freeze!" he shouted.

If the man heard the command, he ignored it. With one of his hands now locked on the woman's wrist, he attempted to drag her toward the rear of the store. Sobbing, she struggled against his hold, her stumbling steps weaving her body from side to side as she fought for freedom.

Still running, Carrie jammed the phone into her coat pocket, and kept her weapon pointed at the ground. She knew the victim's frantic movements were the reason Linc hadn't drawn his Glock. If either of them took a shot at the knife-wielding assailant, there was no guarantee the woman's next scrambling movement wouldn't put her in the path of the bullet.

The knife blade caught light as it slashed. The woman's sobs turned into a shrill wail when the blade dragged across her throat. Carrie could almost hear the breath strangle in her lungs.

Linc hurled himself against the man's back. The impact sent the suspect stumbling sideways, breaking his hold on his victim's wrist.

With blood pouring down her neck, she dropped to her hands and knees, gasping and sobbing. She crumpled to the blacktop just as Carrie reached her.

Carrie jerked off the plaid muffler anchored beneath the parka's hood. Giving silent thanks she'd put her leather gloves back on, she wadded the muffler and pressed it hard against the pumping wound. Blood had already stained the collar and one shoulder of the white parka a deep crimson.

''You'll be okay,'' Carrie said automatically. In truth, she had no real hope of that. She'd worked enough stabbing scenes to know the woman would die unless she did a damn good job at slowing the bleeding. Which meant she had to keep hard, constant pressure against the wound—instead of backing up Linc.

The knife-wielder's snarled curse jerked Carrie's gaze up.

Linc faced off with the suspect a couple of yards away. The man looked fierce and strong and solid. The cop in Carrie kept the muffler pressed steadily against the woman's neck, doing what had to be done. It was the female in Carrie who could not disconnect her emotions. Her stomach knotted and her breath shallowed while she watched the suspect advance toward Linc, the knife's blade slicing little arcs in the frozen air. In a split second of time, she vividly understood the anger, even fear that Parker Jackson must have felt that long-ago night when the juvie physically assaulted her.

A cold sweat of fear misted Carrie's skin while awareness rose inside her. Every instinct she possessed told her that Linc Reilly mattered in ways she hadn't realized until this instant.

"Police!" Linc shouted again. He stood braced and ready, his arms wide in a wrestler's stance as he faced the cursing, spitting, knife-wielding assailant. "Drop the damn knife."

"After I kill you!" the suspect roared, his breath whooshing like smoke on the icy air. In the dim light his eyes looked drug-glazed and wild. With a savage curse he lunged at Linc, thrusting the knife as if it were a sword. Sidestepping the blade, Linc sprung like a cat and chopped the man's arm, dislodging the knife. Linc yanked the suspect's arm back hard and kneed the back of his legs, shoving him facedown to the blacktop.

"Cuffs," Carrie shouted, then tossed her handcuffs to him.

Linc snagged them out of the air with one hand. With his knee in the middle of the man's back to control his struggling, Linc clamped the handcuffs onto his prisoner's thick wrists.

Relief loosened the fist around Carrie's heart just as a patrol car's siren wailed. Dropping her gaze, she saw that her hands were trembling against the wadded, bloody muffler.

Allowing herself an unguarded, pulse-hammering moment, Carrie admitted her feelings for Linc ran deeper, much deeper than even she had suspected.

Too damn deep.

Dangerously deep.

Chapter 11

At three the following morning, Carrie stood on Captain Patricia Scott's front porch where two brass carriage lamps cast overlapping puddles of light. As the IA commander had instructed when Carrie phoned and rousted her awake, Carrie knocked instead of ringing the doorbell.

A frosty mist had enveloped the city about an hour ago, turning the air so cold it made Carrie's lungs burn. Attempting to take her mind off her discomfort, she hunched her shoulders inside her heavy coat, snuggled her chin into her ice-blue wool scarf and gave her surroundings a slow once-over.

The Internal Affairs commander lived in a well-manicured upper-class neighborhood in the far northwest part of the city. Illuminated by porch lights and gas lamps, the nearby houses and adjoining lawns appeared spacious and well maintained. As did Captain Scott's two-story Tudor with its tall rectangular windows that looked out onto the porch like black, empty eyes.

When a light snapped on behind one of those long windows, a pool of light formed around Carrie's booted feet. She had the brief sense of being surveilled through the peep hole before the door swung inward.

Dressed in a brocade robe in a patchwork of jewel colors, Captain Scott opened the glass storm door. Visibly shivering from the cold, she took a quick step back to allow Carrie to enter.

"Good morning, Sergeant McCall." Instead of her usual topknot, the captain's salt-and-pepper hair hung in a sleek frame that softened her face and made her look a decade younger.

"Morning." Carrie stepped into a wood-paneled foyer with glossy pine floors. "Sorry to wake you," she added, repeating the apology she had given on the phone. "This is important."

"I doubt you'd be here if it weren't."

"No, ma'am."

"Let me take your coat, then we'll talk in the kitchen. I made coffee after you called."

Carrie slid her coat off and blew on her bare hands. "Coffee sounds wonderful."

Scott arched a brow. "Why aren't you wearing gloves?"

"I ruined the ones I had on earlier tonight at a stabbing scene." Carrie thought with regret about her favorite leather gloves that she'd discarded in the haz mat container in the ambulance that had transported the victim. "I forgot to grab another pair from home."

Scott hung Carrie's coat in a nearby closet. "Since you don't appear to be suffering from any knife wounds, I have to assume you weren't the victim."

"No. Linc and I spotted a man attacking a woman in a convenience store parking lot. The guy sliced her before we could get to her. I did what I could for her while Linc took down the scum.''

''Why was the man chasing the woman?''

''He's a jealous ex-boyfriend who couldn't accept she'd found someone else. He had a noseful of dope, so he didn't hold back when he cut her. She lost a lot of blood, and the doc isn't sure she'll make it. The suspect has a rap sheet that reads like the Oklahoma Penal Code, so he's going to jail for a long time, no matter what happens to her.''

''You've had an eventful night.''

''Yes.'' Carrie followed Scott down a pine-floored hallway in which faint wisps of lavender haunted the air. Passing an open door, she glimpsed a study that was warm and vibrant with thick rugs, polished brass and heavy furniture. If she hadn't felt such a sense of urgency she might have paused to admire the cozy setting. Instead, she struggled to hold on to her patience.

At the end of the hall they stepped into a wood-toned kitchen with hanging copper pots, hunter-green curtains and a butcher-block island. Minutes later, Carrie was settled on a long-legged stool at the island on which file folders and a laptop computer sat. Clearly this was someone's work space.

''So, Sergeant, why are you here?''

''I searched Linc's house tonight,'' Carrie said, her hands thawing around the mug of steaming coffee the captain had poured.

Dark eyes intent, Scott slid onto the stool beside Carrie's. ''I assume you found something that ties him to the Avenger murders?'' she asked before sampling her coffee.

''No disrespect meant, Captain, but since this assignment began you've *assumed* Linc is guilty. That's a mistake, in my opinion.''

''Point taken, but my assumption is based on facts.

We're investigating Sergeant Reilly for the Avenger murders because we did a computer run on the victims and his name came up way too often for comfort. He's the most probable suspect because he is the SEU detective who's handled the majority of the murdered victims. All of those victims being career criminals who have at some point evaded punishment in the criminal justice system. Further, Sergeant Reilly's wife was murdered by a man who has so far avoided apprehension. By all accounts the sergeant was deeply in love with her.''

A series of images she had catalogued while searching Linc's house clicked in Carrie's brain. The downstairs rooms were the only ones that had the feel of being lived in. Just walking up the broad oak staircase with the Siamese slinking after her like a silent witness, she had felt a crushing sense of emptiness. Aloneness. Upstairs an elusive sadness settled around her as she opened each closed door lining the hallway. Every room was immaculate, the air inside cool. As she stood in the doorway of the master bedroom, she had noted a musty odor redolent of a long-sealed crypt. It was clear Linc seldom, if ever, ventured into the bedroom he and his wife had shared. Carrie's suspicion of that had been verified when she opened the closet in the downstairs study and found it filled with his clothes.

''The Avenger began his killing spree a short time after Kimberly Reilly died,'' Scott continued, pulling Carrie from her thoughts. ''This wouldn't be the first time despair has turned a grieving widower into a killer.''

The knots in Carrie's stomach tightened. ''You're mixing facts with supposition and forming unprovable assumptions.''

''Yes.'' Scott sipped her coffee. ''Despite that, I feel confident making the assumption that you found *something* when you searched Sergeant Reilly's home. Otherwise you wouldn't be drinking coffee in my kitchen at 3:00 a.m.''

"I found something," Carrie concurred. "But it's not the evidence you're hoping for. It's proof that has me even more convinced of Linc's innocence."

"I'm listening."

"We know for sure Linc was in Claremore the night Arlee Dell was shot. Proof of that is the credit card charge he made when he took his in-laws to dinner."

"Yes," Scott agreed. "Claremore being a mere twenty minute drive from Tulsa, the scene of the murder. Taking the time recorded on the charge slip into account, Sergeant Reilly would have had plenty of time to drive to the murder scene after leaving the restaurant."

"You told me if I found anything pertinent to the investigation during my search I should photograph it." Carrie reached into the pocket of her slacks, pulled out a diskette and nodded toward the laptop. "Does that have a software program that displays digital photos?"

"My husband is a computer guru. He's loaded all the bells and whistles on every computer we own."

"There," Carrie said a few minutes later as she swiveled the laptop the captain's way.

Scott leaned in and peered at the screen, then shook her head. "My glasses are upstairs. It looks like some sort of invoice."

"It's Linc's most recent Pike Pass usage bill," Carrie explained, referring to the Oklahoma Turnpike Authority's electronic toll collection system. "The invoice shows that on the Saturday Arlee Dell was murdered, Linc took the Turner Turnpike from here to Claremore, not to Tulsa."

"If memory serves me, there are several routes from Claremore to Tulsa that aren't toll roads. He could have driven to Tulsa on one of those." Scott nudged her coffee mug aside. "We already know Reilly's whereabouts because of his credit card bill. I don't understand why you think his Pike Pass invoice will help clear him."

"It won't," Carrie said. "But seeing Linc's bill started me wondering how the Avenger got to Tulsa."

"On the off chance that Sergeant Reilly is not him?"

Carrie gave Scott a level look. "You ordered me to get close to Linc. I've learned a lot about the man. One thing being that he's a sharp, cool thinker. If he had gone to Tulsa to cap Arlee Dell, Linc wouldn't have left a paper trail for the cops to follow. Any kind of trail, for that matter."

"He could have intentionally left that trail as a facade. Reilly knew no one would believe he'd be so careless. Blatant. So that's exactly what he was."

"Not Linc," Carrie said with certainty. "The Avenger is on a mission to get rid of the baddest of the bad guys. Maybe he earns some applause for saving a lot of good, honest citizens, but that's not the point here. The point is the Avenger is a cop who has decided his badge gives him the right to kill. That implies a man with a whole lot of arrogance. That's not Linc."

"You seem sure of yourself."

"After tonight I am," Carrie replied. "During that stabbing, the scumbag told Linc he was going to kill him, then lunged at him with the knife. At that point, Linc would have been totally within the law to shoot him. *I* would have shot him. Instead Linc went a few rounds of hand-to-hand and took the knife away." Carrie shook her head. "The Avenger shoots people. That's what he does. By now he's got to be pretty comfortable pulling the trigger with a human in his sights. If Link were the Avenger, do you really think he'd have given a second thought about popping a round into a guy coming at him with a knife?"

"Maybe not." Scott pursed her mouth. "I take it you found nothing else during your search of Reilly's house?"

Carrie thought back to the file folder she'd seen in Linc's room at the Drop Inn. At no time during her search had she found a file anywhere near the thickness of that one. Which meant he must have taken it with him to the fleabag motel tonight. What, she wondered, was in the file that he kept so close?

"Nothing," she said, meeting Scott's gaze. "I found nothing that implicates Linc in anything. Which brings me to the reason I rousted you out of bed. Captain, I want a subpoena for the Pike Pass records that cover the two days before Arlee Dell's murder through two days after."

"You're thinking the Avenger has a Pike Pass? That he would be careless enough to let his name show up on those records?"

"You're ready to believe Linc would leave a trail like that as a ruse." Carrie raised a shoulder. "Look, there's a turnpike that slices through the north part of this city, so tons of people have a Pike Pass box affixed to their vehicle's windshield. I'm one of those people. It's there, and I never think about it except when I get my monthly bill. Maybe the Avenger is just like me. Maybe he overlooked that and we'll find his name in the turnpike's records. Bad guys get caught sometimes because they make a stupid mistake. This could be one of those times. We'd be negligent not to look at the records."

"I agree."

Relief came to Carrie in a wave. "If you're willing to make a phone call and get a judge's approval, I'll do the paperwork and deliver it," she said. "Then serve the subpoena to the Turnpike Authority. If everything runs smooth, I can have the records of Pike Pass usage by noon. I'll take them home and start going over them."

"I guess you didn't hear the news last night?"

"What news?"

"A virus has invaded all the state government computer systems."

Carrie's heart dropped. "A virus?"

"A hacker planted some sort of bug in the state's computer system. According to the news, every agency from the governor's office to the historical society is off-line."

"Great. Just great."

"When I get to the office I'll call a judge I know and advise him we need a subpoena. You get the paperwork ready. You can deliver it to him after you hear from me. Then you serve the subpoena to the Turnpike Authority. You won't get your information today, but they'll be ready to run the printout for you as soon as they're back online."

Scott paused, giving Carrie an assessing look. "You've been up all night, Sergeant, and you look beat. After you deliver that subpoena, go home and get some sleep."

"I will." Carrie nudged her mug aside. "Thank you for agreeing to get the subpoena."

"You're a good investigator, McCall." Scott's eyes narrowed, pulling at the tiny network of lines around her eyes. "If your hunch about the Pike Pass records takes the suspicion off Reilly, he'll have you to thank."

Carrie slid off the stool. "No matter what turns up, when Linc finds out I'm IA, the last thing he'll do is thank me."

"The key to getting to buy dope here is to order a Grasshopper at the bar," Linc explained late that night when he and Carrie walked out of The Hideaway.

"A grasshopper?" She eyed him over the Arctic-blue scarf that muffled the lower half of her face against the cold. "One of those icky green drinks?" she asked as they wove their way through the sea of cars in the bar's parking lot.

"Right." Linc aimed the remote on his key ring at the SUV. The click of the disengaging door locks sounded brittle on the dark, freezing air. He climbed behind the wheel and started the engine while Carrie slid into the back and tugged the scarf away from her face. Unearthing the laptop from its hiding place, she pulled off one of her gloves and pressed a button. Seconds later, the light from the monitor illuminated her face in a ghostly hue.

"The grasshopper concept is clever when you think about it," Linc continued. "It's a drink made with both green and white crème de menthe. No one in their right mind is going to stroll into a dive like The Hideaway and order a drink like that."

Carrie met his gaze over the laptop's monitor. "True."

Her lips were slicked with a murderous-red gloss; generous amounts of kohl liner and smoky shadow made her eyes seem enormous. Beneath her black coat was a snug hot-pink sweater and jeans that molded tight to her hips and thighs. Her hair was a wavy mass of fire. Gold hoops glinted at her ears. The overall look was one that kicked a man in the gut.

Linc was no exception.

Just looking at her had need rising inside him. She moved something in him, no matter how hard he tried to stand against it. Dammit, he'd had his hands on her. His mouth. He wanted more.

"So when a customer *does* order a grasshopper," she reasoned, "the bartender knows someone on the inside has approved that person to buy drugs."

"Exactly." He rolled his shoulders in an attempt to dispel the tension. "While you and the cowboy were upstairs shopping at Howard Klinger's stolen goods boutique, the waitress named Yolanda gave me the password. I went to the bar and ordered a grasshopper. Zeke didn't bat an eye, just told me to have a seat in the back booth, open the armrest, put my 'donation' inside and wait for a knock. I did. I kept my hand on top of the armrest and I could feel something move, like a section of its bottom sliding open.

After I heard a knock from below, I opened the lid.'' He reached inside his leather jacket and dug into the pocket of his shirt. ''My money had been replaced by this,'' he said, holding up a clear baggie of white powder.

''Cocaine.''

''I imagine that's what the lab will say, too.''

''It doesn't get much slicker than that. You bought drugs, but there's no way you can testify from whom.''

Linc slid the baggie back into his pocket. ''What I can testify to is that there's one or more persons in the basement just beneath the back booth taking care of the sales.''

''I guess we'll find out his, her or their identity during the raid.'' While she spoke, Carrie toyed with the computer's toggle switch. ''I don't know about you, Reilly, but I'll be glad when we get this assignment wrapped up. The Hideaway has lost its charm for me as a place to hang out at night.''

''Imagine that,'' Linc said, studying her. Something niggled at him, an uneasiness or maybe even an awareness that this assignment would be their first and last together. He had no idea what was behind that feeling. After all, he had Quintana's assurances that he and Carrie would continue working as partners. Since they both had put the skids on whatever the hell was going on between them chemistrywise, there was no reason for Quintana to change his mind. Linc scowled. Outwardly, he had put on the skids. What he felt on the inside was a whole different matter.

For two years he had felt dead. Numb. Twenty-four months with nothing inside him but cold anger and a vicious, impossible wanting to have his past returned undamaged.

Then, Carrie McCall had strolled into the squad room. Since that instant she had been a fire he couldn't put out. Over time she had cracked the hard ice inside him, made his blood heat again. Now, God help him, he wanted to resurrect the part of him he'd buried with his wife.

Knowing that, feeling it, sliced him with sharp stabs of guilt. He realized the only way to live with the guilt was to close the door on the past before focusing on the future. He had stood at Kim's grave and vowed he would find the scum who'd tortured, raped and killed her. He had failed her as a husband by not protecting her. He wouldn't fail her as a cop, too.

While he waited for the engine's temperature gauge to creep up, Linc felt tension tighten his spine. He jerked off one of his gloves and began rubbing his neck. Dammit, it had to be the emotion knotted inside him—the least of those knots being his feelings for Carrie—that had his thoughts a half beat out of sync and his instincts skewed. Why else would he walk into his house after spending a night at the Drop Inn and imagine he smelled the same vanilla scent that had pulsed off her skin at the spa?

He flicked on the heater's fan switch. The first surge of warm air breezed across his face while he reminded himself *this* assignment was like no other. Never before had he worked with a partner who he desired worse than he wanted even to breathe. That alone might drive a man to carry her scent with him, maybe even imprint it on his brain. He had also never before had reason to purposely string out an investigation, delay wrapping it up.

He did this one.

"I hope the camera Wade Crawford planted in this brooch worked." As she spoke, Carrie touched the pewter pin anchored on the left lapel of her black wool coat. Linc glanced at the pin. He had to hand it to Crawford—the only way *he* could spot the pinprick-size lens in the Celtic knot was because the Vice cop had pointed it out to him.

"You don't have to worry about Crawford's equipment screwing up," Linc said, although tonight he wished the opposite were true. An equipment malfunction would be a viable way for him to string out the operation.

"You're so right." Carrie's lips formed a satisfied curve while she studied the monitor. "The camera in the brooch picked up everything. Just going by memory, I saw about six pieces of jewelry that were in Zepeda's sample case when it was stolen in Dallas. Klinger also had some Rolex watches, a stack of laptop computers, cell phones, TVs and other items that have serial numbers. Hopefully we'll get tons of hits after the raid when we run those items through the stolen-property database."

"Yeah."

While he waited for Carrie to shut down the computer, Linc pictured The Hideaway's smoky back room with its twin pool tables. Each time he made a shot at one of those tables he felt the adrenaline, the hunting hormone flow into his veins. It was as if he sensed how close he might be to the tattooed bastard who'd killed Kim. Now he and Carrie were days away from shutting down the bar. Severing the one lead he had to his wife's killer.

"We got a lot accomplished tonight, Reilly," Carrie said after relocating into the front passenger seat. "You made a buy, so now we know how drugs are being distributed through the back booth. I've got Howie baby on a variety of possession and distribution of stolen goods charges, which will overflow to The Hideaway's owner. All that's left before we plan the raid is to write reports on what we did tonight."

"I want to make more buys." Linc knew he'd said the words too sharply when he felt Carrie's attention shift from the job to him in a fraction of a second.

"Why?"

He moderated his voice. "The more dope we buy, the tighter our case. Plus, it's better to have both of us in the position to testify in court as having purchased drugs in the back booth.''

''So maybe we spend another evening here. Two max.'' She kept her gaze locked with his. ''We still need to get with Quintana tomorrow and bring him up to date. He's the one who makes the final decision on when to schedule the raid. Once he does, we have to coordinate with state liquor agents, SWAT, Intelligence, Patrol. The mayor's office also has to be contacted. He'll want to be on-site when the raid goes down so he can make a statement to the media about how he's cleaning up smut and crime. Setting everything up is going to take time.''

''We'll brief Quintana on the Monday after Thanksgiving.''

''Thanksgiving is the day after tomorrow.''

''You think I need a calendar, McCall?''

''What I think, Reilly, is that you've got some reason for us to hang around this dive longer than necessary. Why don't you come clean and tell me what's going on?''

''Why don't you just trust me?''

''Because you haven't given me reason *not* to go to Quintana.'' She shook her head. ''Look, I'm new to the SEU. Quintana views me as some sex bimbo because of the fiasco in Patrol with that rookie and his jealous wife. I have to prove myself in Quintana's eyes. Earn my stripes. Using delay tactics during my first assignment isn't going to earn me anything but my boss's contempt. You keep pointing out that partners back each other up. I'm not saying I won't do that. Just give me a good reason.''

He gritted his teeth. ''All right. I'm looking for a bad dude spotted here by a snitch. The dude isn't a regular. As far as I know, he's only been here once.''

''Why are you looking for him?''

''He killed someone and needs to pay for it. The Hideaway is the only lead I have. I want to keep the place open until I find him. Is that good enough for you?''

''You don't work Homicide. Why are you after a murderer?''

''The case is cold. The boys in Homicide have their hands full dealing with active cases.''

''What's the guy's name?''

''I don't know. If I did, I'd have already found the bastard. This place is my only lead to him. I need more time to find him. And I need you to give it to me.''

She stared out the windshield at the crowded parking lot. ''And I need to know why you're looking for this specific person,'' she said quietly.

A weariness shuddered down through Linc and he struggled to fight it back. He wasn't just physically tired, he was mentally spent. Lying to bad guys was his business. Doing so was a game, and the side who told the best lies came out on top. But the past weeks of mixing lies with the truth wore at him. Carrie wasn't one of the bad guys, and working with her was no game. She was his partner, and she was smart. If he offered an explanation that was a mix of lies and truths, she would quickly see through the layers of coincidence to the cold calculation on his part.

What was more important, she deserved the truth. He cared too deeply about her to continue to hold back.

Accepting that fact was a huge admission, one he was barely able to make to himself. The thought of voicing it was a whole different matter. So he would keep his feelings to himself and deal with the other issue in a simple, straightforward way.

''Okay, McCall, you win.'' He kept his voice soft and even, pulling her gaze back to his. ''Explaining will be easier if I show you the reports and photos I've got at home.''

She stared back at him, her face tense, her eyes cheerless. ''Then that's where we need to go.''

Chapter 12

Secrets, Carrie thought when she paused inside Linc's front door a half hour later. How well she understood the shift in a person's voice when the territory got touchy. Linc was no exception—his words had taken on a honed edge the instant she had recommended they talk to Quintana about the raid on The Hideaway.

Now, in order to delay that raid, Linc was ready to share information he'd kept from her about a killer he sought. His doing so implied a two-way street, but there was no way she could share her secret with him.

"Have a seat in the living room." He shrugged off his leather jacket, then took her coat. "What I need to show you is in the study. I'll bring it here."

"All right."

He was wearing his cop face, as emotionless as a mask, but that did nothing to settle Carrie's raw nerves. Intuition told her the information he was about to retrieve was in the file folder she'd spotted at the Drop Inn. That night, her knee-jerk reaction was to wonder if the folder held information on the Avenger murders. Maybe even a list of future victims. Perhaps a game plan on where and when to make each kill. But with the passage of time she had convinced herself she'd been wrong. About the file's contents. About her original suspicions toward Linc. She knew him now. Had spent enough hours in his presence to feel sure he was a good cop, a moral man, one who believed in fair play. He didn't go around executing people.

Yet he'd just confessed that during their time at The Hideaway he'd been hunting a killer. Lying in wait. Didn't that mirror the Avenger's MO?

In a slow-motion passage of seconds, her belief in Linc's innocence tugged and tangled inside her. Had she been terribly wrong about him? Dangerously naive? Was he the Avenger?

"You want coffee?" he asked quietly. "Something stronger, maybe?"

She met his waiting gaze and felt the lines between role and reality sharpen and converge. It was her heart that had first refused to believe him guilty. Now every cop instinct she had developed after years on the job told her that, too. She had no solid evidence to back up her feelings. He wasn't the Avenger. She just *knew*.

"No coffee. Nothing stronger, either. Thanks." With her stomach churning, she gave a wistful thought to the roll of antacids she'd left on the small desk in her bedroom.

"Make yourself comfortable."

She stepped into the living room while Linc's footsteps echoed down the hallway. Her gaze swept over the leather volumes crammed into the bookshelves on either side of the brick fireplace, the matching hunter-green leather couches that faced each other from either side of the coral area rug. The room looked neat and tidy, just as it had late last night when she'd searched it.

A strident yowl and Linc's muttered "Dammit!" had Carrie looking back toward the door in time to see the Siamese streak into the room, claws skittering on the wood floor. Its graceful feline leap onto the coffee table between the couches sent magazines flying.

"Sounds like somebody got stepped on," Carrie murmured while gathering the magazines and replacing them on the table. When she settled onto the closest couch, the cat immediately slunk onto her lap, meowing piteously. Carrie stroked the soft fur between its ears, wincing when kneading claws pierced her jeans-covered thigh.

"I still don't know your name," she said softly. Last night the Siamese had been her silent companion while she moved from room to room. Now here she was again in Linc's home, this time by invitation.

"What is it with you and that cat?" he asked from where he'd paused just inside the doorway.

Carrie's gaze swept his tall, lanky frame. Even scowling he looked good, his thick black hair still wind rumpled, a beginning shadow of stubble darkening his cheeks and jaw. A man shouldn't be able to make a worn shirt the color of old silver, faded jeans and scuffed boots a fashion statement. Linc Reilly did.

Her thoughts shifted from the man to the job when her gaze dropped to the thick file folders he carried.

"Your cat clearly has good taste." Glancing down, she noted the cat had lowered its ears to half mast and was staring at Linc with regal feline disdain. "I don't think she likes you."

"Feeling's mutual."

Carrie scratched the cat's furry neck and was rewarded with a contented purr. "When I was here before I never heard you mention her name."

"Fabiani." Linc strode across the room and settled onto the couch facing the one on which she sat.

"Strange name for a cat."

"Kim had her before we got married. Fabiani is the name of some interior designer whose stuff Kim liked. Fuzz face—which is what I call the beast—took an instant dislike to me for encroaching on her territory." While Linc matched the cat's gaze stare-for-stare, something akin to regret, only more complex, flickered in his eyes. "When Kim died, fuzz face and I agreed we'd stay here and put up with each other," he added quietly.

Carrie said nothing. She knew she wasn't looking at the tough cop right now, but at a man who had loved his wife so much he couldn't bear to let go of even one piece of her.

The next instant Linc's eyes cleared of emotion. "Kim stumbled on to that gas station robbery two years ago today," he said without preamble, and settled the file folders on the coffee table. "The M.E. estimates the bastard kept her alive about forty-eight hours, torturing her, raping her, before he killed her."

An ache punched into Carrie's stomach over what he must have suffered. Was still suffering. "I'm sorry—"

"I'm not telling you this because I want sympathy. We're talking about Kim because the bastard's still out there. Probably raping. Still killing, maybe."

Carrie's eyes widened. "That's who you're looking for at The Hideaway, isn't it? Kim's killer?"

"I stood at her grave and swore to her I would find him. I intend to do that." He met Carrie's gaze across the small span of table, ruthless determination glinting in his brownish-gold eyes. "About a month ago my snitch spotted the murdering scum playing pool at The Hideaway. Since the bastard wasn't a regular, no one knew his name. My snitch hasn't seen him again. Neither have I."

Carrie frowned while her mind pulled back details about the robbery Kim Reilly had walked in on. "I heard the killer got caught on a surveillance tape. That he wore a ski mask."

"That's right. No one had a clue what he looked like until my snitch saw him. Even now all I have is a general description—medium height, muscled build, dark hair and eyes."

"The killer wore a ski mask. What makes your snitch think the man he spotted at The Hideaway is the same person?"

Linc flipped open the top file folder. "During the robbery, the clerk made a lunge for the suspect's gun. Their struggle shoved up the right sleeve of the bastard's sweater, partially exposing a tattoo." Linc picked up a photo, handed it to her. "That's a blowup of the lower part of the tattoo. The surveillance equipment at the gas station was cheap and the tape was poor quality. That picture isn't great, but it's all I've got."

Narrowing her eyes, Carrie studied the grainy black-and-white image. The photo's poor quality made the tattoo's edges seem slightly out of focus. "It looks like a coiled tail," she said after a moment. "A snake's, maybe."

"Everyone who's seen the picture thinks so. The guy who my snitch spotted playing pool had on a sweatshirt with the sleeves shoved up, just like in the surveillance photo. According to my informant, the tattoo is a faded-green color."

Carrie returned the picture. "I take it you've searched law enforcement databases for tattoos of green snakes?"

"I've run *all* snake tattoos through both local and federal systems." Linc laid the photo aside and picked up a ream of papers. "At first, I restricted my record search to white males with a snake tattoo on the right forearm. I got hundreds of hits.'' When he used his thumb to fan through the stack of papers, Carrie saw flashes of color mug shots and photos of what she imagined was every type of snake tattoo conceivable.

''Nothing close?''

''Actually, some were damn close. I spent months running checks on the owners of similar tattoos, even ones that had only a vague resemblance to the killer's. His tattoo looks professional, so I sent out inquiries, asking if anyone recognizes the artwork. So far nothing's panned out.''

Carrie looked at the second file, twice as thick as the first. ''What's in there?''

''When I couldn't find a snake tattoo that matched the killer's I expanded my search to white males with *any* tattoo on their right forearm.'' Linc opened the folder that was the same thickness as the phone book's yellow pages. ''Some tattoo parlors have Web sites with pictures of sample tattoos. I've printed every picture off the Internet I could find.''

''There must be thousands of pictures in there.''

''I've looked at every one.''

''Did Kim have anything on her the guy could have pawned? Jewelry, maybe?''

''She'd broken the little finger on her left hand. To stabilize it, the doctor taped her broken finger to her ring finger, so she didn't have on her wedding ring that day.'' Linc looked away. ''I'd had a pair of gold and emerald earrings made for her. An anniversary present. She has them on in the robbery video. They were missing when her body was found.''

''I'm sure you notified all the pawn shops?''

''Sent out a flyer with a picture of the earrings I'd taken when I added them to our insurance rider. The earrings haven't turned up.'' Linc laid the pages down, his gaze locked on Carrie's. ''The Hideaway is my only lead to the scum. As long as there's a chance he'll show again, I need that lead. That's why I want to draw out our investigation. Put off the raid, which will shut the place down. I'm asking you to help me do that.''

Slipping a hand beneath her hair, Carrie rubbed at the tension in the back of her neck. Something didn't add up— some shadowy, something that lurked just out of reach.

''We've been undercover at The Hideaway nearly three weeks,'' she pointed out. ''You haven't spotted the man you believe to be Kim's killer. What makes you think he'll ever show?''

''I don't *think* that. I just hope it.''

''Suppose I say no? Suppose I tell you I'm going to Quintana and recommend he set up the raid? What will you do?''

Linc's mouth tightened. ''Meaning, if you tell me no, do I plan to cuff you, toss you into a closet and keep you here until I find the scum? Hardly.'' He raised a shoulder. ''If you're determined to go to Quintana tomorrow, there's not a damn thing I can do to stop you. I'd just appreciate you hearing me out before you make a decision.''

''I'm listening.''

''I'm not asking you to break any laws, Carrie. All I'm asking you to do, as my partner, is give me time. A couple more days…maybe a week at The Hideaway, during which you and I rack up additional drug buys. Those buys will strengthen our case. There's no downside to that.''

She agreed. Still, there was that shadow gnawing at her. Since she thought better on her feet, she nudged the cat off her lap, then rose and wandered to the fireplace. ''This city has a lot of bars scattered around,'' she said almost to herself.

''True.''

That was the shadow, she thought. There were simply

too many bars for fate to have dealt all the cards in this instance.

Turning, she braced a shoulder against one of the floor-to-ceiling bookcases. ''Your wife's killer and a snitch you're working wound up playing pool at The Hideaway. A coincidence, but things like that happen.''

''This is proof of that.''

''Uh-huh.'' She shoved up the sleeves of her pink sweater. ''What about the other part? What are the odds you happen to snag a totally unrelated undercover assignment at *that* same bar?''

''About five-hundred billion to one, I'd say.''

''I'd say they're a lot more. Chance had nothing to do with our assignment, did it? You somehow arranged for us to go undercover at The Hideaway so you could look for the guy who killed Kim.''

''I couldn't be at The Hideaway watching for him while I was working another case somewhere.'' Linc eased back on the couch, his eyes steady on hers. ''I need to spend as much time at that bar as possible, so that's what I arranged to do. I'd do it again.''

Carrie thought back to the briefing he'd given her the first day in the SEU. ''You said some thirteen-year-old boy found skin magazines in the Dumpster behind The Hideaway. That his mother called the mayor's office, promising her church's congregation would vote against him if he didn't shut down the bar.''

''You know what goes on at The Hideaway, McCall. Don't tell me you believe it's impossible some kid might find porno magazines in the Dumpster. Worse things, in fact. Or that there's a lot of nice, churchgoing people living in the area who'd prefer not to have that den of sin nearby.''

Carrie narrowed her eyes, wondering what woman he'd gotten to make the phone calls to the mayor's office.

Maybe his former partner, Annie Becker? "That all sounds real good, Reilly, but you didn't set this up to help those people rid their neighborhood of smut. You did it to serve your own agenda."

"Damn right. And you might want to think things through before you have a snit over that."

Her chin lifted. "I don't have snits."

"Surprising, taking into account all that flaming red hair," he said mildly. "Consider this, McCall. If there hadn't been anything illegal going on at The Hideaway, you and I would have packed up long ago. As it is, a lot of unsavory people will get swept up in our raid. That's because they've freely chosen to engage in illegal activities. And the bar that attracts those disreputable types and condones those activities won't be a blight on that neighborhood much longer. No one has gotten their rights violated during this investigation."

"Not yet," she agreed, her heart pounding against her ribs.

Linc raised a brow. "Yet?"

Now, she thought, they'd come full circle. She'd been ordered to work with Linc, to watch him and find out what he would do if he had a killer in his sights. She hadn't considered the possibility that the killer might be the vicious piece of trash who'd murdered his wife.

"You've searched for Kim's killer for two years." Carrie swept a hand toward the coffee table. "Spent hundreds of hours poring over pictures of tattoos."

"Your point, McCall?"

"What he did to her, to Kim… Linc, what will you do to him when you find him?"

She watched his face darken, a subtle change of expression that went from unreadable to deadly in the blink of an eye.

He rose, crossed to her. "I saw Kim's body after the

cops found her," he said, his eyes hard and flat and flickering with pure hatred. "I know exactly what the son of a bitch did to her. How he tortured her." A muscle in the side of his jaw clenched. "What I want to do is kill him. I mean that, Carrie. I want to rip him apart with my bare hands, then throw him in a sewer, chunk by bloody chunk. He deserves that, for what he did."

Carrie couldn't bring herself to disagree.

Linc scrubbed a hand over his jaw. "That's what I want to do to the murdering scum. Problem is, doing that won't bring Kim back. Won't change the fact I let her down. Nothing can. So, when I get my hands on him, I'll haul him in and lock him in a cage. Then make sure there's a cell on death row in his future." He angled his chin. "Is that why you don't want to extend our time at The Hideaway? Because you're not sure what I'll do when I get my hands on the bastard?"

She let out a careful breath. "It's a concern, considering."

"Understandable, considering. Carrie, I give you my word, he'll wind up in a cell, not in a sewer."

Without question she believed he was as good as his word. She also felt certain that if he did find Kim's killer, Linc's doing what was legal and correct would go far to underline his innocence in the Avenger murders. And she was in just such a position to help clear his name.

"Okay, Reilly, I see the logic in taking time to make a few more drug buys before we go to Quintana. We'd be negligent in our duty if we didn't hold off on the raid until we have the strongest case possible."

His eyes stayed steady on her face, measuring. "Glad you agree." He smiled, just the faintest curve of his lips. "Thanks, McCall. I owe you."

"No. It's our job to catch bad guys. The scum who

murdered Kim needs to get caught. If stretching our investigation gets him locked in a dark cage, it's worth it.''

Linc waited a beat, then took a step forward. ''I didn't like holding back information from my partner. Not telling you until now that I have a secondary agenda.''

Carrie winced inwardly as the words stung with an implication he could in no way be aware of. ''I understand your reasons,'' she managed.

''I intend to make good on my word to Kim,'' he said quietly. ''I'll find her killer, no matter how long it takes.''

''I don't doubt that.'' With Linc standing so close, the familiar spicy tang of his cologne filled Carrie's lungs. It was the same scent he'd worn the night at the Drop Inn, and for a moment she was right back on that sagging mattress, feeling his hands skimming across her flesh, his mouth feeding on her throat, her breasts. An instinctive caution had her taking a step back.

He angled his chin. ''When that's done, when it's all over, you and I should reevaluate our partnership.''

''Don't…you like working with me?''

''Yes, but I can't be your partner and do the other things I'd like to do with you. Want to do,'' he added softly. ''I had a feeling earlier that maybe The Hideaway would be the first and last case we work together. I told myself my thinking was off. Now I'm hoping it wasn't.''

''Linc…'' Her legs had gone weak and her bones ached with wanting him. But her need didn't lessen the guilt that sat in her stomach like a huge, jagged rock. When the truth about her came out, would he understand? Could he ever accept she had lied to him every day because she was following orders? Doing what she'd been assigned to do? Had no choice but to do?

He mattered so much, she realized. So much it was almost too much. The prospect of his walking out of her life tightened a cold fist of apprehension around her heart.

"Let's just concentrate on what needs to be done right now." She looked back at the coffee table. "You said you've gone through all the pictures of tattoos."

"Several times." He watched her for a few seconds before asking, "Why?"

"I'm a new set of eyes. Let me go through the pictures. I might see something from a different perspective."

"It could take weeks for you to do that."

"Doesn't matter." She had it in her mind to scoop up the files and carry them home when a thought hit her. "You want the pictures to stay here, don't you?"

"Yes. It took me a long time to get them. I don't want any lost." He checked his watch. "It's past midnight. I should take you home. You can come back tomorrow. We'll spend a couple of hours on this before we go to The Hideaway."

"If I go home now I'll just sit in front of the TV until I'm tired enough to go to bed." She settled on the couch. "Might as well spend that time looking at pictures of snakes." She glanced back up at him. "That is if you don't mind driving me home later?"

"I don't mind. How about I put on a pot of decaf?"

"Sounds good," she said, and began fanning out photos.

The snake slithered closer, hissing viciously in Carrie's ear. She jolted awake, a scream tearing up her throat as she swung at the greedy slitted eyes looming a half inch from her face.

She sat upright in time to see the Siamese land on the coffee table. Its feet thrashed for traction as color photographs of tattoos flew in every direction.

"Holy…" Gulping air, Carrie huddled in one corner of the couch and waited for the last murky depths of the nightmare to fade. She wasn't in some dark, snake-infested pit like she'd dreamed. She was in Linc's living room, the morning sun beaming bright through the windows.

She plowed her fingers through her hair. The last thing she remembered was her mind going numb and her eyes drooping while she leafed through unending pictures of snake tattoos.

No wonder she'd had a nightmare about the slimy, belly-crawling creatures!

She noted the plaid throw that had been draped across the back of the couch was now tangled around her legs. Linc had covered her up. And left her clothes on, she thought as she inventoried her rumpled pink sweater and jeans.

''What the hell's going on?''

Her head swung around and the air thickened in her lungs. He stood in the doorway, clad only in a pair of cotton drawstring pants that hung low on his hips. His dark hair was rumpled from sleep, his cheeks and jaw shadowed by a night's growth of stubble. The Glock gripped in his right hand was aimed at the floor and made him look seriously dangerous. The fact she wanted to leap off the couch and jump his bones had Carrie clenching her fingers on the plaid throw.

''I'm sorry I screamed,'' she said. ''I had a nightmare. About snakes.'' To keep her gaze off Linc's hard-as-marble chest, she untangled her legs from the throw and began folding it. ''I guess I mistook Fabiani's meow for a hiss. I awoke suddenly and there were these narrow, slitted eyes an inch from my face.'' She glanced around the living room but saw no sign of the Siamese. ''I knocked her off my chest and onto the table.''

''Miserable cat.'' Linc laid the Glock on the wing chair inside the door. ''She gets hungry, she's right in your face, letting you know about it.''

''I'll have to buy her a treat so she'll know I didn't

intentionally turn her into a cat Frisbee.'' Twisting sideways, Carrie draped the throw over the back of the couch. When she turned back, Linc was standing a few feet away. She knew how that impressive chest felt. Those muscled arms. Knew the taste of his mouth. His flesh.

With desire thudding in the pit of her stomach, she slipped off the couch onto her knees and began gathering up the blizzard of paper the cat had scattered.

"So much for having the pictures I've looked at separated into a stack from the others," she mumbled.

Linc hunkered down and scooped up a handful of paper. "Fuzz face has always been a big help around here."

Carrie's hand froze as she reached for more papers. She blinked, then eased out a breath as she retrieved a sheet of paper that was half-hidden beneath several others. "I…" She stared down at the page that displayed a man's mug shot and tattoo. "Linc, I need the picture."

He glanced across his shoulder. "Which one?"

"From the gas station. The black and white photo off the security tape." Still on her knees, she turned to the table, plowing through the disordered pages with focused determination. "The one of the killer's tattoo."

"Here." Linc snatched it from under the table and handed it to her.

Carrie held the two pictures side by side, comparing the color tattoo with the grainy one from the crime scene.

"Linc, I think Fabiani just earned herself a lifetime of treats. I think…she found your guy."

His eyes went razor sharp. "Who?"

"The way this page landed on the floor, the way it was partially covered by another piece of paper, I saw only the bottom of the tattoo. The tail. A dragon's tail that's coiled at the end," she added, handing him the paper.

Linc studied the photo. Using one hand, he covered the dragon's body, leaving only its tail exposed. "Let me see the one off the security tape,'' he said, his voice deceptively soft.

Carrie handed it to him, then waited in silence while he compared the photos.

After a moment he closed his eyes. ''It never was a snake. For two damn years, I've looked for a snake.''

''All you had to go by was a grainy black-and-white photo of a partial tattoo taken by a cheap surveillance camera,'' she reminded him. ''What you had looked like the hind end of a snake. That's what I thought it was. What you said everybody thought.''

''Yeah.''

''The important thing is you now know who owns that tattoo.'' Carrie leaned in, peering at the mug shot of the tattoo's owner. Frank Young was a medium height, muscled man with dark hair and narrow, arrogant eyes.

She placed a hand on Linc's bare shoulder. His flesh felt heated, his muscles bunched tight. ''I'll call records and dispatch to get a background check started on Young. If luck runs with us, we'll have him locked in a cage by the end of the day.''

Chapter 13

Experience had taught Linc how swiftly a stalled investigation could shift into high gear. That a wisp of a clue could turn a cold case hot in the time it took to strike a match.

What he hadn't known was that learning the name of Kim's killer would hit him with the impact of a sledgehammer. A hit so bone deep that six hours after Carrie handed him the photo of the dragon tattoo, he still felt unsteady. Shell-shocked.

It seemed almost surreal that, after two years of searching, he knew the name of the ski mask-clad bastard who'd raped, tortured and murdered his wife.

Frank Young.

After a series of background checks, interviews and phone calls, he and Carrie had yet to get a lead on Young's current whereabouts. But they did have a whiff of his scent. Maybe more than a whiff, Linc amended, considering he and Carrie now sat in the single-wide going-to-rust trailer where Frank Young had lived two years ago.

"I don't got lots of time." Olivia Diaz spoke in a clipped mix of accent and misplaced grammar. "I'm meetin' my boyfriend for dinner," she added, then slid off her stilettos and settled onto a sagging armchair.

"This shouldn't take long," Linc responded, his tone light. From interviews he and Carrie had conducted, they knew the woman with whom Young had shared the trailer was a party girl. She got along better with men than with members of her own sex, whom she considered competition. Knowing that, he and Carrie had devised a cat-and-mouse strategy that initially had her staying in the background while he took the lead. That was subject to change, depending on what—if anything—came up during the interview.

Linc eased forward on the couch, encroaching slightly on Diaz's personal space. He positioned himself near enough to her chair to invite confidence, to suggest support rather than intimidation. "I appreciate your answering my questions about Frank Young," he said while studying his quarry.

In her late twenties, Diaz had big, dark eyes and a thick, straight fall of black hair that reached her waist. Her electric-green dress was low cut and clung to her bulging breasts, flat belly and trim thighs. A cloud of cheap perfume hung around her.

"Frank's a grade-A bastard." Studying Linc, Diaz swirled the drink she'd been sipping when she answered the door. "Why you asking 'bout him?"

"When was the last time you saw Frank?" Linc continued, ignoring her question.

"Been two years. What's he done this time?"

"This time?"

"He was in the joint for burglary. That was 'bout five years before I met him." She raised a shoulder. "You're police, you already know that, right?"

"Yes." The picture of Young's dragon tattoo had been taken when he was booked into jail on charges of residential burglary.

"Anyway, while Frank lived here he started breaking into houses again." Unconcerned, Diaz sipped her drink. "I came home one day and found him cramming all his stuff in his car. I figured he was blowing town 'cause the cops was on to him for the burglaries."

"Did he tell you that was the reason he was leaving?" Linc asked. "Because the cops were after him?"

"He didn't tell me squat." She flicked a hand tipped with pink fingernails that could double as claws. "He didn't come home the night before. Didn't call. Lucky I showed up when I did, or he'd have filched everything I had of value." Her mouth formed a smug curve. "When I seen he was walking out, I let him have it. We had a big fight right in the street."

"You said that was two years ago. Do you remember the exact date?"

"Day before Thanksgiving. I know 'cause he'd promised to take me to a party the next night. I'd bought a new dress and shoes. Frank messed up my holiday."

Linc's jaw set against the boiling hatred searing through his veins. He knew Young hadn't made it home that night because he was raping and torturing Kim.

Diaz sent an impatient look at the battered plastic clock on the table beside her. "Listen, I stopped giving a rat's behind about Frank when he took off. Meaning, us talking about him is wastin' my time. I gotta finish getting ready to go out."

Her petulant tone had Linc tamping down on emotion. He'd waited too long to find Kim's killer to let his lingering grief and burning need for justice mess up this interview.

"A couple more questions," he assured her. "Did Frank tell you where he intended to go when he left town?"

"No, and I didn't ask. Man walks out on me, I don't care what happens to him."

"What about his family? Do you know anything about them?"

"Me 'n' Frank only lived together a couple of months. I never met none of his relatives." She drained her glass. "Maybe he mentioned having an aunt around Chicago, but that could have been some other guy I dated said that." She gave Linc a slow, head-to-toe assessment. "You got a really great build, *novio*. I bet you can dance. You ever go out dancing?"

"On occasion." In other circumstances he would have ignored the come-on, but when a subject had something you wanted, the rule was treat him or her with respect and importance. Linc intended to get every piece of information this woman had on Young.

"Did Frank leave any property here?" Linc continued.

"Some papers." Diaz checked the clock again. "I trashed them."

"Nothing else? No other property?"

"No."

"You said you haven't seen him since he walked out. Have you heard from him? Heard anyone else say they've seen or talked to him?"

"No. Look, I got things to do." Diaz leaned, set her empty glass on the table. Her dark hair swung out from her cheek, fanning across her shoulders. Gold dotted with emeralds caught the light and glinted at her ears.

Linc's chest tightened until he could barely breathe. *Diaz was wearing Kim's earrings.*

He exchanged a look with Carrie. This morning she had studied a picture of the one-of-a-kind anniversary gift he'd had made for Kim. The awareness now in Carrie's eyes

signified she'd also spotted the earrings on Diaz, which
Kim had been wearing when she walked into the gas station. Linc had to fight the urge not to rip them off Diaz's
lobes.

Carrie gave a slight nod, a silent message passing, partner to partner. They had agreed if they saw an opening
that might force Diaz to help them find Young, Carrie
would go into action. The earrings were that opening.

Surging off the couch, she pulled handcuffs out of her
coat pocket. "Forget your dinner plans, Diaz." Carrie's
shift into bad-cop mode included a somber expression and
a curt, official tone. "You're going to jail."

"Like hell!" Diaz's dark eyes bore into Carrie like a
pair of heated lasers. "All I done is answer questions."

"The earrings you're wearing were reported stolen,"
Carrie informed her. "Stand up and put your hands behind
your back."

"Stolen?" Diaz's hands flew to her ears. "I didn't steal
them."

"Doesn't matter, they're in your possession. That means
you win the grand prize. Stand up."

"They were Frank's!"

Linc leaned forward, invading her space. "You told me
he didn't leave anything here." He darkened his expression. "I don't like being lied to—"

"I told you the truth! Frank didn't *leave* them here, not
on purpose."

"On purpose?" Linc softened his tone, easing into his
good-guy role, willing to listen to explanations.

"When I drove up that day and saw all Frank's stuff in
the trunk of his car, I dug through everything to make sure
he wasn't stealing from me. That's when I saw the earrings. I hid them in my purse when Frank wasn't looking.
Bastard owed me over five hundred dollars. Me taking the
earrings evened that." Diaz's chin jutted in defiance as she

glared up at Carrie. "How was I supposed to know they weren't Frank's?"

Carrie narrowed her eyes. "What, you thought he bought them to go with his new green suit? On your feet, Diaz."

"You got no warrant," she wailed, color sweeping into her face. "You can't take me or nothin' outta here without one."

"Wrong," Carrie said mildly. "You invited us into your home of your own free will. You've got stolen property hanging on you in plain sight. We got you cold, Diaz, we don't need a warrant."

"I got rights—"

Carrie stuck a warning finger in her face. "Which I'm about to read to you. *Stand up.*"

Figuring Diaz was amply primed, Linc rose, placed a restraining hand on Carrie's arm. "Take it easy, Sergeant McCall. Maybe we should rethink this."

Carrie shrugged off his touch, her blue eyes glinting with annoyance. "What's there to think about, Reilly? She's *wearing* stolen property. You waiting for the jail to issue her an engraved invitation?"

Linc took a second to admire his partner's acting skill. "Let's not forget our interest lies more in Frank," he said reasonably. "I suspect he's the person who stole the earrings from their rightful owner."

Carrie gave an unladylike snort. "So Diaz claims."

"It *was* Frank!" Diaz's flushed face began to crumple, tears welling in her eyes. "My mama'll kill me if I have ta spend Thanksgiving in jail."

"That would be a shame," Linc said, dropping his voice to a murmur.

Carrie flung up a hand in seeming disgust, the handcuffs dangling from her fingers. "You suddenly go soft in the head, Reilly? *She's a collar.*"

''You haven't read her rights to her yet.''

''I'm about to remedy that.''

He held up a placating hand. ''I'd appreciate it if you'd hold off for a minute.''

Carrie rolled her eyes and said nothing.

Linc looked down at Diaz, as if giving additional thought to her plight. ''We have to take the earrings into evidence,'' he said finally.

''I didn't steal them!''

''That doesn't change the fact they're in your possession.''

He waited while she took off the earrings, then handed them to Carrie. ''It's my opinion Frank took advantage of you.''

''He did,'' Diaz sobbed. ''Bastard.''

''So, I'm willing to help you on the possession charge,'' Linc continued. ''But you've got to help me first. If you cooperate, I'll see about getting you a walk.''

Diaz sprung to her feet, grabbing the sleeve of his leather jacket as if it were a lifeline in a boiling sea. ''I'll cooperate all you want, but that still don't mean I know more 'bout Frank. I swear, I haven't heard *nothin'* from him, not in two years.''

''You lived with him,'' Linc countered. ''Worked for the same company.''

''Not out of the same division. He drove a beer delivery truck. I did filing in the office.''

''Doesn't matter,'' Linc said, easing his sleeve from her grip. ''You know a lot of the same people, right?''

Sniffing, she nodded. ''Some.''

''Sergeant McCall and I need a list of those people before we leave here. If Frank is in town like we heard he might be, he could be bunking with one of them. Maybe calling around to see if anybody will loan him money.''

''You got that right,'' Diaz shot back. ''Frank's good at asking for money.''

Linc reached into his pocket, withdrew a business card. ''Start checking around tonight with people who know Frank. Find out if they've heard from him. Make sure you don't let on that the police are asking about him.'' Linc handed her the card. ''My office and cell phone numbers are on there. Call me day or night if you find out anything about Frank.''

Diaz shot Carrie a wary look before shifting her gaze back to Linc. ''I do that, you won't let her put me in jail?''

''You get me a lead on Frank, I'll make sure of it,'' Linc said. ''When it comes to those earrings, my business is with him.''

Twenty minutes later Carrie slid Linc a look as he steered the SUV through the early-evening gloom. Although he'd done a good job camouflaging his reaction when he'd spotted his dead wife's earrings on Olivia Diaz, Carrie knew the pain had to be there, buried deep inside. And as he hadn't spoken since they'd driven away from Diaz's trailer, she decided to tread lightly.

''So, Reilly, what do you think?''

''You deserve an Oscar for your rendition of a hard-edged cop.''

''That was no act, pal, I *am* a hard-edged cop.'' She tapped a fingertip against the glowing numbers of the clock on the dash. ''A *hungry* one,'' she added. ''We worked through lunch, remember?''

''I'll have you home in a couple of minutes.''

Knowing he intended to drop her off had Carrie frowning out the passenger window. She remembered the emotional upheaval Grace had experienced the night two patrol cops nabbed the scum who'd murdered her husband. As for Linc, Frank Young wasn't yet in custody, but Carrie

suspected her partner felt equally shaken over learning the
identity of his wife's killer after a two-year search. She
knew the smart thing to do was to let Linc drop her off
and drive away, but she couldn't. Not when the thought
of him spending the evening alone tightened a fist around
her heart.

"What about you?" she asked looking back at him.

"What about me?"

"You've got to be hungry."

"I have things to do. I'll pick up something later."

"Later, meaning after you drive downtown to the cop
shop? After you spend a couple of hours waiting for a clerk
in Records to check those names on the list Diaz gave us?"

"You're not just hard-edged, McCall, you're perceptive." Linc swung the SUV into her driveway, leaving the
engine running. He nodded toward the dark-windowed
two-story house painted a cool blue with gleaming white
trim. "Looks like you're the first one home this evening."

"The only one. Grace is working the graveyard shift.
Morgan's at my parents' house, helping Mom bake for
tomorrow."

Linc rested a wrist over the steering wheel. "You
headed there, too?"

"Not until morning. I'm the daughter who grew up
barely knowing her way to the kitchen, remember? I show
up tonight, I'll be assigned to napkin-folding detail with
Pop. Happens every Thanksgiving."

"Honest work."

"It is, but this year Morgan's engaged and she dragged
Alex Blade along. By now he's settled in front of the TV,
folding napkins while he and Pop exchange cop stories and
watch some sporting event. I don't want to get in the way
of all that male bonding."

"Since we're taking a break from The Hideaway, that

gives you a free night.'' Linc glanced at the clock. ''Have a good holiday. I'll call if I get a lead on Young.''

''Okay.''

When she made no move to open her door, he raised a brow. ''Something on your mind?''

''Spaghetti.''

''Spaghetti?''

''It's this Italian dish, Reilly. Has pasta and—''

''I know what spaghetti is, McCall.''

''Not true, since you've never tasted Morgan's spaghetti sauce. There's a bowl in the freezer, so tonight is your chance to find out how truly awesome spaghetti can be.''

''This from a woman who barely knows her way to the kitchen.''

''I know how to boil water and toss in pasta.'' Carrie angled her chin. ''You any good at uncorking a bottle of wine?''

His gaze drifted back to the house where slender, ivy-wrapped columns stood guard on either side of the small, tidy porch. Studying his profile through the evening gloom, Carrie saw the lines of stress at the corner of his eye and mouth.

''I can't stay,'' he said without looking at her. ''I *have* to find Young.''

''*We* will find him. It'll be easier for us to plan our next move if we take a couple of hours to refuel.''

When Linc's gaze remained on the house, she leaned in. ''Pay attention, Reilly.'' She lowered her voice to a purr. ''I'm about to proposition you.''

He looked back at her, gave her a fast, assessing scrutiny. ''You make it damn hard for a man to ignore you, McCall.''

''It's a gift.'' She shook back her hair. ''Here's the proposition,'' she said, tugging on the collar of her hot-pink sweater. ''I showered this morning at your place, but I've worn these clothes for twenty-four hours, and that's my limit. We go in, I head upstairs, take a shower and change. Meanwhile, you settle in the study—that's where the fax machine is. Call the Records Bureau, tell the clerk you're sending the list of names Diaz gave us. We both know it'll take the clerk a couple hours to check criminal and traffic records on all those names. You and I use that time to kick back and refuel on some awesome spaghetti and fine wine. After that, we plan the next step we take to find Young. Sound good?''

After a few silent moments, Linc scrubbed a hand over his face. ''So good I can't come up with a reason to say no.''

''Then don't,'' she said, and swung open her door.

Carrie made short work of her shower then, opting for comfort, pulled on slacks and an oversize sweater. In under an hour, she stood at the kitchen's butcher-block island, stirring spaghetti sauce while waiting for a pot of water to boil.

''You look like you know what you're doing,'' Linc said, striding through the doorway.

''Now who's perceptive?'' She inclined her head toward the bottle of merlot and stemmed glasses she'd placed near the stovetop. ''Corkscrew's in the far right drawer.''

While he uncorked and poured the wine, she stirred sauce. ''I take it Records got the fax okay?''

''Yes.'' He handed her a glass, then pulled one of the tall stools away from the island and propped a hip on it. ''The clerk will call my cell when he's finished running the names.''

''Good.'' Carrie sipped her wine, found its smooth, dry taste almost as revitalizing as the time she'd spent beneath the shower's hot spray.

Linc leaned toward the stovetop, sniffed. "That sauce smells like heaven."

"Wait until you taste it." He looked more relaxed now, Carrie thought, though she wondered if that were truly possible after the day's emotional upheaval. She sipped her wine, unable to even fathom what he must be feeling. A bittersweet, undeniable longing had her wishing she were free to wrap her arms around him and offer the comfort he surely needed.

"Can I help with anything?" Linc asked.

She tamped down her emotion. Since she couldn't comfort him in the way she wanted, she could at least keep the mood light.

Determinedly nonchalant, she leaned against the island, mimicking the slow, head-to-toe assessment Diaz had given him. "You got a really great build, *novio*. I bet you can wash dishes. You ever wash dishes?"

"Consider me the clean-up crew," Linc said, his mouth twitching. "You're good, McCall." The grin he flashed her was reckless and irresistible and slammed fierce, hungry need into her.

Not good. Turning away, she took plates from a cabinet and slid them into the warming drawer in the island. She was long past trying to convince herself that Linc Reilly didn't affect her. Long past telling herself she didn't want him.

She did. And it was her bad luck all it took to shove that want into the searing, desperate category was one damn grin.

You can't have him, she cautioned in something akin to a silent chant. Can't sleep with a partner, especially one you're investigating. She knew the key to staying sane while working Internal Affairs was to keep a distance. Don't let things get personal. Don't get involved. Don't cross the line.

Any way she looked at it, sleeping with Linc would be a huge step across that imaginary line.

Still, she wanted him.

Clenching a dish towel in one hand, she snatched up her glass and took a long swallow. The wine poured through her system, yet it couldn't numb the regret washing over her. Where might life have taken her and Linc if they had found each other under different circumstances? If their paths had crossed some other way? If every move she made, every word she said wasn't based on a damn lie?

Watching her, he set his glass aside and rose. ''That's some stranglehold you've got on that towel. And you suddenly got real thirsty. What's going on, McCall?''

Before she could make up an excuse, his cell phone rang.

Keeping his eyes on her, Linc answered, listened. After a few moments, his gaze shifted and his face went bleak. ''I'll come by tomorrow and take a look,'' he said quietly, then thanked the caller and hung up.

Carrie sat the towel aside. ''Bad news?''

''Yeah, and it's the third time this year I've gotten it.'' He blew out a breath. ''That was the caretaker at the cemetery where Kim's buried. Some kids in this city get their jollies vandalizing tombstones. Kim's grave is in an out-of-the-way corner of the cemetery that's easy to get to from the street. The kids sneak over the wall, and bam.''

For a moment Carrie was back in the SEU's conference room listening to Don Gaines berate Linc. *A guy who buries his wife in the cheapest plot at the cemetery doesn't give much of a damn about her.*

But Linc *did* care. Carrie had seen it in his eyes, heard it in his voice when he talked about Kim. ''Why…?'' she began, then stopped herself.

His eyes filled with awareness as he gazed down at her. ''Why did I bury her so close to the street?'' he asked, as if reading her thoughts. "Do you want to know out of curiosity? Or because you're one of the people Gaines has told I didn't care about Kim because of where she's buried?"

"He told me, but that's not why I'm wondering. I know you cared. I've seen in a hundred ways how much you loved her."

He looked away. "I did."

"I don't mean to pry." She put a hand on his arm, squeezed.

When she started to move away he snagged her fingers, folding them in his hand.

"Other than Kim's parents, I haven't told anyone why I buried her where I did. It's no one's business. But what you think matters, Carrie. You know that."

"What you think matters to me, too, Linc." She also knew she should pull from his hold. Step back. Instead she let the warmth that flowed from his hand to hers keep her in place while a flood of sensation washed over her.

"I buried Kim where I did because it was the closest I could get her to home."

Carrie spent a moment looking into his eyes while a swell of tenderness tightened her chest and she struggled to breathe. She was too worn down by having to maintain a constant facade around him, her emotions too raw to fight the feelings assaulting her.

Absurdly touched, she felt her hand tremble in his. "You know, Reilly, women are sentimental creatures. Romantics. When we hear a man say something like you just said, we get all weak. Shaky. That's because there aren't a lot of guys like you around. And when we stumble over one, our resistance takes a hit."

"Carrie…" He cupped a palm against her cheek.

"I mean, how's a girl supposed to resist a guy like you?"

"Don't resist."

"I have to. Need to…"

"A guy like me finds a gorgeous girl like you, I've got a problem with resistance, too." He wrapped his arm around her, tugged her against him. "A big one." Pressing a kiss against her temple, he worked his way down her cheek, her jaw, then to her throat. "I'm tired of trying to keep my hands off you. I want them on you. All over you."

With the last of her willpower, she fisted a hand against his rock-hard chest. She felt as if she were dangling over a cliff above a very deep, very rocky chasm. Sleeping with him while lying to him would be unforgivable. A betrayal. How the hell was she going to handle this? As a woman? As a cop?

She was afraid… Dear God, she was afraid she loved him. If she succumbed to temptation before she had a chance to tell him the truth, the fall she would surely take would likely be fatal. "Linc, we…have…to…talk."

"Later." His mouth settled on hers and he kissed her long, slow and deep until her body shook and her legs went weak.

When a ragged moan rose in her throat, he lifted his head. He gazed into her face, his amber eyes hot with emotion. "You're the first woman I've looked at in two years," he said, his voice low and rough. His fingers raked through her hair, tugging her head back. "You make me feel alive, Carrie. You make me feel alive when all I'd wanted to do for so long was die."

His words rocked her, hinting at a vulnerability, a need, she never would have suspected he felt. *Need for her.*

His mouth roamed across her cheek, down her jaw. "Let me have you. All of you."

Need blasted through her, toppling defenses, wiping away her agonized chain of thoughts. Surrender was the only way to describe how she felt. She'd lost the battle and given herself up to her searing desperation to have him, to feel him inside her.

For now nothing mattered but being with him.

Chapter 14

With Carrie's teeth savaging his throat, Linc's last coherent thought was to switch off the stove's burners.

"Where's your bedroom?" he managed while sharp-tipped arrows of need speared into him. He couldn't think past the outrageous hunger or the brutally keen desire to give and take. All he knew was he wanted every inch of her and wanted her to crave him every bit as fiercely.

"Upstairs," she answered before fastening her mouth to his in a kiss that turned quickly desperate, quickly ravenous on both their parts.

One of her hands locked on the back of his neck while the other fought to open the buttons of his shirt. "First...door on...right," she added against his mouth. *"Now."*

"We're going." His hands slid down, cupped her bottom and lifted. With her arms and legs wrapped around him like silken rope, he started out of the kitchen, ran into the stool he'd been sitting on and knocked them both back against the doorjamb.

He muttered an oath. "You okay?"

Her response was to shove his shirt off one shoulder and replace fabric with teeth.

Desperate to feel her, he shifted her weight to one arm and streaked a hand beneath her sweater. He sent up silent thanks when all he found was hot, bare flesh.

With his hand closed possessively over one soft breast and their mouths fused in a tongue-tangling kiss, he carried her up the narrow staircase, arms and legs banging against the banister. When they surged into the dimly lit hallway at the top of the stairs, Linc jerked the sweater over her head, pressed her back against the wall and fastened his mouth on one hard, tight nipple, suckling greedily.

Her low, throaty moan filled his senses, as potent and drugging as the wine he'd consumed.

While he fed on her, she shoved the shirt farther down his arms, then dug her nails into his shoulders. "Aren't... going to make it...to bedroom," she breathed.

"Don't bet on it." He pushed away from the wall and bumped into the bedroom door. "I've waited a hell of a long time to get you back into bed."

"Hurry." She nipped his jaw, then scraped her teeth down his throat while the word pumped like a pulse in his blood. *Hurry. Hurry.*

The room he reeled into was dark and airy, lit by slashes of silver moonlight. He could see the silhouette of a bureau, desk and bookshelf. Beyond them, the bed was a lake of smooth, cozy blankets. Here the scents that were uniquely Carrie were stronger than ever; he could smell her smoldering perfume, a cunning female fragrance meant to make a man lose his mind.

It was working.

With her clinging to him like a burr, he crossed the room, tumbling with her onto the bed.

If he'd gone insane with need, so had she. As though

in silent agreement, neither gave thought to gentleness, to soft words or slow hands. They tore at each other, kicking off shoes, dragging off clothes while feeding on each other with greedy kisses.

Rising over her, he kneed her thighs apart. He was keenly aware of every inch of her heated flesh, of every soft, supple curve, all there for his exploration and taking. Feeling a primitive need to conquer, to possess, he caught her wrists in one hand and stretched her arms over her head, arching her breasts upward. He dipped his head, suckled.

The feral purr that sounded in her throat went straight to his head like hot whiskey.

Their want of each other, *need* for each other was huge, ruthlessly keen. Right now, it was all that mattered.

To please her, and himself, he skimmed his free hand over her belly, down between her spread legs. He cupped her, found her wet and hot and unbearably arousing. *Mine,* he thought, hunger for her pumping inside him. His fingers plunged into her while he gorged himself on her flesh. Yet, when the fiery essence of her raced through his veins, he realized it was she who now possessed and conquered.

He was hers. From this moment on, he was hers.

Her breath strained as her head tossed restlessly back and forth within the frame of her upstretched arms. When she breathed his name, heat saturated him, as though a furnace door had been thrown open and the roaring blaze enveloped the room.

With his fingers impaling her, he could feel every pulse beat, hundreds of them, pounding in her flesh. His thumb circled the bud between her thighs, an erotic massage of her throbbing flesh.

His fingers withdrew, entered her again, then again. Sweat slicked her lush curves; he felt her muscles clench, the spasms boil swiftly upward.

"Again," he murmured. He sensed himself edging toward the boundaries of control while his fingers continued moving inside her. His thumb stroked her flesh until he shot her back up that slippery, heated path. When the second climax ripped through her, he shifted, braced himself over her.

She looked like a pagan goddess with her fiery wild mane spread over the pillow and the sheen of moonlight on her damp skin.

"Look at me. Look at me, Carrie."

Her eyes fluttered open, drugged, sated and smoky blue.

"I want to see your eyes while I take you."

"Now." Her lips trembled. "I want you inside me now."

She held his gaze as he thrust inside her, his heart crashing like thunder. He slid deeper, each move fueled by increasing urgency, increasing greed.

Need tore at him, clouding his mind, his vision. She arched higher to take him fully in, her hips meeting his, thrust for thrust, as their bodies mated. Her muscles clenched around him at the same moment his body convulsed.

With the earth moving beneath him, he buried his face in the fire of her hair and surrendered himself to her.

Carrie woke to a drab Thanksgiving morning with weak light filtering through the curtains, the sound of rain pattering on the roof and a man wrapped around her.

Simultaneous surges of sated contentment and anxiety swam through her as she turned her head and watched Linc sleep.

He was sprawled on his side, one arm and leg tossed across her body in firm possession. The gray morning light splayed across his stubbled jaw and firm mouth; his dark hair was rumpled from the fingers she'd tunneled through it during the night.

On a swell of emotion, she knew with certainty she was no longer in possession of her heart. Sometime during the long, exquisite hours they'd spent making love, she'd given it away to this man.

She was in love with Lincoln Reilly.

At the same time, she was lying to him, deceiving him. She couldn't bring herself to regret becoming his lover, but she did lament the fact she had let emotion sweep away logic and reason. Instead of plunging with him into crazed oblivion, she should have stepped back and told him the truth: she was Internal Affairs, assigned as his partner solely to find out if the murder of his wife had turned him into an out-for-revenge killer.

She had known for some time Linc was innocent. Her heart had been first to tell her that, then her cop instinct eventually sent the same message. After receiving Captain Patricia Scott's surreptitious phone call yesterday, Carrie knew the turnpike records the IA captain had subpoenaed contained tangible proof the Avenger was indeed a cop in the SEU. They still had no idea of the cop's identity, but the records alone were almost certain proof Linc wasn't the murderer Carrie sought.

She grazed a fingertip across his tousled hair while emotion tightened her throat. The hold he had on her was alternately comforting and frightening. Now, the latter feeling intensified, settling into a prickle of cold panic at her decision to tell him the truth. She sent up a silent, heartfelt prayer that Linc would understand she was merely doing her job. As ordered.

Cautious and quiet, she disengaged from his hold and slipped out of bed. With a last furtive glance his way, she padded soundlessly across the bedroom to the shower.

* * *

His face buried in the pillow, Linc muttered a pungent oath at the phone's insistent ring. He fumbled for the receiver on the nightstand, grabbed it up and, in a cop's conditioned response ground out, "Reilly. This better be good."

When silence greeted him, he fought his way out of the last throes of sleep and opened his eyes. It took his brain a half-second to register that he was in Carrie's bedroom. In her bed. Answering her private phone line in a voice fogged with sleep.

So much for discretion.

He shifted enough to discover he was alone. Carrie's warmth, her scent, was still there—on the sheets, on his skin. Inside him. His blood heated at the thought of her. She was a fascinating woman. Gorgeous. Passionate. In the space of a heartbeat, he acknowledged last night had steered his life in a different direction. One he hadn't thought he would ever take again. He wasn't entirely sure what he wanted from Carrie, but he knew it was more than just a body in the night.

"Good morning, Reilly." The female voice coming over the line was filled with humor and friendly warmth.

"Morning." Shifting, Linc propped himself up on the pillow, fervently hoping the voice belonged to someone other than the matriarch of the McCall family. If not, Carrie's invitation to Thanksgiving dinner at her parents' house might prove touchy.

"This is Grace."

Linc let out a breath. He didn't know Grace Fox well, but figured in his present situation, Carrie's sister might cut him more slack than their mother. "Morning, Grace. How you doing?"

"Just dandy. How about you?"

"Don't have any complaints. What's going on?"

"I'm in the kitchen at my parents' house, up to my

elbows in ingredients for dressing. What's going on with you, Reilly?''

His gaze swept over the side of the bed Carrie had occupied. ''Nothing at the moment.''

''Glad I'm not interrupting. Is Carrie around?''

For the first time, Linc was aware of rain pattering against the roof, of the muted sound of running water coming from beyond the closed bathroom door. ''She's in the shower. Want me to have her call you?''

''It'd be better if you'd just write down a couple of things while they're fresh in my mind. It's stuff Mom forgot at the grocery store. Carrie has to stop and buy bags of ice on her way here, so she can add a few more items to her list.''

''Let me find some paper.''

''Check Carrie's desk.''

Linc gave Grace points for not even trying to act as if she didn't know he had taken up residence in her sister's bedroom.

Tossing back the covers, he headed across the room, the air cool against his bare flesh. He gave thought to heating up in more ways than one by joining Carrie in the shower when he got off the phone.

He moved into the alcove off the room that held one thin bookcase and a small, dark wood desk with spindly legs. There was only a lamp on the top of the desk, so he pulled open its sole drawer. He retrieved a pad, then a pen. ''Shoot.''

''One can of condensed milk,'' Grace began.

When the call ended, Linc ripped the list off the pad. He shoved it and the pen back in the drawer, his fingertips skimming a manila file folder. His eyes narrowed. Then everything inside him froze when he spotted his name typed on the folder's label.

* * *

With her wet hair wrapped in a towel and her thick terry robe belted at her waist, Carrie emerged in a wave of steam from the bathroom. She glanced at the bed, then frowned, expecting to find Linc still asleep.

"Behind you."

His hard-as-quartz tone had her whirling. Clad in his jeans and sweater, he leaned against the front of her small desk, a file folder open in his hands.

The dark fury in his eyes told her exactly what file it was.

She felt the blood drain from her face. Felt her heart shoot into her throat while dread settled over her.

"Linc, listen to me—"

"Grace called. She asked me to jot down a list of things for you to pick up at the store. I needed paper, so I looked in your desk drawer." He sent her a bitter look. "Wouldn't want you to think I intentionally invaded the privacy of an Internal Affairs cop."

His cold, flat words had her stiffening in defense. "I'm asking you to give me a chance to explain."

Using a thumb, he fanned through the contents of the file. "Your paperwork is self-explanatory." He dropped the folder onto the desk, then speared her with a look that was so immensely damning it ripped at her heart. "You have enough yet to pin the murder of seven do-wrongs on me, McCall? I see in your notes you're calling the killer the Avenger. Am I him?"

"No. I know you didn't commit the murders."

"That why you're *investigating* me? Why you're undercover as my *partner*? Doing all that because you *know* I didn't cap seven scum, most of whom I've handled in the past? All of whom have files in the SEU?"

"Had you already picked up on this?" She wrapped her arms around her waist, forcing herself to stay calm despite the premonition of disaster that hammered in her head. "Had you spotted the pattern to the murders?"

"Wouldn't be much of a detective if I hadn't, would I? Especially since it's possible someone's setting me up to take the fall for the murders." His brownish-gold eyes were as icy as his voice. "You know what's ironic? I talked to Quintana the other day about these killings. I told him I was surprised IA wasn't crawling all over the SEU by now. How wrong I was." His jaw tightened. "Does Quintana know you're a plant?"

"No. His boss, Captain Vincent, called us in. Since the department leaks like a sieve, he felt the fewer people who knew about me up front, the better." Drawing a careful breath, she clenched her trembling hands on the robe's belt. Somehow, someway, she had to make him understand.

"Linc, IA had solid reasons to put me with you. Your wife was murdered by a man who has yet to be caught. That's motive for you to go after other scum who've evaded justice. The seven dead victims are career criminals with files in the SEU. Like you just said, of all the cops in the unit, you handled most of the seven. You knew firsthand they were lowlifes who would never reform into sterling citizens. Left alive, they all would have continued preying on decent, honest people. Like Kim." Carrie paused. "Plus, the Avenger began killing right after her murder. That timing didn't bode well for you, either."

He crossed his arms over his chest. "Sounds like you've built yourself a great circumstantial case against me."

"A great *statistical* case. Your name came up too often for you not to warrant a hard look."

"The one glitch is, I'm not your Avenger."

"I know. You must realize we would have been remiss *not* to look at you for the murders."

"I'm realizing a hell of a lot of things this morning."

He swiped his hand over the file, snagged the document on top. "Here we have a photo of my Pike Pass bill for last month. Whenever I pay a bill, I write the date and check number on the invoice. That's what's on this, which means you didn't get this from the Turnpike Authority. You took this picture at my house."

"Yes."

"When?"

"The first night we went to The Hideaway, I left my purse in your car." She marveled at how her voice could sound so strong and clear with her throat nearly closed. "Later I told you I needed to fix my makeup so you gave me the keys. I had a small box of clay in my purse. When I went out to the car, I made an impression of your house key."

"You broke into my home?"

If she had been faint of heart, the steel in his voice would have had her taking a step back in defense. "I used the key made off the clay impression to unlock the front door," she qualified.

"How'd you bypass the alarm system?"

"I had a recorder in my coat pocket the night Wade Crawford met us there to talk about installing the camera in the jukebox. Before you and I left to go to The Hideaway, you entered your alarm's security code. The recorder picked up the tones."

"And some electronics geek translated the tones into my code."

"Yes." Her hands began to tremble, so she shoved them into the pockets of her robe. "I searched your house the night before last when you stayed at the Drop Inn."

Awareness snapped into his eyes. "When I came home the next morning, I smelled your scent on the air. I thought…" He looked away, a muscle in his jaw clenching. After a moment he turned his head, met her gaze. "That search was illegal, unless you had a warrant."

Seeing the mix of hurt and anger in his eyes had a fist of regret clenching around her heart. "Captain Scott, the head of IA, got a covert entry warrant for the search of your unoccupied residence. It authorized me to look for certain evidence linking you to the Avenger murders. If I found any, I was to photograph it, then leave. For this type of warrant, notification can be delayed up to a certain number of days after the search. You'll be notified. Eventually."

He tossed the photo back onto the desk. "Why'd you take a picture of my Pike Pass bill?"

"When I saw your invoice, I snapped to the fact that the Avenger had to have driven from here to Tulsa, too. There's a chance he has a Pike Pass. If so, we needed to check the turnpike records."

"You think a guy who's killed seven people and left no trace would be careless enough to let his name show up on those records?"

"I think anything's possible. You and I both know that some people get caught solely because they make mistakes." Her lungs were working overtime now, making her voice sound thin and foreign. "I convinced Captain Scott that the Avenger might have screwed up, too. That we'd maybe get a break if we subpoenaed the Turnpike Authority's records."

"Did you get a break?"

"Somewhat." She took another step toward him, close enough to see the small lines of tension fanning from the corners of his eyes and mouth. "Because there's a turnpike slicing through this city, the OCPD has a Pike Pass account. Almost every vehicle has a Pike Pass reader Velcro'ed to its windshield. Those readers get swapped around when a vehicle gets replaced or goes down for maintenance. Because of that, there's no way to be sure what vehicle a Pike Pass is on at any given time.''

''Go on.''

''The SEU is like every other unit—it has a certain number of Pike Pass boxes. One of its boxes was used the day of Dell's murder on a vehicle that left Oklahoma City about a half hour after yours. Neighbors of your in-laws remember seeing you pull into their driveway about the same time the vehicle with the SEU's Pike Pass went through the turnpike reader in Tulsa. You couldn't have been in both places simultaneously.''

''So you think I'm off the hook for the murders?''

''Yes. Linc, what about Don Gaines? He loved Kim and blames you for stealing her away. For her death. Would he go to these lengths to set you up?''

''I have no idea.''

Carrie thought about her other potential suspect, Tom Nelson. The affable cop was once suspected of planting evidence in a rapist's residence. ''What about—''

Linc held up a hand, cutting her off. ''There's other things I'm interested in addressing right now. Like how good you've done your job.''

''That's the point. I'm doing my job. As ordered. Linc, I'm sorry. I couldn't tell you I was undercover, please understand that.''

''I'm a cop, I damn well understand that part of it,'' he retorted. ''What doesn't add up is your claim you believe I'm not the Avenger.''

She tried to gauge where he was going with the comment, but his eyes were flat, cold and unreadable.

''It should add up because it's true.''

''If it were, why not tell me the truth before you climbed into bed with me? Why let me touch you when that lie stood between us?''

''I wanted to tell you.'' Her voice faltered. ''That's…

what I intended to do in the kitchen when I said we needed to talk. I should have told you then.'' Her legs were shaking now, and her stomach roiled against waves of sick dread. ''Things just heated up so fast between us. Got out of control. You can't know how sorry I am that I didn't step back and tell you. Didn't tell you a lot of things.''

He studied her with eyes that were like ice over a deep, empty pit. ''I have to hand it to you, McCall, I'm not often fooled. I knew you had some sort of secret, but I didn't get anywhere near thinking you were IA.'' As he spoke, his expression set in almost savage lines, and those icy eyes sharpened like sabers. ''Now I have to ask myself, if you're that good, how do I know your spiel about Pike Pass records is on the level?''

She blinked. ''Why wouldn't it be?''

''You say you're convinced I'm not the Avenger.''

''I am—''

''Last night, you worked your damnedest to get me to come in for dinner. Were you planning then on us having a go at each other? Hoping once I was inside you I'd be so swept away I'd confess I'm the Avenger?''

''How can you even think—''

''And you were real insistent about how *we* need to make plans to track down Frank Young. You thinking I'll put a bullet in his head, making him my eighth victim? If you're around to witness that, you'll have a hell of a lot more than a circumstantial case.''

She stared at him while her pent-up emotions coalesced into a fury that had a hundred curses trembling on her lips. ''Don't,'' she said, her chin angling with a warrior's challenge. ''Just don't. I know you're angry and hurt that I had to keep the truth from you. I understand you maybe won't ever forgive me or absolve me for doing my job, for following orders. Fine, I knew the risks and I'll accept the outcome. But don't you dare try to turn what we shared last night into something contemptible. It wasn't. You *know* that.''

When he made no comment, her fury seethed even hotter.

''All right, Reilly, you caught me in another lie. I *did* lure you in for dinner.'' Bunching her hands into fists, she sent him a smile sharp enough to drill holes. ''I asked you to stay because I remembered how unsettled Grace was when Ryan's killer got nabbed. The last thing she needed then was to be alone. Yesterday we identified the man who killed your wife, and I suspected you must feel a lot of the same emotions as Grace. I asked you to stay because I didn't want you to be alone.'' She jerked the towel off her head, used a shaky hand to shove at the damp hair that cascaded over her shoulders. ''Dammit, I didn't *plan* on us going to bed. Didn't realize until later….'' She stopped herself, her lungs heaving.

''Didn't realize what?''

That I love you. He was slipping away from her. She was standing two feet away from him, watching the distance grow by leaps and bounds. She dug her fingers into the towel.

''Doesn't matter,'' she answered. ''What matters is I didn't know you when I got this assignment. When that changed, when I saw the kind of man you are, the most important part of the job became proving your *innocence*. I intended to tell you last night I was IA, even though I was afraid you wouldn't understand. That you'd think I had betrayed you. Looks like I was right.''

''Like I keep saying, McCall, you're perceptive.'' He pushed away from the desk. ''You'd better let IA know your cover's blown. They'll have to figure out a new way to come at me.''

Watching him walk toward the door shot a skitter of

panic up her spine. "Linc, the last thing I meant to do was hurt you."

He paused in the doorway and looked across his shoulder, his expression grim. "When you're a cop, knowing something is always better than not knowing. Can't say I feel that way right now."

Chapter 15

It was still raining late that afternoon when Linc parked outside the large fieldstone house surrounded by bare-branched oaks. Although he wasn't in the mood to explain anything to anyone, that was the reason he was about to intrude on his boss's Thanksgiving.

Quintana's wife, a tall, sleek blonde, led him down a hallway ripe with rich holiday scents. She showed him into a paneled study with leather chairs and a massive desk. Linc apologized for intruding, then declined her offer of pumpkin pie. Excusing herself, she slid the door closed behind her.

That didn't do much to block out the murmured jumble of voices that filled the air. Judging from the cars crowded in the driveway and along both curbs, Linc figured all five Quintana kids were there, along with the swarm of grand-kids whose pictures the lieutenant constantly passed around.

Linc muttered a curse when he found himself wondering

if a similar holiday frenzy was taking place at the McCall household. Just the thought of Carrie's deception had his anger and resentment bubbling all over again.

Hands clenched, he strode to the window. The rain fell from low, gunmetal clouds that seemed to press against the glass. He didn't want to think about the quiet resignation he'd heard in her voice. Didn't want to picture the pain he'd seen in her eyes. He was too mad, *too hurt,* to care about her feelings.

Dammit, he knew she'd had a job to do, orders to follow. He didn't blame her for carrying out those orders—life as an undercover cop was mostly about deception, after all.

It was her sleeping with him while a lie stood between them that rankled. It wasn't just because the hurt he felt was huge. What if the accusation he'd tossed at her was right? What if she'd withheld the truth because she believed him guilty of the Avenger murders? What if she'd hoped sex would lower his defenses and he'd spill his guts? For all he knew, IA had her bedroom wired in case he confessed!

A part of him rejected the notion as absurd. But another part, the part that grew out of a cop's instinctive, ingrained paranoia, held on to the idea. He knew full well cops could be treacherous. *He* could be when necessary. Why not Carrie?

He'd seen her acting skills at The Hideaway. Hell, she had West Williams so dazzled the cowboy bought her jewelry and tailed her to another man's motel room like a love-starved puppy!

Linc had no reason to trust her. No reason to think she'd slept with him for any purpose other than to reel him in to make a confession.

And that was the problem, he thought, his mind circling back to the source of his pain. He was close to falling in love with a woman who'd maybe slept with him for the purpose of looking for something rotten inside him. Who quite possibly believed him capable of cold-blooded murder.

He went still when he realized where his thoughts had veered. No, he countered, he cared about her. A lot. That was a long, safe distance from the close-to-falling-in-love category.

And the way he felt right now, each passing minute put more distance between them. He had his wife's killer to catch. He didn't plan to waste time thinking about the red-headed cop who'd thrown him for a loop. About things he'd begun to wish for.

He turned when the study's door slid open.

"Sorry to make you wait," Quintana said, moving into the room. SEU's commander looked relaxed and well fed with the flannel tail of his shirt hanging over his chinos. "I had four grandsons climbing on top of me when you got here."

"No problem, Lieu," Linc said, exchanging a handshake with his boss. "Sorry to bother you on a holiday. A situation's come up that'll probably drop into your lap when we get back to work on Monday. Maybe before. I don't want to be blindsided."

Wariness crept into Quintana's eyes. "Doesn't sound good."

"It's not."

Quintana waved Linc to a group of leather chairs. "I'm listening."

"McCall works for Internal Affairs."

Quintana dropped into the chair beside Linc's, his expression coalescing into an uneasiness that Linc understood. Internal Affairs: two words that drove a heat rash to the back of the neck of even the most honest and upright cop.

As if experiencing that sensation, Quintana scrubbed a hand across his nape. "Captain Vincent must have set this up," he theorized. "He called, said Annie Becker had been transferred to the Homeland Security task force, and McCall was taking her place. Vincent said he thought you and McCall would work well together." Quintana paused. "I guess that verifies they suspect you're the rogue cop whose killed seven pieces of scum."

"Right."

Quintana bounced a fist against the arm of his chair. "You *sure* about McCall? This isn't just your cop instinct at work?"

"No," Linc said. "This morning I stumbled over the IA file she's keeping on me."

"Stumbled over it, where?"

"At her place," Linc said evenly.

"This morning." Quintana's gaze narrowed. "Since we're all off duty today, I figure you weren't there on business."

When Linc made no comment, Quintana shook his head. "I knew plenty was going on between you two that day in the stairwell."

Linc didn't want to think about those heated moments. Didn't want to think about Carrie in any capacity but as a cop on a mission to take him down. "The other day when we talked about the murders, you said you'd talked to the captain over at IA."

"Couple of times." Quintana's gaze focused out the window where the rainy afternoon gloom was quickly transforming into a dank evening. "Captain Scott didn't tell me McCall was hers."

"Did she mention Pike Pass records?"

Quintana's head whipped around. "No. Why?"

Linc tightened his jaw. Scott's failure to tell Quintana about the turnpike records wasn't proof Carrie had invented the story to get him to drop his guard. Didn't disprove it, either.

"Dammit," Quintana said after Linc ran down the information. "When those turnpike readers aren't in a vehicle, they're tossed in a drawer. Everyone in the unit has access to them."

"Yeah." Linc scrubbed a hand across his jaw, a stubbly reminder he hadn't shaved for two days. "Lieu, even if IA considers me in the clear on the murders, there's another reason they can come down on me. You need to know."

Quintana pinched the bridge of his nose between his thumb and finger. "If my grandchildren weren't here, I'd have already downed a Scotch. I'm not sure I want to hear more."

"It's about The Hideaway. Because McCall knows, I figure IA knows, too," Linc added. He then explained he'd set up the operation at the bar to find his wife's tattooed killer. He moved on to Olivia Diaz, summarizing his and Carrie's interview with Frank Young's former girlfriend. He ended with, "If Diaz calls and tips me to Young's whereabouts, I'll have him."

"And I'm having that Scotch." Quintana rose, headed across the braided rug that pooled color over the wood floor. When he reached a mirror-lined nook built into the wall, he took down glasses, filled them from a decanter, then retraced his steps.

"Drink up," he said, handing Linc a glass.

The Scotch spread through Linc's system like molten lava. He realized the last time he'd eaten was when he and Carrie left her bed long enough to fix spaghetti. Thinking about her, about all they shared had something moving inside him, struggling against the anger he felt. He tightened his fingers on the glass. He wanted to hold on to that anger—it was the only thing capable of numbing the hurt.

"Lieu, McCall knows you had no idea I set up The Hideaway investigation. You won't get burned on this, I'll take the heat. I wanted you to know so you can be ready when everything hits."

Quintana drained his glass. "Dammit, I've got no problem with you going after the slime who killed Kim. I just wish you hadn't involved the mayor's office when you set up the deal."

"Needed to make the investigation a priority."

"You did a hell of a good job." Quintana fell silent, then said, "You've got Young ID'd, with Diaz as a way to find him. You no longer need The Hideaway. I'll schedule the raid to go down Monday night when everybody's back at work."

"I've got in-service training that day," Linc said. "You want me to pass? Come to the office to help with calls?"

"No. In-service is required for all cops. With IA breathing down your neck, I don't want to give them anything to hammer you on." Quintana met Linc's gaze. "You've always done a good job for me, Reilly, so I'm going to bat for you. The Hideaway's a blight. We close it, arrest customers on drug, gambling and sex charges, the mayor'll be pleased. Chief, too. IA comes at you over the way you set up an operation that makes this city a better place, I'll back you."

"Thanks, Lieu."

Both men rose, shook hands. "I appreciate you warning me about all this." Quintana shook his head. "McCall needs to be in on the raid. She's observed a lot of the violations. She knows who needs to go to jail and can help the Intelligence guys with IDs of suspects." Quintana raised a brow. "Knowing she's IA, can you manage to pair with her one more time?"

Linc's jaw hardened. "Whatever it takes."

* * *

Carrie put on a brave face and got through Thanksgiving without anyone in the family picking up on the turmoil going on inside her. She then went home, sequestered herself in her bedroom and began reviewing Avenger homicide reports. Now, late Sunday night, she was still propped up in bed, plowing through files with the determination of a woman on a mission.

Her blunt concentration on the Avenger murders had kept her from thinking about Linc.

Mostly.

Whenever she took a break, her mind would drift and she found herself agonizing over the prospect of calling him. Maybe even dropping by his house. She'd ultimately dismissed doing either. He wouldn't believe her, no matter what she said. She'd done a fine job of damning herself, after all. She repeatedly called herself a fool for allowing him past her defenses, for dropping her guard and sleeping with him before telling him the truth about her assignment. Fools usually paid a price for stupidity; hers was a heart that felt as if it had been shredded.

You make me feel alive, Carrie. You make me feel alive when all I'd wanted to do for so long was die.

The memory of Linc's words had tears burning her eyes. Those words alone had told her how deeply he'd cared. The way he'd touched her, held her throughout the night had echoed those feelings.

Regret swelled inside her. She loved him, and she'd maybe lost him because she kept the truth from him. Nothing she could say to him would change that. But she could show him she had been honest when she said she believed him innocent of the Avenger murders. To do that, she had to find the rogue cop who'd put a bullet into the head of seven criminals. A cop who might possibly intend to frame Linc for those murders.

With that sobering thought in mind, she propped her

pillow against the headboard, and shuffled the reports she had read uncountable times. As always, she put the Avenger's homicides in order, the report on the first murder on top of the stack.

She'd never worked a homicide, but Bran had spent a couple of years in the PD's Homicide Detail. More than once her oldest brother had talked about the significance of the first victim in serial crimes. The first was generally the one handled carelessly. Murder was like everything— practice made perfect. First murders were sometimes sloppy, hasty. It was only later the criminal mind thought to start making better preparations, to plan more carefully.

Carrie rescanned the top report, frowning when nothing jumped out at her. Because there was nothing sloppy about the murder, she realized. If the Avenger had acted hastily, he'd managed to cover his tracks.

Or maybe this wasn't his first murder?

Her mind racing, she leaned back into the pillow. When first ordered to work undercover, she'd been handed copies of all homicides believed to have been committed by the Avenger. The first of those occurred soon after Linc transferred into the SEU. Only weeks after his wife's murder. Avenging her had been cited as his motive for turning rogue and killing bad guys.

Were there murders with the same MO that had occurred *before* Kim Reilly's death? Similar homicides where the victims didn't have files in the SEU? Victims whom Linc had never had contact with? *Had anyone even bothered to check?*

Trying to contain her excitement, Carrie grabbed the phone.

At nine-thirty the following morning, Linc stood amid a group of cops in the break room at the PD's training center. Sipping coffee, he listened to several classmates grouse over having to spend an entire day on in-service training.

The feeling of being watched had Linc glancing across his shoulder. His gut tightened when he saw Carrie standing in the doorway. Her fiery hair was piled on the top of her head. She wore slacks and a jacket that made her look soft and feminine. Seeing her, he wanted nothing more than to drag off her clothes, to lose himself in her again.

He looked away. So much for the hours he'd spent telling himself he didn't want a woman who'd deceived him so thoroughly.

He rolled his shoulders to twitch out the tension. He figured his continuing attraction to her was due to the fact something about the woman cross wired the circuits in his brain.

He dumped his foam cup in the trash, then moved to the door. Up close, he saw shadows of weariness beneath her eyes, an unnatural paleness to her cheeks. He felt dark satisfaction that she'd maybe lost as much sleep over him as he had over her.

"Something I can do for you, McCall?"

"We need to talk."

"Thought we got everything said the other morning."

Her fingers tightened on the black coat draped across one arm. "I think I know who the Avenger is," she said, her tone urgent and low. "I'm here because if I'm right, he's close to you. If he's out to set you up, he can do it. Easily."

Linc clamped a hand on her arm. "Let's talk."

Minutes later they settled into chairs in a vacant room.

"I've apologized for how I handled things between us," she said quietly. "I meant that. Just as I meant it when I said I took you off my Avenger suspect list some time ago. That's why I've been poring over the homicide reports IA gave me when I snagged this assignment." She paused, frowned. "I kept thinking I'd missed something. That if I stared at the reports long enough, I'd see it." She pushed wispy strands of hair off one pale cheek. "Last night it hit me that maybe I didn't have all the reports. That when IA focused on you, tunnel vision kicked in and no one dug to see if any Avenger murders occurred *before* Kim's death. Turns out I was right."

"There's more?" Linc leaned in. "I spotted the pattern of the murders. My computer run came up with seven."

"You looked solely at victims who had SEU files, right? Who'd been handled by someone in the unit?"

"Right."

"I had Homicide do a run on all unsolved head-shot killings. It came back with one that wasn't included in the reports I had. The murder of a professional robber with the last name of Eby."

"Eby," Linc repeated. "Doesn't sound familiar."

"He doesn't have an SEU file. I checked." She narrowed her eyes, as though organizing her thoughts. "Eby was shot in an alley. No witnesses. No evidence. Judging from his rap sheet, the person who killed him prevented untold violent crimes."

"The Avenger," Linc said grimly.

Carrie nodded. "Eby was more than a robber. About five years ago he was arrested on a triple-homicide charge, but walked on a technicality. I pulled the file on those murders. The victims were a man, his wife and their small son, all shot in the head at the restaurant the man managed." She closed her eyes. "I saw the photos. From the position of the bodies, it's obvious the little boy was shot last."

The bleakness in Carrie's eyes moved something inside Linc. He laid a hand over her wrist, his fingers throbbing with the memory of how her skin felt under them. "Carrie—"

She slipped her arm from his grasp. "Let...me get through this. Let's just get through this."

"All right."

"The cop who nabbed Eby tied him to the murders because of a partial tag number a snitch got off Eby's car. All parties considered the arrest solid. But Eby's public defender cited some point of law over the way the cop used the information on the tag the snitch gave him." She raised a palm. "I don't know details, just that the judge dismissed the charges."

"Hard to swallow, especially for the cop."

"Yes. A few years later Eby's name came up as the suspect in the murder of an old lady who was beaten, then shot in the head. Wasn't long after that Eby wound up dead in the alley. Two days later, the cop who arrested Eby for the three homicides became commander over the SEU. Do-wrongs with files in that unit began dying of gunshot wounds to the head not long after that."

Surprise hit Linc like a fist. *"Quintana?"*

"None of this proves he's the Avenger. But it makes sense when you put everything together." Carrie furrowed her brow. "Is there bad blood between you? A reason he'd set you up?"

"No." Linc clenched his fist. "I talked to him about the murders. I talked about them at his house the other day."

"He called me this morning, said he's setting up the raid on The Hideaway for tonight. I'm expected to be there." Her mouth curved. "Judging from his tone, you told him I'm IA, right?"

"I figured you'd tell your boss I set up The Hideaway operation. I wanted Quintana to know he was in the clear."

"I haven't told IA. Don't intend to." She kept her eyes steady on his. "The way you carried out the operation was a little off the wall. Still, the only people who'll get hurt are the ones who deserve it. I wish I'd been as smart about my own undercover assignment.''

Linc sat in silence, conscious of her fatigue-shadowed eyes, her pale cheeks. She had walked into his life only a short time ago, yet she had begun to soften the edges and warm the shadows. He was well aware his refusal to accept at face value everything she'd told him might be the biggest mistake of his life.

Just then, his cell phone rang, cutting off his thoughts. Welcoming the interruption, he flipped it open, answered.

''Hey, Reilly, it's about time you got sent to school.''

''What's up, Nelson?'' Linc asked, letting Carrie know it was Tom Nelson, the scruffy SEU detective calling.

''Your partner called earlier, looking for you. I told her I'd let you know.''

''Carrie's here now. Any other messages?''

''A chick named Diaz called. Has this accent—''

''Did she leave a message?''

''Started to tell me about some guy named Frank. Then Quintana walked up. When he saw the names I'd jotted down, he said he'd take the call. I still got her number if you want it.''

''I do. Is the Lieu there?''

''Saw him leave right after that. Hold on.'' Nelson's voice faded and Linc heard mumbled chatter. Nelson came back, saying, ''The Lieu's taking his lunch hour early to work out at his gym.''

Linc hung up, told Carrie what Nelson had said while punching in Diaz's number. A minute later he had her on the phone. Their conversation was short and blood-chilling.

''She said she gave the address of where Young's staying to Quintana,'' he told Carrie. Rising, he ripped the page off the pad on which he'd written the address. ''I'm headed there.''

"*We're* headed there." She was out of her chair like a shot, pulling on her coat as they rushed down the hallway. "I take it Quintana knows about Young? That he killed Kim?"

"That's something else I told the boss," Linc said, then bit back a curse. He checked out at the training center's office and retrieved his bomber jacket while Carrie called Quintana's gym.

"The receptionist said Quintana scanned his membership card into the reader a half hour ago," she told Linc when he joined her at the front door. "She hasn't seen him leave yet," she added as they stepped into an icy wind and dashed to Linc's SUV. "I asked her to page him," Carrie added after sliding into the passenger seat. "Nothing. She sent a trainer to look for him. As far as they can tell, Quintana's not there."

"According to Diaz," Linc began, cranking the powerful engine to life, "Quintana said he would call and give me Young's location. He hasn't. Which means he might be going after Young himself. If Quintana is the Avenger and out to frame me, popping the guy who murdered my wife would do it."

"So, if we're right, we have to get to Young before Quintana."

"Yeah.

Carrie clung to the handle above the passenger door as he wheeled out of the lot at a high rate of speed. "Why you, Linc? If there's no bad blood between you and Quintana, why would he set you up?"

"Hell if I know," Linc said, slicing the SUV through traffic. "I'm blowing the doors off every car I pass so I can maybe save the life of the guy who murdered my wife. Explain that to me."

"I'll pass," Carrie said levelly, tucking her ice-blue

muffler into her coat's neckline. ''My record at explaining things to you isn't too hot.''

''Yeah.'' Linc studied her out of the corner of his eye. In the days since he'd learned the truth, his anger at her had lessened. He hadn't yet sorted out his feelings for her, but he had to admit how good it felt to have her sitting beside him again.

Damn good.

Chapter 16

Carrie unholstered her automatic when Linc parked the SUV down the street from the address where Diaz said they would find Frank Young. The neighborhood was old and rundown with paint-chipped framed houses and grass-bare yards.

They'd driven a four-block perimeter around the house, but hadn't spotted Quintana's car. Carrie knew viewing him as the Avenger was based on theory, not evidence. As was the idea he might come after Young. For all they knew, the lieutenant was still at his gym. He simply might have been in the shower when she had him paged and the trainer looked for him.

Carrie studied Linc's grim profile while his gaze swept the street. She couldn't imagine the emotions he must be feeling over the prospect of finally taking down his wife's killer.

"You okay?" she asked, sliding her gun into her coat pocket.

"Yeah. Let's do this."

"No car in the drive," Linc said as they traversed the cracked sidewalk. "Hard to tell if anybody's home."

With adrenaline pumping through her veins, Carrie hardly felt the wind that was sharp enough to penetrate steel.

"I'll take the front," Linc said. "You get the back in case Frank makes a run for it."

Nodding, she veered up the driveway. Hand locked on the gun concealed in her pocket, she kept close to the house, stooping when she passed each window.

The single-car detached garage—its overhead door closed—sat behind and to the left of the house. A basketball hoop with paint peeling off its backboard faced the street.

She came abreast of trash cans overflowing with plastic bags just as she caught movement at the side of the garage. She crouched beside the cans, her throat closing when she spotted Quintana easing his way from the rear of the garage to its side door. He was dressed in pitch-black workout sweats.

Drawing her weapon, Carrie jerked her phone off her belt. She punched in Linc's cell number and whispered, "Lieu's here. Garage."

She watched Quintana peer through the door's window. Easing back, he drew a gun from beneath his jacket.

The instant he shoved through the door, she sprinted to the garage, snugging her back against the wall beside the door. She struggled to take in enough oxygen to keep up with her heart rate. She saw Linc race around the corner of the house just as Quintana barked, "You're dead, Young!"

Certain the man was seconds from a bullet in the head, Carrie burst through the open door. "Drop it!"

Maintaining a defensive crouch, she swept the area with

both her weapon and her gaze. Stacks of boxes, piles of collapsible lawn furniture and rusted garden tools left no room for a car.

Standing in front of a workbench was a man dressed in jeans and a red flannel shirt with its sleeves rolled up. Beside him was a chest-high toolbox, its lid raised. He had his hands lifted in surrender; his face was white, his dark eyes brimmed with terror. Carrie recognized Frank Young, not just from his mug shot, but from the dragon tattoo on his burly forearm.

Quintana stood across the garage from Young, an automatic aimed at his quarry. The muscles in his face looked hard and tense, his eyes feral. She could imagine his cop's mind assessing her presence, figuring how to defuse the situation.

"Drop it!" she repeated. "No one's going to die."

"She's right," Linc said, stepping through the door. "Drop the gun, Lieu."

"He's a cop?" Young snarled, eyeing Carrie's and Linc's badges. "He breaks in, says I'm *dead!* You better arrest him."

Linc slicked Young a menacing look. "Keep your mouth shut," he commanded, the words dangerously soft.

Carrie had a second to wonder if the grieving husband might override the fair-minded cop. No, she countered. She *knew* Linc would disconnect from emotion. Walk the moral line.

"Lieutenant, I know why you've done what you have," she said evenly. "I saw the photos of the family Eby killed at that restaurant."

At the mention of Eby, Quintana's chin jerked up.

"I *understand* why you killed Eby," she continued, taking a step toward him. Her knees shook and sweat prickled her skin. "And the others. They were slime. You saved a lot of innocent people. But, it's time to stop now. You have to stop.'' She edged in another step, a sick sense of dread pushing at the base of her throat. ''Just drop the gun—''

''Stay back!'' Quintana's nostrils flared and his eyes glittered like black marble. ''That little boy in the restaurant—he had blond hair, just like my oldest grandson. Looked just like him. He was lying there, a bullet in his head…''

Carrie nodded. ''I know.''

''Eby's arrest was righteous!'' Quintana was sweating now, his chest heaving beneath the black sweatshirt. ''I did *everything* by the book. Then some scum lawyer got him off and Eby kept killing.''

''You stopped him,'' Linc said. ''He deserved it. But you can't stop them all—''

''Killing Eby was the only way I could make things right for that little boy! The only way he'd get justice.'' His finger locked on the trigger, Quintana jabbed his automatic at Young. His movements were so sharp and jerky, Carrie marveled that the gun didn't discharge.

''You know who this guy is, Reilly?'' Quintana asked.

''I know,'' Linc said through his teeth. He exchanged a look with Carrie, then took a sidestep toward Young. She knew Linc's intent was to get close enough to the man to shove him down and remove him from Quintana's range of fire.

''You want to make things right for Kim?'' Quintana taunted.

''That's my plan,'' Linc answered. ''Put down that gun, I'll cuff the bastard and haul him to jail.''

''You think he stopped with Kim?'' Quintana jeered. ''You think after he tortured, raped and murdered *your wife* two Thanksgivings ago Frankie here stopped having fun?''

Awareness jumped into Young's eyes. His raised arms

framed a face that drained of all color. "I never touched your wife!"

"Shoot him, Reilly!" Quintana spit out the order while jabbing a finger toward Young. "McCall's got it bad for you so she won't turn you in. I sure as hell won't. You do this pig, we all have a secret to keep. We agree to that, we walk away."

"You're cops!" Young howled. "You can't kill me!"

"Shut up!" Quintana roared, then sent Linc a hostile look. "What's with the sudden Boy Scout act? You just spent two years tracking this scum. Risked your career setting up an undercover op to find him. For what? So you can stand over Kim's grave and tell her you let the dirtbag who murdered her *walk?*"

Linc's eyes narrowed to slits. "A cell on death row isn't a walk."

"Isn't justice," Quintana countered. "Justice comes at the end of a gun. No jury. No trial. That's the only way to stop some bleeding heart judge from putting trash back on the street."

Quintana used a shoulder to swipe sweat off his jaw. "Reilly, maybe your problem is you think I tried to frame you. I didn't. Things fell that way, is all."

"That why you made the hit in Tulsa on a weekend I was nearby?" Linc asked. "Why else would you use an SEU pike pass?"

"Dammit, I didn't *know* you'd be seeing your in-laws that weekend! If I had, I'd have waited to make the hit. As for the turnpike pass, I didn't realize it was in my briefcase." He barked a laugh edged with panic. "I paid my toll with cash, never knowing I had the electronic pass until I got back from Tulsa. Supposedly the turnpike readers can't scan a pass unless it's on the car's windshield. I had to hope that was true."

Quintana swiped again at the sweat dripping off his jaw.

''When you told me McCall was a plant and IA found the turnpike record, I had to do something to get the heat off. Both of us.'' He gritted his teeth. ''When Diaz called this morning, I saw a break. You were at in-service training with cops to alibi you. As far as anybody else knows, I'm at my gym.'' He dipped his head at Young. ''This bastard gets offed with the same MO as the others, your alibi clears you. I'm covered, too, so I don't even get looked at. IA's got no other strong suspects, so they back off. The case goes cold.''

Linc nodded grimly. ''Won't work now, Lieu. Drop the gun.''

''Reilly, for God's sake, shoot him!'' Quintana demanded, his eyes bubbling with desperate panic. ''We'll say he tried to escape. We keep quiet about what we know. *Everybody's fine.*''

Tightening her grip on her gun, Carrie eased closer. ''Give me your weapon, Lieutenant.'' Her heart roared in her head. A few more steps, she could deliver a disabling chop to his wrist. ''We'll work—''

Blurring movement at the corner of her eye brought Carrie's chin up. She swiveled in time to see Young lunge at the chest-high toolbox. Wrenches and screwdrivers clattered to the floor. His arm swept up, gun aimed.

''Gun!'' Linc's shout was punctuated by the weapon's blast.

Something slammed into Carrie's right arm, sending her automatic flying. Fear locked in her throat, she dove for cover, rolling across the floor toward a stack of boxes.

Another shot exploded, its thunderclap almost deafening. Then silence pressed like fingers against her eardrums.

''Carrie!''

Ears ringing, she squeezed her eyes shut. Linc was alive. ''I'm okay.'' Pushing up on her knees, she peered around the boxes, performing a cop's assessment of the scene.

Quintana lay on his back, face toward her. She'd seen that same glassy stare on the faces of corpses at crime scenes. One of his hands was clenched in a death grip against the center of his chest. His other arm was flung to one side, his hand empty. She did a quick scan but couldn't find his gun.

She spotted her own weapon behind her; when she grabbed it, pain sizzled through her arm. Looking down, she saw blood coursing from beneath her cuff, dripping down her hand onto her weapon. A small, ragged hole marred her coat's upper sleeve. The slam she'd felt had been the bullet Young had fired. She theorized it had grazed her, then hit Quintana.

Leaning farther around the boxes, she spotted Young's body draped facedown over the tall toolbox. A gun dangled by its trigger guard from his right index finger.

His own weapon held steady, Linc kicked the gun from Young's hand, then pressed two fingers against his neck. That Linc made no move to handcuff Young signified his condition.

Intending on checking Quintana, Carrie levered to her feet. Instantly little dots circled in front of her eyes.

Linc rushed toward Quintana while giving her a swift look. "You're sure you're okay?"

She dipped her head. "I think the lieutenant's dead."

Linc crouched, checked for a pulse. "Yeah." He holstered his weapon, then scrubbed a hand over his face. "Dammit."

Carrie blinked away stars. "Better call...this in."

"Already done. I requested backup after you spotted Quintana." Linc gazed down at his boss's body. "Guess he didn't get around to checking Young's toolbox for a weapon."

"Linc, I know you didn't come here intending to shoot Young," she said, leaning against the boxes for support. "You did what you had to do."

"Yeah. Otherwise, we'd both be dead." When he rose and turned, his eyes instantly flashed. "Christ, you're shot!"

"I...think it's just a nick."

Rushing to her, he gripped her good arm. "Dammit, McCall, shot is shot."

Tugging the automatic from her hand, he set it aside, then forced her to the floor. Crouching in front of her, he dragged off her ice-blue scarf and looped it around the oozing hole in her sleeve, his eyes boring into hers. "You plan to bleed out before mentioning you caught a bullet?" he said roughly while jerking the ends of the scarf into a series of hard knots.

The choppy movements seared pain through her arm so intense it made her eyes cross. She sucked in air, felt sweat pearl on her forehead. "Reilly, I know...you're still...really mad at me. But could you...not jerk my arm off?"

"Sorry." His hand cupped her cheek. "I'm sorry."

Her chest tightened while emotion she couldn't read stormed through his amber-flecked eyes. She loved him. She desperately wanted a chance to try to make him accept her love but knew that was something she couldn't force.

Linc dropped his hand when two strapping uniform cops burst through the garage door. Flashing his badge, he barked orders to radio for an ambulance.

He looked back at her, his face grim. "You're right about one thing, McCall," he said quietly.

"What?"

"I'm still mad at you."

Chapter 17

Late that night Linc propped a thigh against the scarred table in the SEU's interview room and gave Carrie a measuring look. Shadows of fatigue clung beneath her eyes, and her cheeks were too pale for his liking. The black sling that cradled her right arm added to her aura of vulnerability.

This was the first time they'd been alone since paramedics had swept her out of the garage. Any officer-involved shooting required the surrender of one's weapon, a half-dozen interviews and a mile of paperwork. He and Carrie were on routine paid suspension until Homicide and Internal Affairs completed their separate investigations of the events surrounding the deaths of Lieutenant John Quintana and Frank Young.

Linc felt a swell of remorse over his boss's death. Having worked in Homicide, he knew there was nothing worse than working a child's murder. Though Quintana had crossed the line, Linc couldn't quite think of the man as a monster.

Frank Young, on the other hand, had been human garbage. Linc felt no qualms over having shot and killed him. Young had murdered Kim, and if Linc hadn't acted, he knew damn well Young's next shot would have more than just winged Carrie.

Now, leaning against the table, studying her, Linc felt all over again the chilling realization of how close he had come to losing her.

"You got shot eleven hours ago, McCall." Despite the tight rawness in his throat, he kept his voice level. Controlled. "You ought to be at home in bed."

"I got *grazed*," she corrected. "And I'm leaving in a few minutes." Looking up, she closed the folder on the report that detailed the raid on The Hideaway. "I wanted to finish going over this."

Earlier, representatives of various law enforcement agencies had swooped down on the bar. The surprise raid garnered a large number of arrests. Hundreds of pieces of stolen property, illegal gambling equipment and an eye-popping amount of drugs were taken into custody. Due to their suspensions, Linc and Carrie could not officially participate, so they observed the raid from the Intelligence Unit's surveillance van.

"That report makes for good reading," Linc commented.

"It does." Looking satisfied, she leaned back in her chair. "We got Howard Klinger on more than two-hundred counts of concealing stolen property. Including him, the troops made forty-nine arrests tonight."

"Would have been fifty if you'd let them nab the cowboy."

"That wouldn't have been right. All we had on West Williams was one count of possession of stolen property— the silver lapis bracelet he bought from Klinger. If I hadn't laid things on so heavy, West would never have bought it.''

Linc crossed his arms over his chest. "Guess his only problem now is getting over the fact you lied to him." Which, Linc acknowledged, gave him something in common with the cowboy.

Carrie gave him a long, considering look. "You ever going to get over being mad at me, Reilly?"

"Don't know. But it is something I've given some thought to." In truth, he'd thought of little else since he'd seen her pale, trembling and bleeding in that garage.

"Care to share what's in your head?" Shifting in her chair, she cupped her hand beneath her elbow, adding support to her injured arm.

"Some other time. Go home, McCall. Get in bed and rest that arm."

"The doc gave me killer pain pills, so my arm's fine. What I need to do is get things resolved with you." She blew out a breath. "So I'll start by saying I called Captain Scott while I was still in the E.R. and requested a transfer out of IA."

"Why?"

"I don't like lying to people I care about."

"So you care about me?" he asked, easing a thigh onto the table.

"Yes."

He put a finger under her chin, tipped her face up to his. "That's good, because I happen to care about you."

Her blue eyes focused on his like a laser. "Do you?"

"Yeah. I hadn't really figured things out until we wound up in that garage together. And I'll admit that when you got shot, I didn't think about how you were feeling."

"No?"

"There I was, trying to stop you from bleeding to death while asking myself how *I'd* feel if that bullet had hit closer to center." His fingers tightened on her jaw. "How I would feel if you died. Like Kim."

"How would you feel, Linc?"

"Devastated." He stroked his thumb over her lower lip. "I lost one woman I love, Carrie. That's not something I want to go through again."

He felt her tremble against his palm. "You...love me?"

"Turns out I do." He scowled when she eased from his touch and rose, her eyes bleak. "Doesn't look like you're happy to hear that."

"It isn't that." She gripped the back of the chair she'd risen from. "I lied to you. I slept with you, knowing there was a lie between us."

"That hurt," he acknowledged, "like hell."

"I can tell you a million times how sorry I am," she said quietly. "How much I regret not telling you the truth."

"Carrie, I know that," he said quietly.

"You *know*, but can you truly forget? Forgive? Will you ever really trust me again? Totally?"

"You trying to talk me out of how I feel?"

"No. I just need to know you won't wake up one morning and regret loving me."

Leaning, he snagged her good arm, tugged her around the chair to stand before him. "You're looking at a man who knows a hell of a lot about regret. For the rest of my life, I'll regret I wasn't with Kim that day. I loved her, and now I can't think of her without regret being a part of those thoughts."

He shifted onto the table, bringing her closer until she stood between his thighs. "I don't want to regret losing you, too. If things between us end right now, that's how I'll always think of you. With regret."

She cupped her palm against his cheek. "I don't want us to end."

"So, we see where things take us. To do that, you're just going to have to trust my feelings for you." He caught a strand of her fiery hair, toyed with it. "Which circles us back to our problem. Trust. When I found out you were IA, I couldn't be sure you hadn't also lied when you said you cared about me. It didn't hit me until today when I had your blood on my hands that I was in love with you. That I wanted a life with you, and I was just going to have to trust that you'd told me the truth when you said you cared about me."

She pulled her bottom lip between her teeth. "It wasn't the truth."

Everything inside him went still. "That so?"

"Not the total truth. It's more, Linc. So much more. I love you." She slid her fingers into his hair. "I think I fell in love that first night at The Hideaway when the bouncer caught us out back. You kissed me until my toes curled, and I fell in love. You kiss damn well, Reilly."

"Yeah?" Shifting his hands to her hips, Linc savored the sense of rightness that washed through him.

"Yeah."

"Here I was, thinking I need practice in that area."

Curling his hand around the back of her neck, he brought her mouth to his. Her warm, ripe taste charged through his system; he deepened the kiss, taking her mouth as if he were starving for the taste of her. Which he was.

Minutes—or maybe hours—later she locked her hand on his shoulder and levered back. Her eyes were big and dazed. "What…was I thinking?" she breathed. "You're a terrible kisser, Reilly. You need practice. Lots."

"You want to go home with me, McCall?" He nipped his teeth along her jaw, and grinned when a moan rose in her throat. "I could nurse you back to health between practice sessions."

"You're on." She tilted her head. "Does this mean you're not mad at me anymore?"

"Nope." He dipped a finger beneath the neckline of her sweater, traced the hollow beneath her collarbone. "I may hold on to this case of mad for the rest of my life."

She trembled against his touch. "That's a long time."

"You could always work on getting me over my mad."

"That could take the rest of *my* life."

"Sounds like we're both in this for the long haul, McCall."

"Works for me, Reilly."

* * * * *

Look for the story of Grace McCall-Fox in
THE CRADLE WILL FALL,
The third book in the exciting
LINE OF DUTY *miniseries by Maggie Price.*
On sale February 2004,
wherever Silhouette books are sold.

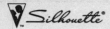

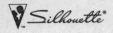

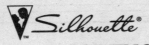

COMING NEXT MONTH